"Look out below!" The cry was accompanied by warning shrieks as those below tried to scatter. There was a sickening thud and a clang and clatter as the euphonium bounced once, twice and settled on the polished oak floor.

The silence was…shocking. Harriet could almost feel the tension in the air.

"Oh, my *God*!" It was Matron who cried out—a cry echoed in muted tones by all around when they realized exactly what it was that the euphonium had bounced off, before it clanged and clattered to the floor.

Christiane Marchant was still seated a little apart in her wheelchair, but now her body was slumped forward and she was hanging out of the chair, her shoulder and the side of her head a bloody, pulped mess. On the table beside her, in stark incongruity, were the smashed and broken remnants of the mince pies, shattered china plates and bloody tablecloth.

MURDER FORTISSIMO
NICOLA SLADE

WORLDWIDE.

TORONTO • NEW YORK • LONDON
AMSTERDAM • PARIS • SYDNEY • HAMBURG
STOCKHOLM • ATHENS • TOKYO • MILAN
MADRID • WARSAW • BUDAPEST • AUCKLAND

With love to Austin, Felicity, Joe, Lyra, Jim, Noah, Jack and Kurt.

Recycling programs
for this product may
not exist in your area.

MURDER FORTISSIMO

A Worldwide Mystery/April 2012

First published by Robert Hale Ltd

ISBN-13: 978-0-373-26796-5

Copyright © 2011 by Nicola Slade

Printed in U.S.A.

ACKNOWLEDGMENT

As Murder Fortissimo is a work of fiction, Firstone Grange is not based on any real establishment, nor are its staff, residents or their guests based on real people. Some of the places mentioned, however, are real, such as the glorious Winchester Cathedral, along with its crypt, and while the village of Chambers Forge is fictitious, it does share a geographical location with its near namesake, Chandlers Ford, near Winchester.

I'm very grateful to everyone who kindly read this book in its various stages, and for their helpful comments: Olivia Barnes, Ruth Beaven, Charlotte Buxton, R J Frith, Linda Gruchy and Joanne Thomson.

Principal Characters

At Firstone Grange

GUESTS

Harriet Quigley A retired headmistress who thinks she could be Miss Marple if only she had learned to knit

Christiane Marchant A Frenchwoman who knows many secrets and gloats too much

Ellen Ransom Remembers the good times in the war but wishes she didn't

Fred Buchan Remembers everything all too well

Tim Armstrong Has difficulty, some days, remembering anything

STAFF

Pauline Winslow A moral matron with a mission

Mrs. Turner A housekeeper with an economical habit

Gemma Sankey A willing worker with a risky secret

FAMILY AND FRIENDS

Canon Sam Hathaway Harriet Quigley's cousin and sounding board

Alice Marchant A daughter who is a drudge

Neil Slater An estate agent who sometimes wears leather shorts

Doreen Buchan Knows that a family history is not always "a good read"

Vic Buchan Don't tell him about "female troubles"

Ryan A nasty little scrote

Kieran A lumpen slowcoach

Gemma's Mum A woman of perception who knows a scumbag when she sees one

PROLOGUE

WHEEE!!! KAPOW!!! SPLAT!!!

Harriet Quigley's hand flew to her mouth to stifle an involuntary whimper but the cartoon image froze on her retina. In the appalled silence an action replay rolled inside her head. The ludicrous object falling, falling, falling as she, and everyone else, stared in horror, unable to do anything. The moment of impact—oh God, that *sound*—a collective shudder and then the... mess. The second shameful thought that crowded into Harriet's mind, despite her horror, was: Jesus, the tabloids will have a field day with this.

From *The Fryern Courier*

FIRSTONE GRANGE

Firstone Grange, which opens its doors soon, combines top-class hotel facilities with discreet nursing care in a brand-new concept. The first establishment of the kind locally, Firstone Grange aims to provide relaxing convalescent care together with short breaks for the over sixties.

Matron and proprietor, Pauline Winslow, says Firstone Grange offers an excellent home-from-home for the independent retired person who wishes to convalesce away from catering and household cares. "We also aim to provide respite breaks for families who will be able to relax knowing their older relatives are happy and comfortable while the younger members of the family take a holiday."

Miss Winslow continued: "Nowadays people are discharged early from hospital and not everyone has family at hand to help during convalescence. At Firstone Grange we can provide that security in the setting of a beautiful country house."

Firstone Grange is independently owned but is next door to Hiltingbury House, a purpose-built facility comprising a residential home together with sheltered housing in a separate block. The proprietors declined to comment on a rumour that they had concluded a deal with Miss Winslow to build further sheltered housing on some of the land belonging to Firstone Grange. Firstone Grange was built in 1900 and stands in two acres.

Firstone Grange was soon fully booked...but the incoming guests brought secrets with them. And among them was someone who found out all those secrets, grave and trivial, someone who knew that power comes from knowing what others do not know. Someone who needed to be eliminated.

ONE

FOR TWO PINS, HARRIET Quigley sighed inwardly, she could go to sleep. Only good manners, combined with the hope that her host would soon top up her glass with some more of that extremely good Merlot, stopped her from dozing off. She could feel her eyes beginning to glaze over as she listened politely to her hostess's monologue about the expense of moving to the new house. "You wouldn't credit, Miss Quigley, how much it cost to curtain this dining room, with those three floor-to-ceiling windows."

"Please call me Harriet," said her guest, casting what she hoped was a look of admiration at the beige velvet curtains. Dull, she sighed, very dull, but then the whole place has been neutralized. The previous owners had obviously watched all those programs about how to sell your house and decorated accordingly, and the interior designer who furnished the house, hired by Doreen, who had no confidence in her own taste, had followed suit. This dinner party was pretty dull, too, she thought, as she stifled another sigh. It was Neil Slater's fault, getting her into it, but her covert glare at him turned into a smile instead. Serve him right finding himself stuck, on either side, with Doreen Buchan's incredibly dull neighbors and for landing her, Harriet, with Doreen's husband, Vic, on one side and on the other a second dull man, one of a pair from Winchester.

At least he required no effort, intent as he was on his dinner, showing no resentment that Doreen had been talking across him.

"Firstone Grange?" Doreen looked up as someone mentioned the name, breaking off from listing her expenses. "Firstone Grange is where Vic's father has just gone to give it a couple of months' trial. He's getting on a bit and rather frail so it seemed a good idea. Of course, you do have to be so careful these days with old people's homes, you hear such awful things. But Firstone Grange is very select. And very expensive."

To Harriet's relief nobody picked up the conversational ball and the topic was dropped. She shot a sidelong glance at her cousin Sam Hathaway, sitting diagonally across the vast polished table. Had he noticed her involuntary reaction when Firstone Grange was mentioned? *I bet he did,* she thought, *even though he looks as if butter wouldn't melt in his mouth at the moment, which is more than I can say about this piece of gristle in mine. Wonder if I can slip it onto my plate somehow?* Some quick sleight of hand and it was nestling under her fork. *I haven't lost my touch,* she thought, *after all those years of slipping bits of disgusting school dinners into my gymslip pocket. Pity I can't...* She contemplated her blue woolen dress from Phase Eight and thought better of it.

"Er, well, Harriet." Doreen Buchan managed the name with a bashful stammer. "I just wondered, at least I didn't catch… Is Canon Hathaway your brother? You do look very much alike, both of you tall and fair, and the way you talk is similar, too."

"Sam's father and my mother were brother and sister," Harriet explained. "So we're first cousins and we were brought up together, next-door neighbors as it happens. But I'm shocked to hear you say you think we're alike. It's always been a great comfort to me that I didn't inherit the Hathaway nose."

She grinned across at Sam, who frowned slightly at her through the glasses perched on the imposing Hathaway beak. He looked puzzled and shook his head as Harriet's impish grin morphed into a bland smile, but went back to nodding sympathetically at Vic Buchan's complaints about red tape and bureaucratic interference in his building company.

When Neil Slater had called her in desperation, she had, as his old friend and childhood babysitter, agreed to his plan with reservations. "Look here, Harriet,' he had wheedled. "Vic and Doreen Buchan have just moved into White Lodge and Doreen's really anxious to meet people. They moved here from Portsmouth and since I made a stonking amount of money in commission from the people who sold them the house I feel I ought to make an effort."

"No," she had pointed out tartly. "You feel *I* should make an effort. What do you want, Neil? Coffee morning or something?"

"Dinner party," he said, adding hastily: "No, no, you needn't glare at me like that, Harriet. *You* don't have to cook, Doreen wants to have a dinner party and invite some locals. She needs to invite her neighbors who are stupendously dull—ditchwater has nothing on them— and I said I'd rustle up a couple more. If I still had a wife I'd have no need to bother you, but now I'm single again I'm a bit stuck. Please, Harriet. If you come, and maybe you could persuade Sam to come as well, it'll be bearable and Doreen will be dead impressed, too. A canon from the Cathedral and a retired headmistress, you'll be bound to add luster to the proceedings."

And now Sam, who knew far too much about his cousin, had, she was quite sure, spotted her startled expression at the mention of Firstone Grange; there was no way he'd leave it alone, he was much too nosy. Curiosity was a family trait, she admitted with a sigh.

"An Oompah Band?" The startled query from Vic Buchan roused Harriet from brooding on the folly of letting old friends blackmail you into tedious social entanglements. "What on earth is an Oompah Band?"

"You might well ask." Harriet began to laugh, then hastily primmed her mouth. Vic seemed pleasant enough in a brick-shaped, brick-faced, moneyed sort of way, but his wife was looking po-faced, and as their conversation had revealed no glimmer of humor, Harriet thought she'd rather not alienate the woman with laughter that was sure to be misunderstood. "It's Neil's latest adventure," she explained. "He's only recently joined the band—you'd better get him to explain." When Neil shook his head she continued. "It's a Bavarian beer cellar act, all brass and oompah-oompah, and knee-slapping. It sounds pretty awful but honestly, it's great fun. Neil forced me along to a session last month. They treat the audience with a mixture of insults and comedy, all in dreadful cod-German accents."

Sam Hathaway was intrigued. "Last month? This must have happened when I was away, christening my new grandson in Melbourne," he said. "So where do you come in, Neil? I thought you were a serious musician?"

"So I was when I was still married," Neil explained. "And in some respects I still am, but I don't have to keep up someone else's standards anymore, so this is just for fun. If you recall, I play the clarinet and I'll have you know I look very fetching in my leather shorts and little feathered hat. We're booked to play at Firstone Grange in a couple of weeks or so."

"Really?" Doreen sounded perturbed. "But are you sure it's suitable for old people? It doesn't sound quite the thing."

"I don't know." Neil was clearly nonplussed. "What do you think, Harriet? Sam? You're both about the right vintage."

Harriet stifled a giggle as she caught Doreen's scandalized expression at this studied insult. Neil knew perfectly well that she and Sam were barely into their sixties and that she at least was vain about her youthful looks, but she addressed the question seriously. "You have to remember that Firstone Grange *isn't* an old people's home," she said thoughtfully. "It's a kind of hotel for older guests who might be convalescent or just want some peace and quiet and a rest from looking after themselves. And as the Baby Boomers are all turning sixty now, things are changing. Didn't you read that article claiming that sixty is the new forty? An Oompah Band won't faze any of them—after all, they survived the Swinging Sixties and there are plenty of people around who coped with much worse in the war, not to mention a few still who were around during the First World War, just about, as children anyway. Older people are usually pretty resilient and not easily shocked, you know."

"Quite right." Sam barged enthusiastically into the conversation. "However old and frail you are you could still take part. How about beating time with your zimmer frame? Or slapping your knees even if you can't get up and dance around? Imagine an impromptu roll of drums created by two spoons and a bedpan." He bowed, acknowledging the laughter with a twinkle, then continued. "Anyone else get an invitation to the champagne reception to launch Firstone Grange? I can't go, got a meeting that night. I expect you'll be going, Harriet?"

Damn, all eyes were on her now. "Nope, I'll be away for a couple of weeks," she announced firmly. "I'm trying a retreat."

As she'd hoped, this silenced the company apart from Sam, who, under cover of the renewed buzz of conversation, leaned across the table. "What do you mean a retreat? That's not your kind of thing at all. What's up, Old Hat?"

The childhood nickname nearly broke down her resolution, but not quite. Sam really didn't need to know. "I'm just tired," she confessed. "Really, really worn-out. This last year has been pretty hard going, Mother dying in the spring and her house to sort out, then the sale and the move to the cottage. A couple of weeks of peace and quiet suddenly seemed a good idea."

Sam's concern made her feel even more guilty about lying to him, but beyond the steadily munching man beside Harriet, Doreen was looking anxious and Harriet turned to her with relief.

"I'm a bit worried about this Oompah thing," her hostess fretted. "I really thought, what with the price they charge, that Firstone Grange would be five star, really exclusive. Don't you think this concert sounds a bit…well, a bit *common?*"

As Harriet soothed and reassured she shot a considering glance at her hostess. Seldom had she come across anyone quite so lacking in confidence, so anxious about the social niceties. Doreen Buchan was a tallish, raw-boned blonde with naturally curly hair that she kept cut short. Were curls common, too, Harriet wondered? In her late forties, married to a successful, wealthy older man, recently moved into a large, imposing house in one of the most sought-after villages in one of the most beautiful and historic parts of southern England; two children doing well, the boy recently qualified as an accountant and the girl a beautician at an exclusive health hydro a few miles north of Winchester. With all these trappings of success Doreen still came over as a woman with an outsize in inferiority complexes, but why?

As for Firstone Grange, Harriet pursed her lips. *I'm almost beginning to regret what I've done. Too late now, though.*

IDEAL STARTER HOME. *IDEAL* Starter Home. Ideal Starter *Home.* Alice typed the words over and over again, the rhythm hammering into her brain, I-*deal* star-ter *home,* dum-dum, dum-dum-*dum.* Suddenly jerking awake from automatic pilot she stared at the words in front of her.

Oh, I wish, oh God, I *wish.*

The anguished whisper bounced back at her, echoing round the empty office, then, with a shiver of guilt, she deleted what she had typed and forced herself back to work.

"Range of fitted floor and wall units, inset one-and-a-half bowl sink unit with mixer taps, wall-mounted gas boiler" and so on, including the estate agent's old favorite, "deceptively spacious," which in this case was close to contravening the Trades Descriptions Act, describing as it did the one and only bedroom, a deceptively spacious eight foot six by eight foot (just).

To Alice it sounded like heaven, even the "easily managed garden" with "decked area and laid to lawns." Correctly interpreting this as meaning that the garden was barely larger than the bedroom she heaved a wistful sigh at the thought of mowing a handkerchief-size bit of grass rather than having to struggle with an acre of tangled shrubbery, wantonly spreading mildewed roses and vast expanses of decaying herbaceous borders. You wouldn't even need a lawn, she gave a sigh of pleasure, it could all be decking.

She expanded her theme. Not to have to lay coal fires, carry heavy scuttles, rake out cold ashes; no scrubbing of stone flags in the Edwardian kitchen and scullery, home to black beetles in spite of her best efforts. No miles of threadbare carpet to Hoover with an asthmatic ailing vacuum cleaner that had been new before Alice was born; no monumental pieces of mahogany furniture that needed endless polishing and feeding with wood restorer. The blissful castle-in-the-air sustained Alice through the drudgery of her days, and the very fact of daydreaming was usually enough for her.

Today for some reason it was more like a knife, a goad, a whip applied to her shrinking flesh. This perfect little house, ideal for just one person; say, for instance, a thirty-nine-year-old spinster living alone, this little house was everything she dreamed of. On second thought make that a single woman, a career woman, not a spinster, definitely living alone and not, absolutely not, living with her mother.

Alice's afternoon job, where she inefficiently typed out details of houses for sale and to let at Williams's estate agency, was the means of her salvation, her only escape into the outside world; without it she thought she would dissolve into a wistful wraith.

Predictably her mother hated it. "I think you might have some consideration for *me,* Alice," she had complained only this morning, a discontented note in her light pretty voice, with the lingering trace of accent from her long-ago Breton childhood. "You know how much I need constant care—it's really too selfish of you. After all, you won't be troubled by me for much longer."

The sweetness and light phase currently in vogue was always fairly short-lived, to Alice's relief. It was much more trying than when Christiane was in full flood as a bullying monster. The sweet little old lady pose, oozing exhausted, neglected resignation was too much like hard work for Christiane, she was too much Ghengis Khan and not enough Mother Teresa to sustain the performance. And that was what made her dramatic acceptance of Firstone Grange all the more mystifying. Alice had shown her mother the newspaper article with no real hope of persuading her to try the place, but what could possibly have made her so suddenly amenable? The anticipated tantrum had never materialized and the sneer, that initial curl of her lip, was replaced by a glee-ful, mischievous smirk which was new to Alice, some-thing she had never witnessed. But what did it mean? Nothing good, that was certain, and Alice found that

Christiane's quiet, satisfied complacency was proving much more alarming than a torrent of abuse.

The previous few days had tumbled over themselves with Alice bobbing along—she fumbled for images, like—like a coracle nearing a thundering, crashing waterfall. Exactly a week ago two things had happened, two earthquakes, two… She ran out of metaphors and similes and reverted to pure astonishment. *What happened? How could something like this, two somethings in fact, happen to* me? *And in one day?*

The first pebble in the avalanche had been the article in the local paper, and the effect it had had on Alice herself. *How did I dare,* she wondered now, a week later; *how did I dare hand her the paper and suggest she should try Firstone Grange?*

Whatever well of desperation had forced her to take that step, she hadn't really expected anything to come of it, so the real avalanche, earthquake—whatever it was—had struck when, instead of becoming abusive, Christiane Marchant had agreed to try a month's respite care.

Her mother, the decision made, had withdrawn into herself a little, brooding though not on any unpleasant topic, Alice thought. There was an air of ripe satisfaction about the older woman, an unpleasant complacency, a sort of *who'd have thought it* about her attitude. Whatever machinations were going on behind the façade, Alice was too tired to investigate, too weary to care and, to tell the truth, too afraid of what she might discover if she did ever manage to lift the lid and see into the seething cauldron of vicious spite that was, she knew, her mother's default position.

Alice had squeezed in a preliminary visit to Firstone Grange, registered her mother for a month's visit starting almost immediately and to include Christmas and New Year, and handed over the enormous sum of money required. Later she went in state with Christiane on a tour of inspection. Normally she loathed the palaver entailed in transporting her mother from one place to another, booking the taxi, washing and ironing, dressing the invalid while picking up one discarded outfit after another from where they had been flung to the ground in a fit of petulance. For the visit of inspection, however, all Alice was required to do was act as lady-in-waiting while the *grande dame* made her stately progress round Firstone Grange, a gracious nod here, a graceful phrase of greeting there, making sure that everyone understood they were shortly to be honored with a Presence.

The bedroom Matron showed Christiane was approved with a faint die-away smile, as was her comment about the bathroom.

"Unfortunately," Miss Winslow explained with a slightly apologetic smile, "we don't have any ground-floor bedrooms but you should find it quite easy to manage the wheelchair in the lift. I'm so sorry you were just too late to secure one of the rooms with en suite facilities, but there it is. The bathroom is just down the landing, fully kitted-out for disabled guests and in the near future I hope it will be possible to have every room en suite."

Leading the procession toward the lift, Miss Winslow failed, unlike Alice, to note the way Christiane Marchant's gaze strayed toward the name card tucked into the brass slots on one of the neighboring bedroom doors. A satisfied, almost feline, smile spread across the plump features, the dark eyes glittered under their slightly hooded brows, and she glided down the landing still smiling.

Scurrying along after her mother and Miss Winslow, an insignificant moon in the wake of two major planets, Alice cast a curious glance at the name on the door. Ellen Ransom. It meant nothing to her nor did she register as significant the way her mother paused for a moment as they passed the open door of the drawing room, her eyes narrowing as she stared wide-eyed, transfixed in astonishment, at a stocky, balding old man hunched over a game of patience. As Alice caught up with her mother, the man looked up, impaled on that dark and burning gaze, and stared back at Christiane, his pale eyes puzzled and wary but showing no recognition. With a weary gesture he turned back to his playing cards.

To Alice's further mystification her mother seemed buoyed up by the visit and the face she turned to her daughter as they clambered and maneuvred her into the taxi was shining with a malicious delight.

"Well, daughter mine," she purred. "You really have excelled yourself this time. I think I'm going to enjoy myself there. For once you've managed to do the right thing, though it's for all the wrong reasons." She fulminated to herself for the rest of the half-mile journey to the large, inconvenient house on the outskirts of the village, and then as Alice settled her in the wing chair for a rest, Mrs. Marchant turned to her daughter.

"Don't think I don't know why you want me out of the way," she spat, reaching for the remote control. "You think, with Christmas coming, that there'll be men on the loose, looking for a good time. Well, don't kid yourself, Alice, so they may be but what they're looking for isn't a thirty-nine-year-old virgin who wouldn't know a good time if it bit her on the nose."

Alice had schooled herself to endure this kind of tirade with a blank face, knowing that her impassive reception incensed her mother, but this time she couldn't restrain a small gasp. Christiane gave a triumphant smirk.

"Underneath everything you're not actually bad-looking. In fact you could be like I was if you put your mind to it, though you'll never have my vivacious sex appeal—you're too like your grandmother, the wicked old bitch." The thought of her mother-in-law, dead for more than forty years, could still inflame Christiane's temper.

Alice turned on her heel, actually biting her tongue to prevent the outpouring of grief and anguish that threatened to engulf her. If only Daddy hadn't died, she wailed to herself. Mother was always careful not to let him see this side of her; the venom of her tongue had been restrained then, unbridled now. Why was she like this? What had made her use people in this manner? A faint memory from her childhood surfaced, an impression of her father telling Alice a story and making her promise not to upset her mother, but what could it have been? Alice felt only the haziest stirring of memory and her father had never mentioned it again, whatever it had been. *The truth is,* Alice thought now, *that I've always switched off when Mother went on at me, it made life so much easier not to hear her diatribes.* Sometimes, though, it wasn't possible to switch off.

"I'm going to work now. I've left you a sandwich in the kitchen." Alice picked up her handbag from the small oak table by the door and made her escape. Out in the garden she scrabbled for her Ventolin inhaler and took a couple of puffs to make the burning in her chest subside, then leaned against the side wall of the house, uncontrollable spasms racking her body, hot tears stinging her eyes.

"Oh God," she railed aloud, but hushed, an agonized but muted howl. "Oh God, please, please help me. Help me to cope, give me the strength to endure. Don't, please don't let me have a breakdown, but please, *please*, God, please make her die."

TWO

"LET'S SEE…" HARRIET Quigley dumped her bag on the bed and ran through her checklist out loud as she started to unpack. "Nighties, dressing gown, sponge bag, spare underclothes, spare outer clothes, four books—which I certainly won't get through in the day or so I'll be here, but they'll be useful later on, when I get to Firstone Grange. Out-of-office message set up for emails, mobile phone switched off. Anything else I haven't done?"

The lie she had told her cousin Sam sat heavily on her conscience, but she shrugged it off. *What he doesn't know won't hurt him,* she thought, philosophically. *Besides, he knows how squeamish I am. He'll understand.*

WHEN ALICE MARCHANT reached the office, she let herself in through the back door and ran straight into yet another earthquake. Barry Williams's rumbling boom could be heard in the front reception area, with a lighter, younger voice interjecting the odd comment or question. *I can't face clients,* she thought, and reached for the kettle. *I need a cup of tea after Mother…* She shied away from her mother's frank appraisal of her, still too agitated to escape into the small sanctuary of her daydreams, even though the brisk walk up the hill had calmed her nerves a little.

"Is that you, Alice?"

Barry Williams was a small, jolly man in his early sixties, his air of eternal optimism at odds with his chronic bad luck. He was currently trying to extricate himself from a financial mess his ex-wife had dragged him into. Only Barry would have been foolish enough to let himself be named guarantor for the enormous loan she had taken out so that she could open a guest-house. "I really thought she could make a go of it," he had confided his disappointment to Alice, his round red face glum and surprised as he reluctantly put his own house on the market to pay off the debt.

"I've got some fabulous news." He beamed at her now. "Is that tea? Splendid, bring three cups in with you, dear, we're celebrating. I've finally sold the business, so come and meet your new boss."

Alice felt her stomach churn and her heart grow heavy as she obediently took three mugs of tea into the main office; she had been dreading this moment. A welcome retirement with his debts paid and just enough to buy a tiny flat would prove paradise for Barry, but what of Alice? *Who else will employ me?* she mourned. *What other employer will put up with my incompetent typing, as well as the time off I have to take when Mother's being more difficult than usual? And a new owner is bound to buy some new computers and I'll have no idea what to do with them.*

The tall, thin man was introduced as Neil Slater. She had heard of him through the local grapevine and knew he was highly regarded. He looked about her own age, with a pleasant smile—a kind smile—she thought with a glimmer of hope, as he accepted the mug of tea she proffered.

"I didn't want to say anything, not a word, till it

was all signed, in case it all went pear-shaped." Barry bounced across the room. "You know one or two of my little ventures have been a bit of a disappointment lately, but we finalized everything this morning and it's all official." Still beaming at his own financial acumen he turned to Neil Slater. "How many branches have you got now, Neil? Four including this one, isn't it?"

Neil gave a pleasant nod and included Alice in his answer.

"I'd like to get this branch established as part of my group," he said. "There's a lot to offer here, plenty of housing and great transport links, with the motorway, airport, trains and the ferry ports. I know there are one or two of the big estate agencies already here but I'm convinced there's room for the kind of customized service a small, independent business like this can provide. Besides, I think it'll be fun."

Alice was touched by the way his long, rather equine features lit up with a boyish enthusiasm at that last assertion.

"Well, it will be." He shot her a shy grin, responding with gratitude to her evident sympathy. "I'm planning to start off here, using this as my base, I think. I've got a good team running the established branches and you and Barry have a good little outfit here. It's not far for me to travel, either."

He answered her look of inquiry, explaining, "My mother died last year and since then I've been converting our old family home into two flats—it's in Locksley just beyond Hursley, no journey at all and I'd be going against the flow of the traffic so the rush hour wouldn't be a problem."

Barry rubbed his hands together, radiating satisfaction, rosy with pleasure. "Well, this is all splendid, isn't it? I'm sure Alice will agree to stay on to help you, Neil, she's a tower of strength."

In spite of her terror at the prospect of leaving her job, Alice could have killed him; she could see that Neil was taken aback though he manfully tried to conceal a flicker of dismay. In the mirror above the filing cabinets Alice could see herself, thin and anxious, dark hair scragged back into a bun, worried grooves ploughed between her brows and—*oh God, not tears, please not tears,* as her eyes began to glitter. *What will he think of me?*

When she dared look up at her new boss she found him biting his lip as he surveyed her. "Look, Miss Marchant," he spoke abruptly, coming to a sudden decision. "Why don't you come out with me now to have a look at some of the properties on your books? Barry says you know all about the business and it makes sense for us to get to know each other. I've obviously gone into the financial side pretty thoroughly and I believe we could have a little gold mine here, but it would be valuable to get your angle on things."

Barry sat down at his desk at the back of the room with the Father Christmas glow happily in place. "Miss Marchant?" He shook his head playfully at Neil. "What's this? Call the girl Alice, for goodness' sake. 'Miss Marchant' sounds much too formal. Now off you go, I'll hold the fort, it's much too near Christmas for anyone to be thinking of moving."

He gave them a genial wave to push them out of the office and settled down to watch the portable television he kept discreetly tucked away on top of the cupboard in the kitchen. If a potential client ventured in through the front door, Barry could flick the remote and be all attention, the snooker or soap opera vanished in an instant.

ELLEN RANSOM LIKED WATCHING television, too, though not soaps or snooker; she preferred something pretty about gardens or an undemanding film, a love story for choice. It had been a struggle today, she reflected, to bag the most comfortable chair in the drawing room, just close enough to the fire for comfort but not near enough to scorch.

One or two new ones these past few days and more to come, they said. Somebody had been eavesdropping past the office, easy enough to do; stop, wheeze, lean on the wall and look pathetic or drop for a rest on the upright hall chair, just by the grandfather clock. Who would question you? They all did it, even the la-di-da ones, though they pretended not to, stuck-up bitches. A sour smile did nothing to lighten Ellen's face. They were no better than she was—money talked wherever it had come from and Ellen's money didn't come from piddling scrimping and saving, not likely; her money had come in a lump sum, a pools win way back, and then Douglas had spoiled it all by dying so suddenly.

She shook her head to get rid of the memory and wondered about the stir there had been this morning. Some woman in a wheelchair had come to view while Ellen had been out in the minibus and the gossip ran that she looked the kind who thought a lot of herself. Oh well, somebody else with a bit of character about her, even some pepper, might spice things up a bit; they were a bland bunch so far.

That old bloke over there—with the scanty tufts

of hair punctuating his bald head—from Room 7 just
down the landing from her; said to be a retired bank
manager shoved in here to give his family a bit of a respite. Look at him staring at the carpet, not all there by
a long chalk.

And then there was that one sitting in the window,
mild as milk with her nose in her book, but watching them all. *She looks younger than the rest of us,*
Ellen decided, though she had to be sixty, that was the
rule, but she didn't look it. There was something about
her that gave Ellen the creeps—a kind of *I know what
you've been up to and it simply won't do* sort of feeling.
Not fair, when chance would be a fine thing, nothing to
get up to; schoolmistress, that's what that one looked
like.

Ellen would have been gratified to know how spot-
on she was with her diagnosis.

HARRIET QUIGLEY SHIFTED to a more comfortable position and congratulated herself on her strategy. No
way, she thought, would she allow friends and neighbors to ferret her out, and the retreat had worked well
enough as a cover story. She felt a pang of guilt about
her cousin Sam. *Maybe I should have told him,* she admitted to herself, *but I can't help being such a wimp
about hospitals and I certainly didn't want anyone else
to know;* hence the sphinx-like silence at that wretched
dinner party.

No, Sam was squeamish, too, and since his wife's
death he was out of touch with "female troubles."
Harriet winced at the memory of the consultant as he
briskly informed her, "It's better out than in, nothing
to worry about but you'll be more comfortable. Start

running marathons? Take up trampolining?" He had spoken only the truth, however. The day or two in the smoothly efficient private hospital, now to be followed by a gentle recuperation at Firstone Grange, looked set to do the trick; none of the lying around for weeks that Harriet remembered from her mother's experience.

Her terror of hospitals had been, well, *lulled* was the word, though not diminished. Although she still felt very tired, Firstone Grange, she considered, was doing her proud so far; pleasant staff, delightful room with its own bathroom, delicious food. So far it was living up to its promise, and so it should considering the cost, but… She cast a discreet glance round the room. *I'm not so sure about some of the other inmates, though. Residents, guests even,* she corrected herself hastily, *not inmates.* Matron certainly wouldn't like that word.

TIM ARMSTRONG STARED miserably out at the garden, bright under the low December sunshine but otherwise dismally bare, lacking in color. The stark black silhouettes of the trees and shrubs against the sky, a few late leaves drifting slowly down onto the damp lawn, all added to the melancholy that seemed to be his constant companion these days.

Why am I here? he wondered, hunching a fretful shoulder and staring back at the strangers in the room behind him. *Where did Jane go? She shouldn't have left me here all by myself. She knows I don't get on with strangers nowadays. And what about the boy? Wasn't I staying at his house? So why am I here?*

His face creased in an anxious frown, struggling with half-remembered images and voices, snatches of conversation that made no sense, and the constant, unsettling apprehension that Jane had abandoned him. Facts and figures that had been his life's work now scrambled themselves into a jumble, people who had been dearly loved and close to him now assumed alien, frightening faces. Words that had flowed smooth and reassuring in his role as a bank manager now lay in meaningless scattered fragments, clues to a crossword puzzle he had no longer any hope of completing.

GEMMA SANKEY STEPPED nervously into the drawing room, breathing deeply and aware of the responsibility, her tongue caught between her teeth as she bore the heavy tray. She was really enjoying her new job. "You're coming on really well, Gemma," the housekeeper, Mrs. Turner, had said after the first week spent helping in the kitchen and laundry room.

"Let's see how you get on taking the guests' tea and coffee to them," she had suggested today. "Don't worry if they want to talk to you. Some of them like to chat so just be polite and always call them Mr. or Mrs.— we don't go in for first names here, Matron's very firm about that, she likes things done properly. Set the tray carefully down on the table and put the cups out, then ask who wants what and pour out for them. You'll soon get the hang of it. Some of them like to get up and fetch their own cups but some of them need to be waited on, the older ones and the convalescent people."

It was nice to be greeted with smiles and words of welcome. Gemma felt her courage rise and it was just as Mrs. Turner had said. "Who would like tea?" she asked and they laughed and put up their hands like a bunch of little kids, and the same with the coffee.

Mum would be pleased when she heard about it at

the end of the week. It was odd at first, being away from home, and that hadn't pleased her mother at all but it was much nicer than Gemma had expected. Instead of Mum shouting at her, saying she was thick and a wicked little slut, there was Mrs Turner, ever so patient and not getting cross if she got it wrong. Mrs. Turner was nicer than Mum.

She clapped a frightened hand to her mouth but nobody had read her mind, picked up on this heresy. *I bet,* she ventured further, *I bet Mrs. Turner wouldn't have said I had to get rid of my baby, I bet Mrs. Turner would have said I could keep it.* Gemma tidied the empty cups and saucers onto the tray, picturing a dear little baby girl, all chubby cheeks and blond curls, dressed in pink, with Mrs. Turner as a fond granny. At this point a vision of the baby's father thrust itself into the forefront of her consciousness and she dropped a cup.

"Here you are." A hand reached down beside her as she scrabbled on the floor. "No harm done, it landed on the carpet and rolled under the table. What a bit of luck, just pop it back on the tray and nobody will be any the wiser."

Gemma gave Harriet Quigley a look of gratitude and scuttled away.

THE FATHER OF GEMMA'S baby was lounging around the playground at the Rec. He drained the last dribble from his can of Foster's, tossed it in the air, caught it deftly on his foot and kicked it into the sandpit. "You know my girl, Gemma?" he asked.

"Yeah?" Kieran fancied Gemma; she had a nice face, not too clever like most girls, always one step ahead of him. She had lovely big tits, too, not that he'd ever dare say anything about that, Ryan might have a go at him; not with his fists, Kieran could handle that and he was bigger and stronger, even though he hated violence. But it might be something worse. Ryan was a bit too handy with that knife of his for Kieran's liking but he couldn't stop you thinking about Gemma. Or about those tits. Kieran had never seen a girl with nothing on, only in pictures, though he kept quiet about it in Ryan's company; no need, either, to confess to being a virgin at seventeen. Still, he had spotted Gemma bending down once and he'd been able to look right down her T-shirt; she hadn't been wearing a bra and the moment was one of Kieran's best memories, treasured and taken out nightly to dream about.

"Listen, will you? What's the matter with you, you big dummy?"

Kieran jerked his head up from a smiling daydream about putting his hand down Gemma's T-shirt and— He had no idea what he would do if he ever got that far; his life up to now was a tit-free zone. Ryan was staring at him with narrowed dark eyes, a scowl disfiguring his handsome Elvis features, with the smoldering look that drove the girls wild, along with the careless tumble of shining dark curls that haloed his face. Kieran had no need to look in the mirror to know that his own amiably stupid face was too fat and too freckled, not to mention too spotty, to make any headway with girls.

Ryan stood on the swing and glared at Kieran.

"My girl. Gemma." He was speaking with exaggerated patience now, the way nearly everyone did eventually. Kieran was used to it, and most of the time he didn't mind. He had heard Ryan only the other day, explaining his friend to somebody else. "Old Kieran's all right, just a bit thick and you have to give him a kick now and then when he has one of his stupid times, but he's a good mate and built like a brick shit-house—comes in handy if there's a fight.'

Kieran beamed now and nodded, glad to be of use, smiling as he remembered Ryan snorting with laughter as he went on: "He's good to take with you if you want to nick stuff, get him in the off-license with that great khaki army coat flapping round and he'll knock cans flying. He doesn't mean to do it but the noise it makes and the fuss means they don't notice me sticking cans and bottles in my pockets."

"I was telling you about Gemma, are you listening?" He took another can from his pocket, flicked the ring-pull over toward the bushes at the edge of the play-ground and took a long swig. "She's only gone and got a job at that Firstone Grange place. You know, down the road with the rich old wrinklies. I told you about it the other day when she was going for the interview. She texted me and told me she's got a live-in job so she'll be away from her old witch of a mother. Might come in handy."

Kieran nodded slowly. Gemma's mum was one of the few who had failed to come under the spell of Ryan's soulful brown gaze. In fact she had threatened him with a knife if she ever caught him near Gemma again and Kieran could tell that Ryan had been impressed by the threat.

"Funny how upset Gem was about getting rid of the baby," mused Ryan, switching moods. "Everybody does it, my mum's done it loads of times, never bothers her. So why did Gemma get in such a state? Besides—"

the scowl was back "—she was supposed to be on the pill. Might have known she'd cock that up somehow. Like I said, she's about as bright as you are."

Kieran accepted the clap on the shoulder but avoided Ryan's eyes. It was only too plain from the lowering frown that Ryan was remembering what Gemma's mum had said. She had called him a "shifty, oily, randy little scumbag who never did a day's work in his life and ought to have his balls chopped off—and would have, if she had her way."

The fat boy had been lurking by the garden gate when he overheard that diatribe and now he trembled for Mrs. Sankey's safety. Ryan's temper had been evil for days after that episode and that meant Mrs. Sankey was on his punishment list.

"Do you handle many period cottages?" Neil asked as he opened the leaded casement window and gazed out at the view from the master bedroom. The cottage, with its immaculate decor, Farrow & Ball of course, and manicured garden—no expense spared—had stood for more than three hundred years against a gentle slope of farmland, halfway between the winding and pretty redbrick village of Hursley and the nearby village of Otterbourne.

Alice leaned beside him on the windowsill, a tight squeeze but a companionable one.

"Cottages?" She shook her head. "Not an awful lot. Barry hasn't really concentrated on what you might call country properties. He's gone more for smaller and cheaper, the first-time buyer and the next stage up."

She cast an approving glance over the garden with its neat vegetable plot, bare now apart from cabbages

and brussels sprouts, with a carefully tended herbaceous border already showing the points of a few fool-
hardy bulbs.

"This has been awfully well done, hasn't it?" She
waved a vague hand. "I mean, the house is obviously
two farm cottages knocked into one and they've managed to keep the cottagey spirit without sacrificing
comfort. The garden is nice, too. I bet they have holly-
hocks and night-scented stocks in the summer, proper
cottage flowers."

Neil gave her a sympathetic grin, obviously surprised at this flight of poetic fancy from the prosaic
Alice, then he called her attention to the splendid clump
of beech trees, tilting precariously in its chalk bed, on
the brow of the hill beyond the boundary.

Downstairs in the low-beamed sitting room of the
cottage they compared notes, Alice adding a quick
scribble to her clipboard, detailing the limed-oak
Smallbone kitchen, then they took their leave of the
owner, who was reeling in delight at Neil's valuation,
and drove back toward Chambers Forge.

"From the sublime to the ridiculous." Neil laughed
as he turned the car into the minute drive of the final
house on their list, built on the site of the old brick-
works that had once provided the village with its main
industry, supplanting its previous claim to fame, the
cherry orchards of the seventeenth century.

Alice heard his remark but failed to respond, lost in
admiration of the tiny house of her dreams, the Ideal
Starter Home. She shook herself and smiled at him, still
shy but gaining in confidence after an afternoon spent
in Neil's undemanding, friendly company. "It's such a
cozy, compact little house." She sighed and saw in his

eyes astonishment that such an undistinguished building should seem like the Promised Land to her. "It's just—" She hesitated. "We've got a big, rambling old house that's falling to bits and costs a fortune to heat. There's an enormous garden as well—it would be wonderful not to have much work to do."

He nodded and seemed to be thinking hard. Alice was aware that several times during the afternoon he had been struck by something she had said, some shrewd comment that had surprised him. She had noticed him stealing covert glances at her, frowning slightly.

"Can you drive, Alice?" he asked now, abruptly.

"Yes, yes, I can. I passed my test years ago, when Daddy was still alive, but I haven't driven for years. We got rid of the car when Daddy died because it was too expensive to run. Why?"

"I was just wondering, thinking aloud, I suppose. You're so knowledgeable about the business, but I don't think…" He glanced down at the badly typed house details in his hand and she felt her cheeks burn. "How would you feel about being my assistant? Training as a negotiator, I mean, and helping on that side of the business? We could get someone else in to do the typing, maybe on a part-time basis."

The glow spread from her burning cheeks to her dark eyes and for an instant a new, very different Alice sparkled at him. He was about to speak when the color faded, leaving her dull and sallow, her eyes bleak.

"She won't let me," she said drearily.

THREE

NEXT MORNING ALICE PACKED under her mother's supervision, knowing she looked as wan and miserable as she felt. Christiane's stream of criticism suddenly dried up and Alice looked up, to intercept an unusual expression on her mother's face. It was almost— No, not affectionate, maternal emotion—that was not something she had met with, not once in her entire life— but instead of the usual contempt, her mother wore an oddly calculating look as if she was weighing up just how near to breaking down Alice actually was. A moment later Christiane was frowning at her nails and the moment, whatever had prompted it, vanished. A clumsy movement destroyed the peace.

"You stupid creature, can't you do anything properly? That's my best silk nightdress, fold it properly, I don't want it creased to blazes."

Stifling a weary sigh Alice refolded the ivory silk, shuddering a little at the touch. *I'll never, ever have a silk nightdress, or anything else silk,* she vowed silently. Somehow the fluid, supple softness of the fabric had come to epitomize her mother over the years. Christiane must wear silk next to the skin because of her extreme sensitivity, no matter what the state of their finances, no matter that during the bad times Alice had been driven to wearing her father's old vests in

winter to keep warm. Christiane must clothe her delicate frame in silk, and silk of the finest quality at that.

Christiane could be like silk, smooth and slippery
and, to strangers, a charming and delightful woman,
but Alice was always aware of the worm at the heart
of the apple.

If I brought Neil Slater here, Alice thought, *and introduced him and told her about his offer of a job,
she'd be lovely to him and he'd be utterly charmed.
That snowy hair in its elegant French pleat, those sparkling dark eyes and that still-attractive* jolie-laide, *all
like a ton of bricks, people always do. And then she'd
put the boot in, oh so delicately, oh so reasonably, and
stop me taking the job and I'd end up looking a callous,
unfeeling bitch for wanting to neglect such a sweet old
lady, confined to a wheelchair, too.* Shocking. As a
child Alice had assumed all mothers were like Christiane; when she found she was mistaken she was wistful but resigned. Her mother was as she was and there
was nothing to be done about it.

The taxi arrived with all the commotion and hustle
and bustle of maneuvring Christiane and her wheelchair. The driver, the same one as on the initial trip to
Firstone Grange, obviously remembered the dear old
lady and her anxious spinstery daughter. Alice caught
his sidelong glance and winced at the pity in his eyes.

As they disembarked at Firstone Grange Alice broke
out in a cold sweat born of a terror that something
would intervene. *Maybe the matron will say they're full
up after all,* she thought, trembling, *or Mother will turn
round with a peal of laughter and say it was all a joke
and she was going home now.* Nails digging painfully
into the balls of her thumbs, she prayed, a fervent, in-

coherent gabble of supplication. *Please, oh please, oh God, don't do that to me, let me have a respite, please, oh please,* please.

No, it was all right, they had negotiated the entrance hall and the matron seemed delighted to welcome them. Up in the lift, out onto the landing, along the carpeted corridor toward Christiane's room, no problems. A door opened and an old woman came out, spotted them and halted, holding back to let them pass, though there was ample room for all on the broad Edwardian landing. Alice suspected the woman of being just plain inquisitive, wanting to suss out the new arrival, and why not? Time must hang heavily on the residents' hands if they weren't great readers or knitters or embroiderers.

"Good morning." Christiane made a point of slowing down and smiling a bright, cheerful greeting.

To Alice's astonishment the other woman recoiled, staring, her mouth open in shock. She said nothing but cowered back in the doorway of her room, reaching out a shaking hand to lean on the door jamb for support.

As Alice followed her mother she caught a faint thread of a whisper. "No, not her, not that one, not after all these years!" It meant nothing to her, caught up as she was in her own dread that even now, her mother might call a halt to the experiment, but no. Christiane Marchant's face radiated complacency and satisfaction, a cat-with-the-cream smirk, an air of delighted malice. Alice trembled even more, she had seen that expression once or twice in her life and it boded no good. What the hell was she so pleased about now? What mischief was she brewing?

Installed in her comfortable bedroom, Christiane turned to her daughter with an airy wave of dismissal.

"Off you go, Alice, I'm sure you have things to do before you go to work. I'll be quite comfortable here."

She held up her cheek for a farewell kiss and Alice bent down reluctantly. Was it her mother's doing, she wondered, that she had such a fear of intimacy, had never been able to bear being touched at school, couldn't stand games where you had to get too close to other people? It had been a relief when her father had decided his asthmatic daughter should be educated at home, although her asthma had gradually become less severe so that she could probably have gone back to school for the last year or two. Luckily the subject had never been broached. An attempt, years later, to join a keep-fit class had ended when the instructor insisted they do lots of partnered activities involving contact with hands, feet, legs and other parts of the body. For once in her life Alice had welcomed her mother's "heart attack" that gave her an excuse to abandon the class without losing face.

Now she braced herself not to shudder as she gave the obligatory kiss and managed to get herself out of the room, out of the building, out of the neatly lawned and graveled garden, though it wasn't till she was nearly home that she began to relax. She was free. *It's going to take the whole of my pitiful "escape fund,"* she reflected, *to keep Christiane at Firstone Grange for an entire month, but, oh goodness, it's going to be worth it. Free!* She savored the word, rolling it round her tongue. Freedom!

CHRISTIANE MARCHANT WAS pleased with herself, too, absently answering the care assistant, Gemma, who was nattering away nineteen to the dozen as she un-

packed, not noticing the look of intense, inward concentration on the new guest's face.

This is going to be fun, Christiane exulted. She was
aware, only too well, just how close to breakdown she
had driven Alice, and this month at Firstone Grange
had offered her the perfect opportunity to back off
without losing face; that, and the knowledge that the
fees would clean out Alice's escape fund completely.
Serve her right, too, Christiane frowned, tucking away
money like that.

"Do you want to rest, Mrs. Marchant?" asked
Gemma, pushing the last drawer shut. "Or you could
come down to the drawing room for coffee if you like,
to meet some of the other guests?"

"That would be lovely, dear," agreed Christiane. "If
you could just help me a bit with my chair? I'm sorry
to be such a dreadful old nuisance."

The practiced pathos she put into this remark had
something of its usual effect, though not all. Her eyes
narrowed as she looked closely at Gemma. *I don't think
the girl is all there,* she decided.

In fact Christiane did the girl an injustice. Gemma
was properly concerned about any nice old lady who
had to get about in a wheelchair and she had never had
any qualms in her previous job at the nursing home
about the bedridden ladies, either; sponging bedsores,
changing soiled sheets without complaint, it was no
trouble. *We all come to it,* she thought with a philosophical shrug.

No, it was something else that was on her mind,
something nagging at her that might upset this lovely
job away from Mum, with these lovely old people, especially that nice Miss Quigley, who really talked to

Gemma as if Gemma was a proper person. That was what impressed Gemma. Mum shouted at her and treated her like a dummy, Ryan said he loved her but she knew that all he really wanted was sex and he was horrible sometimes, like he'd been last night on the phone.

She wrenched her mind back to the present and, as she negotiated Mrs. Marchant and her wheelchair into the lift and out again into the hall, she thought about Miss Quigley, who had taken to having long, comfortable chats with Gemma, chats about all kinds of things but mostly about what Gemma wanted to do with her life. That was something nobody else had even considered worth discussing and it was a pleasant new experience that raised questions and avenues Gemma had never thought of exploring.

"Just push me up by a table, dear," suggested Christiane, glancing round the drawing room with a bright social smile. "Over there will do, by that lady in the pink cardigan."

ELLEN RANSOM FELT NUMB as her past rose up and smacked her in the face. Encased in ice, she heard Gemma give a general introduction; Matron Winslow was very hot on that kind of good manners and Ellen watched as Christiane Marchant smiled and nodded all round. Then came the moment she had dreaded in her dreams, but this was a waking nightmare. The woman was real enough, and so was the memory. And the threat.

"Good morning." It was the same voice, the same accent she remembered so clearly even after more than sixty years. "Pleasant weather for the time of year, isn't it?"

"What?" Ellen jerked her head up, meeting a bland smile. Was the woman going to pretend she hadn't recognized her? Was it possible, by some blessed miracle, that she *hadn't* recognized her? "Um, yes, yes, very nice and sunny today."

As Ellen Ransom sank back in her chair, fiddling with her cardigan sleeve and looking dumbfounded, Christiane nodded pleasantly and turned to her other neighbor.

"It seems very comfortable here. Have you been here long?"

The man hunched in the wing chair came out of his reverie and stared at her blankly, then, as he came to himself, he shrugged.

"A veek, maybe two? I don't know, it's all right. It could be vorse."

He looked away, obviously wanting to discourage any further intrusion but she persisted.

"I see you're another foreigner, just like me," she chirped merrily, her eyes snapping with dark amusement. "Where do you come from? I'm from France, myself, but of course I've been over here for a good many years. How about you?"

He shifted impatiently in the big tapestry-covered chair, trying to ignore her but the high-pitched, sharp voice, with its very slight trace of an accent, bored into his consciousness.

"Well? Cat got your tongue, has it? Where do you come from?"

He stood up and glared at her.

"I am from Eastern Europe and I do not vish to discuss my past vith you." His voice, strongly accented, grated and he shot her a savage glance as he turned on his heel and limped out of the room.

"Oh dear." Matron Winslow had just looked in to check on the new arrival. "I do hope poor Mr. Buchan isn't too upset." She frowned slightly as she spoke but Christiane was oozing sympathy and regret, so Miss Winslow went on. "We ought to have explained to you, Mrs. Marchant. He won't talk about his wartime experiences but it must have been pretty bad. We think he was in a concentration camp, that's what his son told us, but poor Mr. Buchan won't say a word about it."

"Oh, how sad." Christiane sighed, her syrupy tones belying the sparkle of interest in her eyes. "Clumsy old me, putting my foot in it. Mind you, I don't suppose any of us had a very easy time in the war, or after it, either."

She glanced at Ellen Ransom as she spoke and was gratified to see the other woman shudder very slightly. With a tiny nod, Christiane turned her attention to the other occupant of the wide bay window.

"Why, it's Mr Armstrong, isn't it? The bank manager? Remember me? I used to know your wife. Such a pity she passed away, wasn't it."

"Passed away?" Tim's brow furrowed as he looked anxiously at the stranger. He had, up till now, been having one of his good days, engaging in a perfectly lucid conversation with Harriet Quigley for a long time this morning. She had just slipped upstairs to fetch a book from her room, and without her protection Tim Armstrong looked as though his hold on reality was beginning to slip. "Jane is... Jane is going to come and see me soon.... Today, she's coming to..."

Christiane's smile was sweet but with the tail end of a sneer and her victim floundered deeper and deeper. "It's true." The words of protest were blurted out as Christiane allowed a trace of skepticism to show. He clearly struggled to contain his emotions and started to shout at her, hands flailing. "Jane is coming to see me soon. You don't have to look at me like that. I'm not stupid. Or…or mad."

As Christiane assumed her misunderstood expression and opened her mouth to deny the charge, a cool voice broke into the conversation.

"It's all right, Tim, leave it to me. Why don't you come and give me your arm round the garden? The sun's shining for once but I really could use a bit of help." Harriet patted Tim's arm and gave him a nod of approval as he pottered off obediently to fetch his coat, then she turned to the other woman, a stern expression on her pleasant features.

"Look, I'm sure you didn't mean to upset Tim, Mrs., er—" she began. "But it's much kinder not to argue with him. Most of the time he knows perfectly well that his wife is dead but sometimes it gets too hard to bear so he shuts it off. He doesn't harm anyone by it and he has enough other problems to worry about, so please, do me a favor and let him alone, will you?"

Before Christiane could protest her innocence, Harriet smiled politely and went in pursuit of Tim, obviously hoping to catch him before he started to worry about why he was wearing his coat indoors. Christiane was left staring after Harriet, whose words and tone had both been perfectly friendly and reasonable. So why did she have the impression that she had received a reproving slap on the wrist? And why did she feel even more strongly that she should watch her step with that one?

KIERAN WAS SINGING AS he worked. His redoubtable mum had found him a job as a packer and to everyone's astonishment he was good at it, his stubby fingers capable of swift, deft movement, and the rhythmical monotony of the work suiting his temperament. He was proud of his work, proud to have a job and he enjoyed working with the older women who were his workmates.

He worked in a warehouse for a small promotions company, packing items like airline toilet bags, tucking in sample-size bottles of cologne, tiny soaps, mini toothbrushes and toothpaste, and so forth, into the First Class bags. The Grannies, as the women packers were affectionately known, all enjoyed having him there to mother, his slowness and gentle nature reminding them of their own sons as little boys, but with the tarnish of adulthood left off. There was nothing wrong, it was only that he was just a few steps behind everyone else.

Today he was happy. Ryan had let him have a ride on his motorbike last night and it was dead good. *I want a motorbike, too,* he thought, then pouted. *Mum won't ever let me.* His thoughts flickered toward Gemma and he perked up. Tonight Ryan was going to sneak into the garden of Firstone Grange and try to get Gemma to come out. Ryan didn't know it but Kieran was going to follow him and try to watch him with the girl. Maybe they'd, you know, kiss and stuff and he might get to watch. That'd be dead good.

Kieran sang loudly, his split-melon grin and carroty curls a delight to the Grannies.

"Bless him," they crooned.

"I'M FREE," ALICE WHISPERED then, with a tremor of excitement. "I'm *free,*" she shouted aloud. Alone for the first time in years she made herself a cup of tea and a ham sandwich for lunch. This afternoon she would go in to the office as usual but she would be a different person. "I'm free," she said it again, quietly but firmly.

Without thinking at all, her mind a complete blank, she drank her tea and ate her sandwich, then she went into what had originally been the morning room when the house was new. Formerly her father's surgery, for the past few years it had been her mother's bedroom. She stripped the bed and put the sheets into the washing machine.

The room smelled of her mother, a compound of French perfume and a warm, musty smell, the smell of old woman. Alice stared at the bed, her thought processes kicking back into operation. *I simply will* not *think about her,* she decided and, with a determined slam, she shut the door behind her and went upstairs to get changed for work.

The thought of the office sent a shaft of sunshine through the gloom. Neil! She recalled his kindness when she stumbled over the words as she tried to explain her reaction to his offer of promotion.

"I'm not taking that as final," he told her. "I know what it's like, living with an invalid," he had explained and told her a little about his own mother.

Alice's mouth twisted into a bitter smile. Neil's mother and Christiane Marchant sounded as much alike as Maria von Trapp and Lucrezia Borgia, but plainly Neil meant her to take the job, come hell or high water. "These invalids can be tyrants," he had observed as he drove her back to Chambers Forge that day. "But you mustn't let her get you down. You have to try and keep a life of your own."

Neil had given a wry smile then himself, she recalled now, then he had laughed abruptly, shaking his head. "Just listen to me," he conceded. "It's easier said than done—I know that only too well."

Today Neil was expected in the office to discuss the final details of the handover with Barry Williams and to go over some of the files with Alice. Instead of wearing her usual depressed navy, Alice found herself putting on her best jumper, the daffodil-yellow one and the good wool-and-cashmere cocoa-brown skirt that she had found last week in a charity shop in Winchester.

Alice adored clothes, good clothes, and she loved charity shops, thrilling to the excitement of the treasure hunter stalking a designer label. Hitherto, though, she had gone for hard-wearing quality rather than color and beauty.

Idiot, she chided herself, looking at her reflection with dissatisfied eyes, then she squared her shoulders. Why not? What was wrong with trying to look halfway decent? Better, surely, than sinking into a depressed, premature middle-age and withering away.

PAULINE WINSLOW WAS AN evangelical in her chosen field of geriatric nursing, and the unexpected but entirely deserved legacy from a grateful patient, of the large Edwardian house, Firstone Grange, had enabled her to set up her dream enterprise. She had inherited a modest amount of cash along with the house but her financial prayers had been answered when she discovered with delight that an old nursing colleague was already in charge of the existing residential home next door.

"As you know," her friend had explained, "Hilting-bury House caters exclusively for nursing cases at present, which, of course, is why we were happy to make no trouble over your planning permission. After all, Firstone Grange is in a quite different category, comfortable short-stay visits, so there's no clash of interest. However, we would like to upgrade and move into permanent residential facilities for the less infirm—you know the kind of thing, reasonably able-bodied people but too frail to want to go on living alone. Sheltered flats with all the benefits of a community and care at hand but a degree of privacy and independence, as well."

Pauline Winslow had been interested, wondering where this was leading.

"We have plenty of land at the back of the house," explained her friend. "But we could do with more. Our most pressing need is for a decent driveway from the proposed new building out to the main road. We don't want to use the existing entrance. Now do you see what we're after?"

The money from the sale of land at the side and rear of Firstone Grange was a godsend and Pauline Winslow was happy to give all the credit where it was due. "Thank you, Lord," she acknowledged on the morning of Christiane Marchant's first day. "Thank you for giving me this chance, and please, dear Lord, please look after poor Mr. Buchan and don't let him have been too upset."

She frowned and prayed aloud with renewed fervour. "And please, Lord, forgive me for not taking to him—help me to find something likable about him. And the new guest, Mrs Marchant," she added as an afterthought. "Please let things continue to go well, it's all so lovely, so perfect. I'll die if anything goes wrong." The frown deepened. "I think I'd kill anyone who spoiled it."

THERE WAS NO OFFICIAL REST period after lunch at Firstone Grange. "They're not toddlers." Pauline Winslow had been quite fierce when someone suggested it to her. Some of the guests disappeared to their rooms for an hour or so but others preferred to sit in the drawing room, either reading or nodding over the paper until the two-thirtyish time suggested by Matron to potential visitors.

Today Doreen and Vic Buchan arrived promptly on the dot of half-past two and sat down beside Vic's father in the bay window. Stifling an exclamation of dismay, Harriet Quigley shrank back in her corner chair, lest Doreen Buchan spot her, hoping the shadows would conceal her. If her cousin Sam found out where she was holed up he'd be ringing the doorbell in record time, along with friends from Locksley Village, and Harriet was uncomfortably aware of her straggling hair and roots showing gray. Time to fish out the semipermanent wash-in color that was tucked into her sponge bag. It should be possible, she thought, to do that in the hour or so between tea and dinner. In the meantime she twitched the heavy cream brocade curtain and leaned back out of sight behind its loosely hanging folds.

Doreen Buchan gave Fred a cool peck on the cheek and sat down with her back to Harriet, who relaxed into her corner and reached for her book. Vic tried to engage his father in conversation, with little success, so he indulged himself by slipping into his favorite topic, talking about the business.

Doreen sat back and tried to look happy about her surroundings. *I hate these places,* she thought, shuddering, *they're all the same. Oh, I know I've been telling everyone how nice it is here, and I suppose it is, it ought to be, costs enough, but it's still a Home, still an Institution. In the end it all boils down to the same thing, just dressed up pretty. Prettily,* she caught herself up, *it's a place to put people who aren't safe outside, because they're ill, or old, or...not right.* Her thoughts panicked around inside her head. *Don't think about Mum,* she urged, *don't let yourself remember—it's all over, all gone and nobody knows. Especially Vic, he'll never know, he mustn't know. Ever.*

"Hullo? I know you, don't I? From a long time ago?"

The voice was in her head and her head was going to split open at the shock, coming so pat on her tangled thoughts. It *was* in her head, wasn't it? Doreen gasped and looked round, straight into the shrewd, glittering black eyes of an old woman in a wheelchair. A woman whose face had an eager, almost lustful look, curious and waiting for her answer.

"No, no, I don't think so," she stammered, pleating the fine blue wool of her Country Casuals skirt with troubled fingers.

"Oh, I think I do, dear," the woman went on, her voice warm, interested, curious. "Didn't you live in Surrey Road when you were little, dear? In Bournemouth? With your auntie?"

The shock knifed into Doreen, icy fingers twisting her stomach, her heart juddering as she stared, anguish glazing her eyes, at the older woman. Did she know?

What did she know? How could she, how could *any*one
here possibly know? Her aunt had kept herself to herself, never gossiping. Besides, the name had been different, but secrets had a way of seeping out through
the cracks. Doreen said nothing, was hardly capable of
speech anyway, and slumped in her chair in a frozen
terror.

"Not feeling well, dear?" The concern sounded false
to her tormented listener. "I say, excuse me, but I think
your wife's feeling poorly."

Vic turned round. "You all right, Dor? You're looking a bit green."

Wetting her lips, but not capable of attempting
speech, Doreen flapped a hand and shook her head.

"Thanks, love." Vic nodded to Christiane Marchant.
"I'll keep an eye on her. Time of life, you know," he
added, not noticing his wife's cringing at the booming
explanation. "We won't be long anyway, got to go for
a test drive. We're looking at a new Mercedes." Swell-
ing with pride he bent toward his father and raised his
voice. "You hear that, Dad? We're off to look at a new
Merc in a minute, top of the range. What d'you say to
that then?"

Fred Buchan raised his eyes from silent contemplation of the bare-stemmed silver birch outside the
window, graceful and starkly silhouetted against the
pewter sky. He looked out at Vic from heavy, hooded
lids, pale blue eyes faded and chill. "Good, my son,
very good." He went back to staring at the tree and Vic
shrugged. The day Dad took an interest in anything
beside himself would be the day Vic put up the flags.
Mum had been the one to talk to, to praise, to admire.
Never Dad. Vic sighed, raising his eyes to the ceiling;

thank God for Doreen, at least she took an interest. She was a good wife, Dor, a real good sort, never any secrets with Doreen, just straight up front.

RYAN WAS STILL IN BED. No point getting up, nothing to do, not the day for signing on. If Gemma hadn't been working he could have got her to come round; his mum was down the road till three-thirty, had been since breakfast, working in the kitchen in the Blue Boar. Even Kieran, the faithful dog, was working. Stupid dickhead, always going on about that shit job of his. Who in their right mind would want a job? Still, that said it all, didn't it? Kieran wasn't in his right mind really, the great soft pudding. But useful.

Gemma was another great soft pudding, soft in the head, and soft in other parts, too. He lay back, arms folded behind his head, watching the porno DVD he'd liberated from a market stall in Eastleigh, and he thought about Gemma and her soft, yielding body. His eyes glistened in anticipation; he was going round there tonight, to that fancy great old folks' home, and she was to get out and meet him. All that fuss about getting rid of the baby, not "feeling" like it, not going with him, and her bitch of a mother sticking her oar in. Well, it was too long; tonight he was going to get lucky—or else.

STILL IN HIDING BEHIND her curtain, Harriet Quigley watched with interest as Vic and Doreen Buchan gathered up their coats and took their farewells of Fred. Vic clapped him heartily on the shoulder, mumbling empty nothings, clearly anxious to get away, and Doreen repeated her earlier performance, a chilly peck on the cheek, given and received with not the slightest evidence of pleasure on either part.

As the couple walked out to the drive Harriet looked out of the window and was intrigued by the sight of Doreen's pale, ravaged face looking back toward the house. Her shoulders sagged as Christiane Marchant, now being wheeled on the terrace by Gemma, waved gaily at her.

Now, what does all that mean, I wonder, Harriet mused. *That woman has only been here a few hours and already she's upset Tim, got Ellen Ransom sneaking around like a whipped dog, caught Matron on the raw, as well as Fred Buchan, and now here's Doreen Buchan looking as though she's been given the Black Spot. What does it all mean? Why do I have a feeling that Christiane Marchant is trouble?*

FOUR

ALICE WAS CHEERFULLY singing Christmassy songs, slipping from "Jingle Bells" to "White Christmas," when she broke off abruptly as she realized that, give or take an adjective, it was true. She really *was* dreaming, looking forward to the day, though the chances of snow falling then in this part of southern England seemed highly unlikely. Not impossible, though; look at today with its bright, glittering morning, branches rimed with silver, berries bellying red on the holly, a stout robin yelling his head off on the washing line.

It had been different when Daddy was alive; she looked wistfully down the long avenue of the years. After all the childless years of his first marriage, Daddy had been over the moon at the advent of his little princess, his little miracle, but how had his sophisticated little Breton bride felt about her surprise pregnancy when she was already past forty? Had Christiane ever really wanted a child, Alice wondered? There had been murmurs and whispers sometimes in her childhood, sidelong glances that spoke of dark secrets and terrible things, but timid, frail, asthmatic Alice had never dared provoke the temper so carefully concealed from Daddy.

No, temper tantrums had certainly never featured in Christiane's dealings with her doting husband. Alice could remember countless occasions when her father

had been overcome with remorse at the way his "harsh
and unkind" words and actions would set Christiane
off on one of her martyred moments. Far from just
"moments," either; Alice sighed as she recalled weeks
on end when her father had endured sighs and tears
when some ill-advised comment had given Christiane
an excuse. She had favored two particular methods
of punishment for both daughter and husband. Alice,
while her father was still alive, tended to be on the receiving end of gusty sighs and repeated, chilly comments on the lines of: *If you don't know how much
you've hurt me, I'm certainly not going to spell it out
for you.* That had been in Daddy's hearing; in private,
Alice was never in any doubt about what she had done
to offend.

Her mother had used a different ploy with her husband. This had followed an invariable pattern which involved an initial gasp, a frail hand clutched defensively
to her heaving breast, then a torrent of tears, broken
only by references to her "terrible ordeal." What that
ordeal was, Alice was never permitted to know, but all
reference to it had worked like a charm on her father,
who never failed to be contrite and to bring his injured
wife round with offerings of jewelry and chocolate.

The week since Christiane had moved into Firstone
Grange had flown by. Alice had paid a duty visit each
evening after her blissfully solitary supper and found
that absence, while not having any effect on her fond-
ness for her mother, certainly did make it easier to tol-
erate her in short doses.

Work had become increasingly interesting. Neil, still
shuttling between his four branches, had taken to dropping in to the Chambers Forge office every afternoon

for a cup of tea and to check out some point with her, to pick her brains on the district, to toss a suggestion or idea into her lap, seeking her opinion. *He treats me like a human being;* she gave a slight smile as she deadheaded a very late, frostbitten rose on her way back to the house. *And not just a human being, he treats me like an adult woman with a mind of her own and with opinions to be valued and respected.*

He thinks I'm real.

Daddy's precious jewel, arriving just in time for her father's retirement at sixty, had led a sheltered, enchanted life, too poorly to attend school regularly and, secure in her father's companionship and love, never feeling the lack of friends her own age. Whisked into hospital with appendicitis, shortly after his death, Alice had come home to find herself allocated a new role, that of lady-in-waiting and slave to her mother.

A neighbor had greeted her as she tottered from the Patient Transport ambulance and led her indoors to where tea had been laid and Christiane sat, weak and saintly, in a wheelchair.

"Her poor heart," whispered the neighbor, who had thoroughly enjoyed playing Florence Nightingale. "She's so brave, so afraid she'll be a nuisance to you, dear."

Alice was never very sure what, if anything, was wrong with Christiane's heart. Nor was her doctor. "I've no idea," he finally admitted. "The tests all indicate there's nothing wrong with her heart, or anything else. It could be some kind of hysterical paralysis," he suggested, registering with patent concern Alice's pale, drawn face. "There seems to be no structural damage to the legs, spine or muscles, either, that I or anyone else can detect, but the fact remains, Miss Marchant, that your mother seems unable to walk."

Yes, it was a convenient organ, Christiane Marchant's heart, her daughter sighed. It allowed plenty of eating and drinking and other pleasurable activities but prohibited anything strenuous or inconvenient, so Daddy's Princess was now body slave to Daddy's Queen. With her stern upbringing in the tradition of filial duty and her singular lack of self-assertiveness, Alice did what she had to do. But now, with Christiane at a remove and with her talents at work being valued, Alice Marchant was changing, growing, feeling her way.

Yesterday, for instance, she had gone with Neil to check out some commercial premises in the old docks area of Southampton. As they walked back to the car Alice had sniffed the salty breeze coming in off the sea and savored the watery gleam of sunshine over the marina. She turned as Neil spoke.

"Canute Road?" he queried. "Why him? Isn't he the king who tried to stop the tide coming in? He wasn't local, was he?"

"For goodness' sake, Neil." She was impatient. "You should know your local history. Yes, it's King Canute, and no, that's not what he did. Everyone always gets it wrong."

"You mean he's had a bad press all these years?"

She failed to spot the amusement in his voice and tried to explain. "What he was trying to do was demonstrate how hopeless it was to try and stem the tide of invaders, Danes or Normans, I can't remember which. What he did, just here—see that plaque, that was the waterline then—was to point out that it was equally impossible to make the tide stay out."

He raised an eyebrow at her vehemence then leaned on a rail to admire the yachts in the marina. "I like it down here," he commented. "It doesn't take much imagination to picture it in the heyday of the great liners, does it? The boat train coming in laden with wealthy passengers, not to mention the people in steerage." He waved a hand at the blocks of flats, the cinemas and the boats. "It's good that it's still in use."

As they drove away Alice peered into the deepening gloom.

"Looking for something?" he asked.

"I'm trying to see if you can see the French church from here. There, did you see? Just round the corner from God's House Tower, where the museum is."

"What? You've lost me, Alice. What French church?"

"Didn't you know? I suppose not that many people realize it's there." She smiled at him. "It's the old pilgrim's church, St Julien's. Mother and I used to go to a service there every year—a pastor came over from Le Havre to conduct the service in French. He might still come, for all I know, but we haven't gone for years."

"Really?" He was intrigued. "I suppose you speak fluent French?"

"Reasonably fluent." She nodded. "I suppose I ought to have used it and looked for a proper job, but, well, you've seen my typing—it never seemed worth the bother."

"Don't be so negative," he scolded gently, negotiating more traffic lights before heading homeward. "Tell me instead why on earth there should be a French church in Southampton?"

She shook her head slightly at the first part of his remarks, then, "There's always been a lot of trade between Southampton and France, of course, even before the Conquest—well, even before the Romans, too. After that the Normans settled in the west of the town and the English stayed in the east and when the Huguenots fled here in Tudor times they took over the church." Her dark eyes sparkled as she looked at him. "Of course, the Huguenots were Protestant and Mother is nominally a Catholic, but she's not fussy. She liked to go to the annual service, it made her feel special." She blinked, darting a sidelong glance at him. "It made me feel special, too," she said in a startled voice. "I've never realized that. I've obviously more in common with Mother than I thought."

Back at home and warmed by the memory of that outing with Neil, Alice pirouetted round the room then looked at the dingy kitchen more closely. *I wonder how much this place is worth? Maybe we could get rid of this mausoleum and there'd be enough to keep Mother at Firstone Grange and buy something for me, even if it was only a studio flat. I could ask Neil to value it,* she thought; then, with startled realization: *I could value it myself!*

It was a *eureka* moment. She grabbed a pad of paper and went all over the house making notes, gasping at the figure she reached. *I'll have to get Neil to check that,* she thought. *The furniture, too, that might be worth money.* Some of it was enormous Victorian mahogany but quite a lot dated from earlier times, pride and joy of Daddy's great-grandparents. Would that be worth money, too? An appointment for the local auctioneer to take a look was made before reaction set in and she had to sit down and confront the undercurrent of terror that was threatening to submerge her sudden burst of—what? Courage? Lunacy? What would happen when Christiane found out?

MATRON WINSLOW STOOD ON a high pine stool fixing garlands of tinsel and greenery to the staircase's ornate spindles. The entrance hall was now beginning to resemble her dream of a picture-book yuletide and the pitch-pine paneling offered an ideal background for her decorations. Oak logs lay ready in the fire basket; copper pans gleamed along the mantelpiece, highlighting her best arrangement of carnations and Christmas greenery.

Miss Winslow was delighted with her efforts. The house was looking wonderful, a piney-spicy plumminess in the air and a sense of anticipation almost palpable about the residents, even the stolid suet puddings among them. Luckily, she thought, the suet puddings were in the minority; her gamble—to have a short-stay clientele—had proved, by and large, a great success.

Two of the first guests had now signed up to move in to the nursing home next door and one or two had inquired about the proposed sheltered flats; all in all it was very gratifying. She was a happy woman, so why, Matron puzzled now, why did she have this feeling of unease? A shiver ran through her and she almost crossed her fingers, though not generally a superstitious woman. Instead she decided that she would make time to walk up to the village church and lay her problem before the proper authority. God will provide, she thought with relief.

PAULINE WINSLOW WOULD have been even more uneasy
had she known that another woman at Firstone Grange
shared her misgivings. Getting on for forty years of
ruling over classrooms meant Harriet was attuned to
nuances of emotion: little frissons of guilt, private
anxieties an open book to the accomplished reader
of humankind. *There is something going on here,* she
thought, and debated with herself as to the cause and
what, if anything, she could or should do about it.

There was no doubt, she decided, that the heart
of the trouble was Christiane Marchant. The woman
sat in her wheelchair oozing sweetness and light, but
gradually it seemed that everyone had come to loathe
her, even those who had initially responded to her un-
doubted charm. Harriet, observing her closely where
others simply turned away in distaste, felt there was
something repellent about the way the woman savored the little nuggets of information she extracted
so artfully from her victims; her victims who, too late,
cursed themselves for giving away so much more of
themselves than they had intended or indeed realized.

Little snippets, quite innocuous gleanings, such as
the tidbit of gossip about a resident recently departed
to spend Christmas in the South of France. That guest
would have been mortified to know that instead of the
grand upbringing she claimed, everyone now knew that
her alma mater had been not Roedean, but a run-down
school in a city slum.

That guest was safely out of the way but Ellen Ransom was far from all right. Harriet pursed her lips. *I
almost wish I had Sam here, to bounce ideas off him.*
She sighed. *At least I could tell him that the Marchant woman seems to delight in sneaking her well-oiled*

wheelchair up behind Mrs. Ransom and talking at her. It sounds perfectly innocuous, what she says, Harriet recalled, *but Ellen is looking gray and pinched and she looks worse after every conversation with Mrs. Marchant. And now I think the woman has got something on young Gemma.* Harriet frowned. *The girl was so happy when I first arrived, but now she's creeping round like a little mouse.*

HARRIET WASN'T THE ONLY person who was worried about Gemma. The girl had worried herself sick as she scuttled around the house trying to forget what had happened, trying to enjoy the excitement and anticipation that had the residents stirring. It had seemed innocent enough, to start with.

"Go on," Ryan had coaxed. "I want to see you, Gem, and it's too cold to meet down the Rec. I'll bring Kieran. We can say he's your cousin come to see how you are, if anybody wants to know. People always like him."

When he wheedled in that special, sexy voice, she knew, as he did, that there was no way she could resist, but still she felt anxious. Mrs. Turner wouldn't like it, she knew, but the housekeeper was out for the evening and Matron was safely out of the way, entertaining members of the trust who ran the nursing home next door. All Gemma had to do was serve supper-time drinks, and then her time was her own.

She slid back the bolt on the back door, peering out to see two indistinct shapes in the blackness.

"Quick, come in before somebody sees you," she implored, pulling at Ryan's sleeve and prodding Kieran's slow bulk to get him indoors.

"All right, all right." Ryan was in a good mood, boisterous and laughing as he drew her roughly toward him. "Okay, Gem, come here." He kissed her fiercely, hurting her, but she was his, in his power, he could do anything to her and it wouldn't matter. She scarcely noticed that he was propelling her toward the old, disused washhouse, muttering a word to Kieran.

"Stay there and keep watch," he hissed a savage warning, wiping the anticipation off the other boy's bewildered, fat red face. "Make sure we don't get caught!"

Confused by the speed of events, Kieran barely had time to nod before the door slammed in his face. His face puckered; this wasn't part of his plan, how could he see what they were doing, stuck here in the back scullery? Looking round he spotted a gleam of light above the ill-fitting planks of the washhouse door and, feeling very clever, he tiptoed across the flagged scullery floor and picked up a wooden stool. Wicked! He could see everything through a two-inch gap, licking his lips as Gemma protested about the light.

"But I want to check out the goods, Gem, so shut up and get your kit off."

Kieran's eyes were soon bulging as Gemma, with Ryan's increasingly fevered assistance, slipped out of her jumper and then her bra. Kieran was so excited at what he *could* see, and so desperate to see what was out of his line of vision, that he almost got caught out when, surprisingly quickly, it was all over and Ryan scrambled to his feet, zipping up his fly. In a frenzy of anxious haste Kieran tumbled off the stool, shoved it back by the sink and sat on it, reaching for an old newspaper and pretending to read it. Just in time, he managed to give quite a convincing start when the washhouse door opened.

"That's better." Ryan smirked. "You fit then, Kieran? Let's go down the pub. You got any cash, Gem?" He sneered, without comment, at the two-pound coin plus a couple of ones that was all she could offer. "Text me when you get time off." At the back door he turned casually, as though struck by a sudden thought. "You said the old gits have got a concert or something on Friday, didn't you?"

She nodded. "It's on Friday night, there's going to be a sort of comedy brass band, I think. Matron fixed it up, she knows the bandleader or something."

She looked pleased as he pricked up his ears and asked, "Will they all be going to it? Nobody upstairs or ill in bed?"

"Oh yes." She nodded, delighted at his approval. "They're all looking forward to it."

"That's nice," he said, pleasing her even more, glad that she had done something right. "What time does it kick off?"

"The band's booked for half-past seven and there'll be mince pies and sherry and things," she told him. "They're all inviting their families, too. It's more like a hotel, not an ordinary old people's place at all."

He nodded. "Like I said," he repeated, "that's nice." He laughed again but this time his laughter made her uneasy.

After the boys had gone Gemma checked all the doors, straightened up the scullery, then slipped upstairs to her room. On tiptoe along the landing, she jumped out of her skin as a voice spoke softly from a door held ajar.

"Oh dear, what have we here? A naughty, naughty Gemma, I'm afraid." Christiane Marchant smiled sweetly as Gemma's hands flew to her mouth. "I saw you, Gemma," the soft voice cooed, and she smiled at the shocked girl. "You were very careless, you know. Didn't you notice the skylight in the old washhouse roof? I had to go to the bathroom and as I wheeled past the back window I just happened to look down. Dear, oh dear, whatever would Matron say? She's such a religious woman, too, very strict on *proper* behavior, isn't she? I'm sure you wouldn't want to lose your job, would you, dear?"

HARRIET WASN'T DOZING, of course she wasn't, but the drawing room fire was very inviting so she lay back in the comfortable armchair and rested her eyes. A tall figure loomed in front of her.

"Afternoon, Harriet."

"Oh, for heaven's sake! I might have known. How did you track me down, Sam?"

Canon Sam Hathaway grinned down at his cousin, her reaction exactly what he had expected and hoped for, though he wondered for a moment at the fleeting look of relief on her face.

"Doreen Buchan," he explained. "I bumped into her in Marks & Spencer in Winchester and she mentioned she'd seen you. Wanted to know what you could possibly be doing in an old folks' home—and so do I, Harriet, so come clean."

"Oh honestly, Sam," Harriet snapped, her automatic response with Sam, but she was secretly delighted to see him and even more glad that she'd dabbed on a spot of makeup today and that her roots were now impeccable. "This is a terribly upmarket convalescent hotel, the guests might be on the elderly side, but believe me, there's nobody drooling or dribbling here."

She gave him a brief rundown of her health then turned to the much more interesting topic of Doreen Buchan. "You say she spotted me? I'm surprised she was in any condition to notice anything."

"Why? What's wrong with the woman?"

Sam was intrigued, Harriet could tell. She knew the signs and knew, too, that he would treat her ideas with respect—at least until he demolished them with logic. Sixty years of squabbling, closer than brother and sister, best of friends and enemies, closer now more than ever since the death of Avril, Sam's beloved wife, Harriet's dearest friend. Sam was the person she needed to talk to.

"I don't know." She frowned as she stared past him into the garden. "There's a feeling of unease about this place, it's almost tangible and it all stems from one woman." She turned a grave face to her cousin. "There's something very wrong here, Sam, something very wrong indeed."

FIVE

BRUSHING ASIDE SAM'S protest Harriet frowned and tried to explain. "I'm serious, Sam. There are at least three people here, if you count Doreen Buchan, who are terrified of what Christiane Marchant knows about them. I'm sure she has some kind of hold on them, God knows what or how. I'm not kidding, Sam, they cringe when they see her." She frowned again. "What gets me most of all is the pleasure the damned woman displays, she revels in their fear. Oh, she disguises it well, she's an expert actually. I suspect she's had years of practice at being nicey-nasty. She strikes me as a very unpleasant piece of work."

Sam contemplated his old playmate. "You'd better get it off your chest," he said, without further comment, casting a wary look round. "Here, let's go into that little sun parlor, there's nobody in there." Once they were settled, he gestured to her to let it all out.

"Doreen's father-in-law, Fred Buchan," she said, after she'd described Ellen Ransom's reaction to the other woman. "He never speaks to anyone and the story is that he was in a concentration camp during the war. Of course nobody would dream of trying to probe in any case, but Christiane Marchant delights in chipping away at him. I heard her the other day, telling him about her home in Brittany. She said, 'My home village was at the end of a funny little neck of land sticking out into the Atlantic,' and when she said that, Fred Buchan jerked his head up and stared at her, and she went on, 'It was a bleak little place to grow up in, gray stone and Atlantic gales, but even though it was at the back of beyond, it became quite well-known for what happened there.'"

Harriet shrugged. "Fred just got up without a word and stomped out and she sat there gloating. It was horrible. I don't like the man particularly, he goes out of his way to avoid being pleasant, but…"

Sam waited in silence and she sighed. "Then there's Doreen Buchan, she's the proverbial frightened rabbit whenever Mrs. Marchant smiles and greets her, all sickly sweet. And the care assistant, Gemma, she's afraid, too. I've seen her shudder when the Marchant woman speaks to her." She fiddled with the ring on her right hand, her mother's engagement diamond. "The stupid thing is—" she faltered "—it's downright silly but… I almost feel anxious about two or three other people, as well."

"What?" Sam had listened in attentive silence but now he sat up and stared at her. "That's a bit strong, isn't it? You've got four victims already, how many more do you want? And what exactly *are* you talking about? Do you think this woman is blackmailing them?"

She bridled a little then subsided with a slight laugh. "Oh, I know, it sounds crazy, do you think I don't realize that? I've been turning it over and over for the last day or two, since I realized there's a pattern. I just don't know what to—"

"Look." He settled his long frame more comfortably into the wicker chair, taking her seriously, good old Sam, as she had known he would. "To start with, who are these other people you think she might have put the screws on? Let's see what you've got."

Shaken out of herself she reached out and gave his hand a grateful squeeze then, as they both recoiled at such an excess of emotion, she composed herself.

"Well, there's Tim Armstrong, for one." As Sam raised an eyebrow she explained. "You do know him, Sam, he used to be the manager at Lloyds Bank, a lot older, years older, than us. His wife died the day he retired, very tragic it was, a cerebral hemorrhage, I think." He nodded and she went on. "I don't know what she, Christiane Marchant, what she says to him, she's too fly to let me catch her in the act, but I know she whispers away at him and he gets upset." Harriet looked down at her hands. "He's a little… Oh, I don't know, I wouldn't say it was Alzheimer's, or maybe it's just the onset, I don't know enough about dementia, but there are times when he's…a long way away, and she worries him, makes him angry and miserable. But—" she shook her head "—I've no idea what it is that she says to him."

"It couldn't be just that he gets, well, bad patches?" Sam ventured. "Maybe she just jars on him, personality clash kind of thing?"

Harriet's shake of her head was decisive. "No, it's more than that, I definitely sense mischief. And it's not just Tim. I've spotted that she takes a great delight in upsetting her own daughter, Alice. A pleasant sort of girl—woman, I should say—bit of a downtrodden slavey type, but I suspect she's beginning to enjoy her freedom, she's started to look different, more alive, younger. I notice Mother's been skillfully putting the boot in whenever Alice visits, though whether that's par for the course or something over and above the usual I've no way of telling."

She did a mental totting up of the people she believed to be Christiane's victims, coming to the final one with a rueful grin. "The last one sounds even dafter than the others, but I think she's really getting right up Matron's nose." At Sam's snort of disbelief she shrugged and laughed again. "I told you it sounded mad and maybe I'm clutching at straws here, it's just that Matron is one of those rather terrifyingly single-minded souls—you know, she has a vision, tunnel vision in fact, and nothing, and no one, is allowed to interfere with it."

She had his attention now.

"I know exactly what you mean," he spoke eagerly. "That sort can be quite lethal in pursuit of their vision. I had a curate like that once. I remember he decided we needed a crèche during morning service and rock bands in the evening. He went at it like a bull at a gate and offended all the regulars of course. I wasn't too bothered about the crèche idea but nobody had actually asked us to provide one and we already had a Sunday school and children's services, but I was dead against the heavy metal and the rock band, or at least having them in the church. Apart from anything else I was worried the spire might fall! I suggested we should invite them in the summer and hold an outdoor service but there were some pretty heated clashes. If you weren't *for* him, you were *agin* him, kind of thing. At one time I honestly thought he was slightly deranged."

He gave a reminiscent nod, a wicked twinkle in his blue eyes, Harriet noted, that was a large part of the charm that worked on his parishioners and colleagues. "It was all sorted out in the end," he continued. "An Act of God, we all decided. He fell madly in love with the barmaid at the local pub and she told him, in no un-certain terms, that motorbikes and babies were as in-appropriate in a church as a bishop in a brothel. Lord only knows what the attraction was—she was boot-faced but a buxom wench. The general consensus was that he must have been bottle-fed as an infant and was working on overcoming the deprivation."

"Sounds like something from Trollope." Harriet sniffed sarcastically as Sam gave a lewd chuckle. "How-ever, I do wonder just how far she'd go—Matron, I mean—to protect this place. Sometimes she comes across as almost unhinged about it, so the moot point is whether her passionate regard for her treasured creation would be strong enough to contemplate actual bodily harm to something, or someone, who offered a threat."

Jolted out of his amusement Sam Hathaway gave his cousin a stern look. "Oh, come on, Harriet, stop being such a drama queen. I appreciate you're worried and it certainly looks as though there are some unpleasant undercurrents, but actual bodily harm?" He rose to his feet, gathering up his long limbs and his long black overcoat, then a bulge in one of the pockets attracted his attention. With an exclamation of pleasure he drew out a slightly battered book with a gilt and pictorial cover, showing a vapid Edwardian teenager applying a lace-edged handkerchief to her brimming eye.

"Here, something to take your overheated mind off playing at Miss Marple. I spotted this in the Oxfam bookshop yesterday. Have you already got it?"

"Oh, you're a sweetheart, Sam, let me see?" She

flicked through the pages and beamed at him. "Nope, I've never seen it before, *Madcap Mabel and the May-pole,* and I've never even heard of Zamora Pridhoe. What a find. I wonder why she's crying—if she's a madcap, I mean?" She examined the distraught dam-sel's dainty lace hanky. "Madcaps are usually cheer-ful. I expect she's been falsely accused of something, that's usually the problem."

Sam smiled as she riffled eagerly through the gilt-edged pages. Harriet's collection of school stories and his own model railway layout were nonnegotiable areas, not to be laughed at and they both stuck scrupu-lously to the rules. He prepared to take his leave then looked down at her again.

"I hear there's a party here tomorrow night? Neil and his Oompah Band mates, isn't it? I thought it sounded rather fun."

Their eyes met and she pouted. "Oh all right, no need to look so hopeful, of course you can come. We're allowed guests anyway and I know you'll do anything for a free sherry, especially with a mince pie or two thrown in."

He grinned and waved goodbye, taking careful note of the woman in the wheelchair as he made his way through the drawing room to the entrance hall. As he said goodbye to Matron, Sam noticed, out of the corner of his eye, the woman propel herself over to an elderly bald man sitting alone. She said something, only a word or two, and the man lifted his head and stared at her, the bleakness in his gaze sending a chill through Sam.

ELLEN RANSOM WAS IN HER room, her face gray against the pale gold pattern of the Laura Ashley wallpaper, cold despair emanating from her hunched body in spite of the cozy warmth in the square, sunny room with its generous Edwardian proportions and large efficient radiator.

Carol had looked concerned during yesterday's visit. "Are you sure you're all right, Mum?" she had kept asking. "You seem to have lost some of your pep. You're surely not pining for us, are you?"

Ellen couldn't blame her for asking. *I've never been the doting kind of mother,* she thought, in a rare moment of self-knowledge, *too busy poking my nose into other people's business and out earning a crust, until Douglas... Until Douglas had won all that money on the football pools then gone and died a couple of months later. Typical.* She made a face, pushing aside the memory of meek, careworn Douglas and his hangdog face whenever he glanced at her.

Still, the money was a kind of compensation for everything she'd missed out on, all the good times she had never known. Pity it had to come so late. And a pity that woman had turned up here. *Nobody else ever found out about* that *and I'm not letting anyone spoil things now,* she vowed.

WHILE HIS MOTHER TOILED away at her ironing downstairs, Ryan relaxed in the bath, planning. This concert at the old folks' place was a gift: loud music, everyone downstairs, deserted bedrooms with unattended jewelry and money. Perfect.

Kieran had turned chicken, though. Kieran liked old people, starting with his own granny and including everyone else's grannies, it seemed sometimes. He'd even told Ryan off, after that quickie with Gemma the other night. "You didn't ought to treat her like that," he'd complained, and he was angry and suspicious about Ryan's plans for the residents of Firstone Grange.

But Kieran was just fat and stupid. *I can handle him.* Ryan frowned. It was the text he'd received from Gemma, followed by a frantic, hysterical call that was giving him grief now. Some old bag had seen them the other night and was threatening to tell the matron. He really wanted Gemma to keep that job and now, as he soaked in the cooling water, inspiration struck. Instead of the one-off big job he had planned, it would be more fun and probably more profitable in the long run to nick odds and ends, a bit at a time, starting during the concert when he could do a recce upstairs. A few quid here, a ring there, enough to keep him ticking over but not enough to ring alarm bells. If he did it really carefully, cat and mouse, take something then put it back a few days later, the old gits would keep quiet. Which of them would want to risk looking stupid? Going mad?

And why not...? He sat up, pleased with himself. Why not offer to do a few odd jobs round the place, for free maybe? He could spin a sob story about his old gran and be like Kieran. His good deed for the day; that was it, that's what he'd tell them. That way he'd have the run of the place.

As he dried himself he suddenly remembered the old woman who had threatened Gemma. In a wheelchair, Gem had told him, so it wasn't the one who had been looking out of the window of the sun parlor yesterday afternoon. She'd spotted him skulking, talking to Gemma at the kitchen door. Remembering her suddenly alert, cool stare as she had eyed him up and down, he felt uncomfortable, but she could walk all right, and anyway, Gem said she was all right, that one. But the one in the wheelchair, she was the one Gem was afraid of. He chewed at his thumbnail. If she was going to cause trouble he might have to—*do* something about her. His face darkened.

BACK AT FIRSTONE GRANGE Christiane Marchant sat in the sun parlor and narrowly scrutinized her daughter. Yes, she definitely looked better, the risk of a breakdown pushed into the background. It had been worth giving in for once and letting Alice think she was making the decisions. But… She frowned slightly. Was that all it was? An improvement in her mental and physical health? She had noticed the smartening up of Alice's wardrobe but accepted without question the explanation that they were charity shop bargains. Alice didn't know how to tell lies.

"It's nice here, isn't it, Mother?" Alice moved over to the window, perhaps to escape the gimlet scrutiny. "Like a hotel, not with chairs all round the walls like an old people's home." She gestured to the printed paper on the polished mahogany coffee table. "This newsletter is good, too, with all these interesting activities. Have you been to any of the talks, or…or tried the aromatherapy?"

Her voice tailed away as Christiane shot her a darkling look. "It's all right here, but I think I'll—" Whatever she had meant to say remained unsaid as Doreen Buchan thrust her head into the room, spotted Christiane and withdrew, gray-faced.

"Well, well." Christiane wore her gloating smile. "I'll have a rest now, Alice. You might as well go home." As Alice picked up her bag and coat, Christiane fired her farewell salvo. "Make sure you turn up good and early for this concert tomorrow. I want to talk to you. About something important."

She brushed aside Alice's startled query and reluctant parting kiss, then, instead of making for the lift and her own room, she headed straight for the drawing room in pursuit of Doreen Buchan.

Doreen was a sitting duck, her chair a little to the side as Vic chatted at his silent father.

"Hullo, dear," came the breezy greeting. "Nice to see you. My word, you get more and more like your auntie every day. What a coincidence, us meeting here like this after all those years. Let's see now, your auntie, was she your dad's sister, or your mum's?"

Not waiting for an answer, and not getting one, from the woman who cowered beside her, Christiane carried on, pulling the wings off the fly. "Are you like your mum, I wonder? They say heredity is a strange thing, of course, and it's amazing what can be passed down through the generations, but it takes a brave man, I always say, to marry into some families."

An inarticulate sound was Doreen's only response, her features frozen in horror, so Christiane turned her attention to Fred Buchan, nodding cheerfully to Vic as she drew her chair nearer.

"How are you, Mr. Buchan? I see your father's in one of his moods today. Still I suppose it can be hard to cope in another language, I know that for a fact. I was lucky, of course, I've got a good ear and some people have told me they'd never have known I wasn't English. Funny that." She gave Vic a genial smile and indicated his father. "Funny how some people are like me and have no trouble at all learning English and others can be like your dad and still sound really foreign after years and years."

Vic agreed politely and she went on, turning the screw. "Well, we've all had our moments, too, I daresay, I know I have. I bet your dad could tell us a tale or two about what he got up to in the war, eh? And some of the others here, too, no doubt."

With that she nodded gaily and wheeled herself off, leaving a puzzled Vic, flanked by a frozen father and a wife sagging limply in her chair, her face drained of all color.

ALICE HURRIED HOME FROM the shopping precinct and flung herself into her latest bargain, a silk dress of dull cardinal-red silk, an extravagant £14.99 from the Friends of the Hospice shop, and brushed her long shining black hair. Up? Surely not down, no—*I'd look like a superannuated teenager,* she decided, *but I'm not screwing it back in that tight bun.* Finally she managed to pin it up into a more or less secure French pleat, then, with a dab of eye shadow, a quick dusting of blusher on her sallow cheeks, a trace of lipstick, and she was ready.

The woman in her mirror was a stranger. "Goodness," she exclaimed. The stranger was, if not a beautiful woman, certainly an attractive one. When had that happened? It wasn't just the makeup, it wasn't just the dress, in spite of its designer label; this new confident woman had been trying to crawl out from under her stone for several days.

Ever since I walked into the office that day and found Neil there. She shuddered. *Ever since Mother went to Firstone Grange.* And now Neil had asked her out to dinner.

The wheezing chime of the front doorbell was a welcome interruption to her thoughts; she raced down the hall, slowing her headlong rush as she reached the lobby with its encaustic floor tiles.

"Hi." Neil was his usual friendly self but there was a new, surprised glow of admiration in his eyes. "Ready?"

As she went back to the kitchen to pick up her bag Neil took a look round. He was eyeing up the carved and antlered hat stand when she returned.

"That was my grandfather's pride and joy," she told him, turning up her nose. "It's the worst dust trap in the house and that's saying something."

"I think your valuation was pretty much spot-on," he remarked as he handed her into his car. "I wouldn't have said anything very different. Will you sell, do you think?"

He maneuvred the car down the overgrown drive and through the crumbling brick gateposts, then once they were out and driving up past the old flour mill and through the village, he repeated the question.

"I don't know." She turned her anxious brown eyes on him and confessed. "I don't know what possessed me to do it, Neil. Mother will kill me when she finds out. I've told the auctioneer's agent to collect most of the furniture on Monday and I've done all the paper-work to put the house on the market then, too."

Her hands twisted nervously in her lap as she fell silent, retreating into the anxiety that was now constant. Who owned the house? Had Alice any right to sell it? Had her father left it outright to Christiane or to both of them? She bit her lip. *She'll kill me,* she faltered silently as she stared out into the rain.

THE GUESTS AT FIRSTONE Grange had all gone to bed and Gemma was on the late shift. It wasn't difficult; all she had to do was check on each of them to see if they were settled comfortably for the night.

"Don't forget to knock first," Matron urged when they met on the stairs. "You must always respect their privacy, you know, you wouldn't just walk into a hotel room and these aren't senile patients, they're highly intelligent, professional people. Remember not to treat them like children, Gemma."

She smiled as the girl carried on upstairs. It really was working out well, her dream, her vision. Careful selection had made sure that she had a good mix of guests and the odd misfit only made her determined to be a good deal more choosy in future. There were one or two mistakes. She wasn't a snob; money was necessary, of course, Firstone Grange was expensive. She decided, though, that the main requirement was to maintain the harmony she worked so hard to create. She frowned at the thought of Ellen Ransom. Plenty of money there, but Mrs. Ransom was definitely not con- tributing to the harmony of the house and to top it all, she had a sour, spiteful disposition, as well.

And the other one, Mrs. Marchant, pity I can't expel her. Matron gave a small, down-turned smile. *But she's paid up in full for the month and to tell the truth I don't think I could do that to her poor daughter. Especially now, not when she's looking so happy, so alive.* Matron straightened a holly wreath and tweaked a gold-sprayed teasel firmly into place. *I'll not let any-*

thing interfere, though, she vowed, *specially the likes of Christiane Marchant.*

Most of the guests were already in bed and happy to call out in answer to Gemma's knock, but Harriet Quigley beckoned her inside.

"I'm fine, dear," she answered Gemma's look of concern. "It's just that I thought you looked a bit worried earlier on and I wondered if there was anything I could do?" Harriet's shrewd blue eyes noted the slight withdrawal, the anxious frown, the twisting fingers, and she continued. "I'm a very good listener, Gemma, if you ever want to talk about anything."

Well, what did you expect, you silly old fool, she told herself, closing the door behind Gemma, who mumbled something and fled. *I'll be glad to see Sam tomorrow,* she decided, *I don't think there's anything we can do but it'll be good to talk through some of these insane fantasies of mine.*

Gemma hesitated at the end door, tempted to go straight past, but her conscience smote her and she knocked, ready to hare downstairs as soon as she had done her duty. The door opened immediately; Christiane Marchant must have been poised at the ready.

"Well," she smirked. "If it isn't the sex siren of Firstone Grange. Expecting visitors again tonight, Gemma? I do hope Matron doesn't find out, it would be an awful pity to lose your job, wouldn't it?"

NEIL DROVE CAUTIOUSLY along the overgrown drive and pulled to a halt.

"Would…would you like a coffee?" Alice stuttered with nervous tension. Apart from a couple of innocuous teenage forays, she had never been out with a man. Would he think she was pushy?

"That'd be great, thanks." Neil was jittery, too. It had been so long since he'd taken a woman out, other than his ex-wife, and that had been years ago. He'd lost the knack and was terrified of scaring Alice away, afraid she'd think he was bent on seduction. Newspaper stories of dates gone wrong made his tongue cleave to the roof of his mouth.

The evening had so far been a great success. Over a pleasant meal in the Christmassy pub restaurant the conversation had swooped in grasshopper leaps from likes and dislikes to schools and childhood to plans for the business. Both were glad to discover similar interests and shyly delighted to find that a clash of opinions just added to the spice. They had fallen silent as they neared the dilapidated old house and Alice seized on the opportunity to make coffee, leaving Neil to warm up in the drawing room, where she had banked up the fire before going out.

The best Crown Derby cups, Mother, she thought defiantly as she carried in a tray. *And see if I care.*

Prim and petrified, they sat on opposite sofas, bought new from Maples in 1923, the big shadowy room lit only by the fire and a lamp on the piano. She wondered about music, should she play some? On what, though, Daddy's big old radiogram? Christiane's television in her bedroom? Definitely not. Grandpa's steam radio, circa 1935, that didn't work anymore because she didn't know if you could still get spare valves? *I suppose I could play the piano?* She began to rock very gently, wringing her hands in an agony of bashful suspense.

The companionable pleasant feeling of the evening seemed to have disappeared. *What did I do,* she agonized, *was it asking him in for coffee? Don't people do that?* Her coffee threatened to choke her but she fought the urge to cry and tried to make polite conversation. As she dared to look across at him, wondering when he would make his escape, Neil put his cup down.

"Oh God, Alice, this is awful," he said, coming to stand in front of her. "I never meant this to happen."

She gulped and struggled for some kind of dignity. "It—it's all right, Neil, I don't mind. You'd—you'd better go."

"Don't be silly," he said, sitting down beside her. "I don't *want* to go, that's just the trouble."

He took her in his arms, stifling her squeak of surprise with a kiss that started lightly and somewhere along the line turned to desperation. Carried away on a tide of sensation Alice gave herself up to the feeling completely, her lips, and his, frantic with desperation born of years of unfulfilled longing. She gasped with dismay as Neil broke away, panting, "Christ, Alice, I'm sorry. I shouldn't be doing this. What must you think of me?"

They were on the hearthrug now, firelight gleaming on her bare shoulder, her hair a descending tangle of curls. "Don't…" she whimpered. "Don't stop, please, please."

He gasped and turned her face toward him, her eyes glistening with unshed tears. "I think I'm in love with you, Alice," he whispered.

As he pulled her close and she melted into his arms, she had a last coherent thought: nothing must spoil this, not now, not *her,* not ever.

SIX

Harriet Quigley ate her dinner on Friday with an air of attentive interest that completely deceived the guest beside her as he droned happily in her ear. She knew that Pauline Winslow had done some thorough research into convalescent and residential homes and that was why everyone was moved round on a daily basis to encourage socializing. No cliques or cabals for Matron. Mostly, Harriet thought, it worked very well, the shy guests were saved the ordeal of having to introduce themselves; the neat place cards saw to that. This meant that the bores were shared out among the whole company so that nobody suffered unfairly. Today it was Harriet's turn to endure, but only for one day.

"Ladies and gentlemen." Matron was up on her feet. "As you know, the Oompah Band will be entertaining us tonight. I believe it's a mixed program, some Christmas carols and some other old favorites."

She looked puzzled as she caught Harriet's eye. Miss Winslow had obviously spotted that Harriet was concealing a smile at the memory of the recent Oompah offering in her own village, in aid of the organ fund. It was certainly likely to prove a "mixed" concert.

"There'll be wine and beer available from Mrs. Turner, by the door to the kitchen." She acknowledged the ragged cheer that greeted this statement, looking round to make sure nobody was offended. "I'm sure we'll all have a wonderful evening."

There was a mild ripple of applause and she continued. "As I explained the other day, the Oompah Band do a lot of charity work and they assure me that any contributions will be extremely welcome, so we'll be passing a plate round. I do hope no one will take offense at their banter—I'm told they can be quite saucy, but it's all in good fun."

Hmm. Harriet pursed her lips and resolved on a quiet word with Neil. *I can't see Ellen Ransom rising to the occasion if she found herself on the end of a stream of cheerful abuse. No, and not Christiane Marchant, either, she has to be the one doing the abusing.*

She gathered up her book and handbag, ready to go upstairs and titivate, pausing for a word with Mrs. Turner, who was busily decorating her makeshift bar with its stacked bottles and glasses.

"It's going to be fun, isn't it?" Mrs Turner gave her a friendly nod, snipping off lengths of black thread as she tied up an errant strand of tinsel. "Oops, there goes another one. I couldn't find any gold thread but black ought not to show up."

Harriet admired the cheerful display and gestured to the bar, which in everyday life was a side table in the drawing room, used to display Miss Winslow's artistic flower arrangements. "I imagine there'll be some kind of limit on consumption," she inquired, raising an eyebrow, and they both grinned, studiously not staring at Firstone Grange's most glamorous guest, who was teetering past them on three-inch heels, her eyes slightly glazed.

"Where on earth does she hide it? Still, she's always discreet about it," Mrs. Turner whispered. "Oh yes, there won't be any hangovers tomorrow, it's just to add to the sense of occasion, a bit of fun. We checked beforehand that nobody had any strong teetotal views, of course. Matron's very good about that."

Harriet nodded. Matron was very good about everything. Single-minded, as Harriet had told Sam, but good luck to her anyway. Her dream of a specialist home-from-home for the elderly was obviously fulfilling a long-felt want in the neighborhood, to judge by the rapidly lengthening waiting list. So, apparently, was the nursing home next door while the list for the sheltered flats was fully subscribed. *But not for me.* Harriet shook her head. *Not yet awhile.*

Christiane Marchant's door was slightly ajar so Harriet, feeling ridiculous, started to tiptoe past, desperate not to be trapped. *She doesn't like me, though.* Harriet grinned. *I think she's given up on me—I don't give any secrets away.* At that moment Gemma hurtled blindly out of the room, tears pouring down her cheeks, great sobs racking her slight body. Harriet, shoved to one side, clutched at a side table to catch her breath, but the girl was gone, taking the stairs two at a time. At the same time Christiane's door closed quietly but firmly.

Now what? Heaving a heavy sigh Harriet made her way along the landing and shut her door behind her.

Locked in the staff bathroom Gemma sat on the edge of the bath. *How was I to know that my aunt couldn't keep her mouth shut? Mum should never have told her about me.*

"Dear me, Gemma," the hated voice had purred just now, when she was checking on the radiator thermostat. "You've been an even naughtier girl than I realized, haven't you?"

No sound had emerged from Gemma's dry mouth.

"I've been talking to one of the cleaners here, dear. It turns out she's good friends with your aunty and it seems they've had a nice, long chat about you. I hear you're just getting over a little bit of trouble." The woman in the wheelchair smiled sweetly. "The usual sort of 'trouble.' I do hope you're making sure it won't happen again, Gemma, considering what I saw the other night!"

"I—I must—got to go." Gemma had turned blindly toward the door but the wheelchair blocked her way.

"Of course," agreed Mrs. Marchant. "But I really wonder if I ought to tell Matron about it. She's such a religious woman I'm sure she has strong views on abortion, and probably fornication, too. *Extremely* strong views, I shouldn't wonder. Perhaps it's my duty to tell her?"

In the bathroom Gemma's nails dug viciously into her clenched hands.

"I could *kill* her," she moaned aloud.

PAULINE WINSLOW SMILED benignly at her guests as she offered sherry on a silver tray. Mostly dry sherry, too, she noted with a glow of pride; the guests at Firstone Grange were a classy lot, not many requests for dark sweet syrup. Disguising the distaste that Christiane Marchant always aroused in her, she bent to offer the tray.

"Sherry, Mrs. Marchant?"

One of her iron-clad rules was that guests were to be addressed politely and formally. Woe betide any well-meaning employee who bandied around a given name in a disrespectful manner.

"Why, thank you." Christiane smiled graciously then lowered her voice, forcing the other woman into an unwelcome intimacy. "I think I should tell you, Matron, that I'm rather worried about your fire precautions here."

"Eh?" Pauline Winslow let out a squawk, hastily muffled. "I don't understand, Mrs. Marchant?"

"I've been reading up on Fire Regulations." Christiane looked delighted at the effect of her remark. "You've got a copy in the bookcase in the drawing room." She smirked and wagged a finger at the matron. "I'm afraid your fire extinguishers are out-of-date, I couldn't help noticing. If you check the tag on the extinguisher you'll see the next service is ten days overdue." She gave a malicious, tinkling titter. "You're operating illegally, you know, so you'd better get them sorted out."

Miss Winslow had herself in hand now. "I can assure you, Mrs. Marchant," she said stiffly. "I had Firstone Grange stringently vetted by the Fire Brigade before we opened and there is no need for alarm."

In fact Matron had quite forgotten that she was behind with the servicing. There had been so much to do, so many expenses, that it had quite slipped her mind, but now she bit her lip. Of all people, why did it have to be Mrs. Marchant who spotted the discrepancy? A complaint from a "concerned" resident was the last thing she needed just now. The other woman was speaking again.

"I thought you had to have asbestos doors, too, in an

institution like this," she said, her eyes sparkling. "I'm sure those big mahogany doors are a fire hazard."

"As it happens you're quite out-of-date, Mrs. Marchant. I can assure you that asbestos is no longer used on doors." She turned on her heel. "And this is not an institution, Mrs Marchant," she snapped, striding away. *That woman is a menace. I wish something would happen to make her go away. But I won't let her spoil things for me, not now.*

"DEAR ME." CHRISTIANE put on her plaintive face. The evening promised more entertainment than was on the official program, she thought with relish. What next? Aha, her eyes lighted on Fred Buchan, hunched in his chair, a dejected tortoise.

"Good evening, Mr Buchan," she cried brightly, drawing her chair up beside him. "How are you today?"

Not waiting for, and not getting, any reply, she waved a copy of the *Daily Telegraph* under his nose, her bright eyes watchful, gauging his temper. "Did you read the books page yesterday? I saved it specially for you. There's a very good review of a book about the Israeli squad dedicated to rooting out old war criminals? I've marked it here, I'm sure you'd find it interesting."

His hooded eyes flicked open but she met his hostile glare with a broadening smile.

"I wonder if there are any of them left. I don't suppose the Israelis would be too gentle with them, do you? An eye for an eye, and all that?"

Fred Buchan hauled himself out of his easy chair, staggering as he found his feet. As he stalked from the room he shot a glance back at her. "You are an evil bitch," he grated, his accent harsher, more pronounced, than usual.

As Christiane wheeled herself complacently out into the hall to watch the preparations, Harriet, who had watched this exchange with distaste, strolled over and casually picked up the discarded newspaper with its headline helpfully ringed by Christiane Marchant: *Retribution Squad Investigates War Criminals*. She pursed her lips as she scanned the piece about persistent rumors of old Nazis living in Britain under aliases and she pictured Fred Buchan with his strongly accented speech and his grim refusal to discuss his history. With a thoughtful frown she deftly ripped out the article and stowed it in her handbag just as a crowd of visitors arrived.

"You're looking a lot more human." Sam Hathaway hugged his cousin and piloted her toward the bar. "Less like something the cat dragged in. Here, have a drink and tell me all about—" He broke off hastily as she glared at him, seeing Mrs. Turner smiling at them both. "Tell me about the book I gave you," he changed tack smoothly. "Why was Madcap Mabel in tears?"

"It was as I thought," Harriet backed him up. "She'd been unjustly accused, not to mention getting involved with ghosts." He raised an eyebrow and she explained. "Poor but noble owner of a stately home has opened it as a girls' school to make ends meet, but the wimpy wenches are scared of the headless Elizabethan lady who wails around the Great Hall. Mabel eventually banishes her, would you believe, by having a maypole dance indoors and then it turns out she's the noble owner's long-lost heiress. Not a dry eye in the house at the end. It was great, a real find. Thank you, Sam."

"Look at them all," Mrs. Turner murmured. "The families are delighted because they'll have a granny-free Christmas and the grannies are delighted not to have Christmas ruined by shrieking grandchildren and noisy toys. It's so much easier to love your relatives in small doses and with a clear conscience!"

"Quickly, Harriet." Sam spoke quietly but urgently as he steered his cousin into a convenient nook by the stairs. "What's the matter with you? No," he said, as she began to protest. "Don't give me that. You do look a lot better, it's true, but I also know when you're upset. What's happened?"

"It was that *bloody* woman," she hissed. "And don't you look at me like that, Sam Hathaway. She makes me so mad I *have* to swear! She cornered me just after dinner and came out with the old 'concerned friend' routine at me. 'Wasn't it Lakelands Manor School, Miss Quigley? It was all over the local papers and on the television, too. The one where you were head teacher? Oh dear, oh dear, but surely that was the school there was all that dreadful scandal about?' And out it all came, tumbling out in a cascade. She was so keen to tell me that she knew all about the whole wretched mess that she was actually tripping over her words. I tried to stop her but she went on and on. All about the deputy head—'Oh dear, such a terrible thing to happen, interfering with children like that.…' And then the killer punchline—'But of course you must have known all about it, Miss Quigley, after all, you were the head teacher. It was your responsibility to look after the children in your care.' I tell you, Sam, I could have hit the woman."

Looking slightly alarmed at all this vehemence,

Sam gave her a quick, affectionate hug. "For heaven's sake, Hat, the whole sorry affair was investigated thoroughly and you were completely exonerated, never in the frame, in fact. For a start, the offenses had occurred six months before you were appointed and everyone knew it. After all, that's why you were offered the job—damage limitation and to restore confidence—and you did a marvelous job. Ignore the woman, she's not worth getting so worked up about."

Still thrumming with anger Harriet subsided gradually, giving his hand a grateful squeeze. "Oh, I know," she agreed, blowing her nose discreetly. "But…honestly, Sam, that woman is poison, sheer poison."

FED UP WITH CRANING HER neck to look for Alice, Christiane looked for other sport, gleefully making for Doreen and Vic Buchan.

"Evening, dear," she greeted Doreen with a fond smile, receiving only a gasp in reply, as Christiane parked expertly alongside her. Vic nodded politely and offered to fetch them all a glass of wine.

Christiane patted her victim's hand. "This is cozy, isn't it, dear? I was just talking to Matron, saying how cozy it is and she agreed. 'It's not an institution,' she told me."

There was no answer. Doreen had withdrawn into herself, clutching at her handbag.

"Of course, dear, you'd know all about what an institution looks like, wouldn't you? What does your husband think about it all? Didn't he mind?" Her eyes gleamed as the frightened rabbit twitched. "Don't mind me, dear, I mean no harm, you know. It's just that somehow, people have always told me their little secrets and I do have an excellent memory. You'd be surprised how easy it is to make connections sometimes." She paused, then smiled. "You *did* tell your husband all about it, didn't you, dear? When you got married?" Her concerned expression would have been an Oscar contender. "I mean about your mother and what she did. Where she went?"

It was immensely satisfying to hear Doreen Buchan groan, to see her writhe, to have her turn tortured eyes on her tormentor.

"Leave me alone," she gritted, fumbling at the arm of her chair. "Leave me alone, I *hate* you. I could *kill* you."

She stumbled into the darkened dining room just as Vic appeared, carefully toting three brimming glasses.

"Where's Dor then?" He looked mildly surprised.

"She's just gone for a breath of air," Christiane reassured him as she accepted her drink. "It's getting a bit close in here."

Lurking by the kitchen door and hoping to waylay Neil, her insider in the band, to warn him to pick his victims carefully, Harriet was surprised when, alerted by a slight movement in the scullery, she spotted Gemma fiddling with the outer door, looking flushed and guilty. Just then the seven members of the Oompah Band appeared and Neil, nattily clad in lederhosen, embroidered shirt, wide braces and dapper feathered hat, paused for a quick word.

"Don't worry, Old Hat," he reassured her, grinning as she frowned at his use of Sam's nickname for her. "Alice warned me already. I know who can take it and which ones to avoid." Appeased, she let him shoo her back to the audience as the band struck up an Oompah rhythm and marched into the hall, round the room and up the stairs to the minstrels' gallery. As they took their places, the door to the outer lobby opened a crack and Alice Marchant slipped in, tiptoeing shyly to the empty chair beside her mother.

"You!" shrieked the bandleader, pointing an accusing finger. "Vot do you sink you are doink? Vy are you being so late?"

Startled, Alice lifted a blushing face toward the band and caught Neil's eye. At his reassuring wink she smiled and sat down, hoping the bandleader would move on to other prey.

"Ve vill not vait for you again," he threatened her, however. "I sink you shall pay for zis, by giving me a big, sloppy kiss und gettink me a drink in ze interval, *mein fraulein!*"

Alice smiled and nodded, thankful to get off lightly but amused nonetheless, and the band played on, interspersing their pieces with a nonstop series of gags, sketches and slapstick, neatly treading the thin line between comedy and abuse, offending nobody and sending them off into fits of laughter.

Outwardly docile, sitting demurely beside her mother, Alice was enveloped in a glow of remembered bliss. *Nothing can touch me now,* she thought, *nothing can hurt me, not after last night.* It had come as such a surprise. She had known Neil liked her as a colleague and, lately, as a friend, and she had helplessly recognized that her own feeling for him came close to idolatry as the one person in the world who had seen her as a real, adult woman, not a drudge, not just an invisible, dowdy spinster.

That he could have fallen in love with her had simply not entered her head and his awkward declaration had taken her unaware. There had been no time to consider, no room for shyness, carried away as they had both been on that tide of passion, though he had been very gentle, in spite of his urgency, and so her virginity had finally been lost with very little discomfort. Before he reluctantly left her they had made love again and Alice had discovered at last what all the fuss was about; and now she sat in the festive hall at Firstone Grange trying to disguise the adoration she felt for him.

Christiane shifted uneasily beside her daughter, this new, serene Alice, glowing with confidence and happiness. *What's happened to her?* She frowned. *If it was anyone else I'd say there was a man involved, but Alice?* As the band reached the end of their last number before the interval, Christiane remembered a notion that had occurred to her the previous evening, a way to depress any pretension to independence that Alice might be harboring. *I'll put a spoke in her wheel,* she decided, *I'm not having her get any ideas, she's looking far too pleased with herself.*

"You can order a taxi for eleven tomorrow morning." She nudged Alice to make sure her daughter was listening. "I'm not really that struck on this place, the matron thinks a lot of herself, so I'm going home."

She leaned back in her wheelchair waiting for a reaction and was not surprised to see the color drain out of Alice's cheeks.

"No!" The involuntary protest was explosive and Alice was as surprised as her mother at the force of her speech. "No, we've paid in advance and it's too much money to waste. I'm sorry, Mother, but you'll be staying here over Christmas as we arranged. Besides, I've been working nearly full-time lately. We're very busy, rushed off our feet, so I wouldn't be able to look after you properly."

"Don't you dare tell me I can't go back to my own house, madam." Christiane spat out the words during an outbreak of chatter and bustle at the beginning of the interval. "If you won't call me a taxi I'll ring for one myself."

She wheeled herself away, her forehead creased with angry lines, cursing Alice for that surprising show of strength. In fact she was perfectly comfortable at Firstone Grange and had no intention of passing up such a delicious fount of opportunities to meddle and to annoy. *I'll make her pay,* she vowed, *and I'm certainly not letting her off the hook. Just let her sweat it out till tomorrow morning, waiting to see if I carry out my threat.*

Feeling refreshed, she spotted Ellen Ransom sitting beside Tim Armstrong. *Just what I need,* she thought, *two for the price of one.*

Stranded in her chair Alice slumped, trembling with rage and a burning anguish. For a few blissful hours she had almost forgotten about her mother, had spent the day at work exchanging delicious secret smiles with Neil and, when the office was empty, exchanging even more delicious secret kisses. She had felt strong and invincible, able to cope with her mother, able to cope with anything life chose to throw at her. And now— *Oh God,* she prayed, *give me strength. Make her die.*

GEMMA WAS AS ANXIOUS AS Alice. Obedient to Ryan's prompting she had left the back door unlocked while he and Kieran went off to the pub, because he said he would look in later on, "to listen to the band, no harm in that, is there?" What was he up to? Gemma knew his sudden interest in the residents at Firstone Grange had nothing to do with a feeling of festive goodwill. She sighed and hoped Kieran might be able to restrain Ryan, knowing that Kieran, like Gemma herself, was nothing more than his faithful dog.

She straightened up and bustled round the hall collecting empty glasses and neatly avoiding the colonel, who was becoming heavily gallant after a couple of glasses of Merlot. He was exhibiting a distressing tendency to want to pat her bottom, not that she minded really, it made him feel young and handsome, and didn't bother her. As she bent to pick up a glass she felt someone's eyes on her and looked up to meet Christiane Marchant's gaze. The French woman smiled at her and, looking round, spotted the matron, nodded significantly at Gemma and wheeled herself over toward Pauline Winslow.

Gemma gripped the back of a convenient chair, her legs suddenly cotton wool. *I hate her,* she wailed inwardly. *I hate her.*

To Christiane Marchant's satisfaction she spotted that Tim Armstrong and Ellen Ransom were both watching her approach with apprehension written clearly on their faces. Hemmed in as they were by a throng of residents and guests beside the makeshift bar, there was no escape for either of them.

"Very festive, isn't it?" came the merry greeting as Christine rolled up in front of them. "I like those old songs, don't you, Ellen? Reminds me of the time, just at the end of the war, when I came over here—those were the days and no mistake. I had a lovely time. I was something a bit different, you see," she explained to

Tim, who looked both fascinated and terrified. "What with being French and pretty. I was smart and, clever with it, soon had all the fellows round me."

She looked at Ellen with a conspiratorial air. "Good gracious, but we all had a time of it, didn't we, dear? My word, if some of the men who were still in the Far East could have known what their wives were up to! Sometimes you heard of girls who'd got themselves in a fix taking desperate steps to get themselves out of trouble, none of this abortion on tap like there is nowadays, eh? No, you had to take matters into your own hands if you were desperate then."

Ellen lost color and Christiane, satisfied with her efforts, turned her sights on Tim, changing tack. "Of course, lots of people get desperate, don't they, Mr. Armstrong? Not just in wartime, either. Sometimes they have to move house to avoid the shame of what they've done, or the shame of what some member of their family might have done. Still, however carefully you cover your tracks, there's always somebody who finds out about these things, isn't there, Mr. Armstrong? Such a shame."

"I do beg your pardon." A pleasant voice broke in abruptly and a tall man with silver hair loomed over the trio. "I'm Sam Hathaway, Mr. Armstrong, Harriet Quigley's cousin. I think we've met once or twice on committees and so forth?"

"Excuse me." Matron had materialized and spoke at the same moment but she smiled and nodded to Sam to continue. He shook his head and she went on. "Oh, thank you, Canon Hathaway. I'm so sorry, but I shall have to ask you to move, Mrs. Marchant. I'm afraid your wheelchair marks the parquet so I've put down a special mat for you. I do apologize but the floor in the hall here is rather special, so we are obliged to preserve it."

She took a firm hold of Christiane Marchant's chair and wheeled her away to a spot in the corner just in front of the minstrels' gallery and well away from the rest of the seating. "There we are," she said heartily, parking the seething woman on the small rug. "That's much better. I'm afraid you won't get much of a view of the band from here, not that you can see much in this dim light, but at least you're right next to the table with the mince pies. Help yourself if you feel peckish, won't you."

Sam silently applauded Pauline Winslow's masterly strategy, having watched her become aware that Ellen and Tim were under attack from their tormentor. Giving her a mental three cheers, he stooped to give Tim a hand and went on, without waiting for a reply. "Come and join Harriet and me, she's put her coat on a table over there to save it, and gone off to grab us a drink."

Under cover of his gentle flow of talk Sam hoisted the older man out of his seat and hauled him off to join Harriet. He shot Ellen Ransom a speculative glance, wondering what the brief exchange he had overheard could possibly mean. Not really an exchange, if it comes to that, he decided with a wry smile, considering neither Tim nor Ellen had uttered, but the threat in Christiane Marchant's words had been unmistakable, as had the hatred in Ellen's face.

"That woman deserves to die," said Tim, suddenly quite lucid.

SEVEN

"PLACES, EVERYONE, PLEASE," called Matron fifteen minutes later as she fussed over her flock, urging them back to their seats and away from the bar. She cast a rapid look round, counting heads. Yes, Mrs. Marchant was still there, where she'd been parked, thank goodness. Certainly, she had a sullen expression but she was stationary, taking advantage of the permission granted her, and munching her way through some of the remaining mince pies on the long table that separated her from the rest of the audience.

Matron hurried up the gallery stairs to chivy the guests who had gone up to take a look at the instruments. "Come along, Mrs. Ransom," she fussed. "And you, too, Mr. Armstrong. Goodness me, I think almost everyone, residents and visitors, must have come up here during the interval. Mr. Buchan, Mrs. Buchan, please come down now and take your seats again."

Harriet watched appreciatively as Pauline Winslow shepherded them into place then turned to find her own seat. "Anything wrong, Mrs. Turner?" she inquired, seeing the housekeeper searching the makeshift bar.

"What? Oh no, nothing wrong, exactly, Miss Quigley," came the explanation as she ducked down to peer under the table. "It's just that I've mislaid my reel of black thread somewhere and I'll spit if I've lost it. It's one of my silly economies. We all have them, don't we?

I hate spending money on sewing cotton and this is a new one, and button-thread at that, which means it's stronger and costs more." She gestured at the flickering candle bulbs and shrugged. "This is all very pretty and Christmassy but it's hopeless for trying to find something."

Harriet murmured something sympathetic and left her to it while she made her way back to Sam, who had moved her bag and was now saving her chair, Tim Armstrong having declined a drink and wandered off somewhere. "Here, Harriet, take this before I spill it," he urged, handing her a glass. "I made sure we had iron rations to hand for the second half. There's a packet of nuts in my pocket if you're feeling peckish."

"Good thinking, Sam," she congratulated him, sipping her Chilean Merlot and looking round the room. Miss Winslow and her housekeeper made a formidable team, she reflected, admiring the decorations. What a gift, to have both the vision and the determination to realize it. The two women had conjured up a perfect reproduction of a Dickensian Christmas, the scent of pine, the sparkle of the tinsel just touched by the glimmer of candle bulbs, the crackling log fire in the hearth, the tall tree in the corner. There was an evocative glamour to the scene, she mused, like a Christmas card or a Victorian painting, and as a finishing touch, Neil had told her, there would be carols to wind up the concert.

The members of the Oompah Band had returned to the minstrels' gallery, brainchild and folly of the Edwardian industrialist who had built Firstone Grange. Safely tucked away behind the elaborately turned and carved oak railing, the men in leather shorts galloped into a heavily accented version of "Tulips from Amsterdam."

Over to her left Harriet could see a cluster of people, some sitting, some standing, all apparently enjoying themselves as they beat time, sang along or tapped their toes. *Ah, that's where he'd got to;* Harriet was pleased to spot Tim Armstrong leaning against the paneled wall and looking a lot happier now, with Ellen Ransom beside him, actually cracking a smile. They both seemed to have put their antipathy to Christiane Marchant on hold for the time being.

It was too much to hope that Doreen or Fred Buchan might have summoned up a grin but they, too, were standing by Tim and Ellen, flanking Vic—husband and son respectively—and their gloom was clearly not sufficient to put a damper on their companions. Although still fairly close to the woman in the wheelchair, the little group of Christiane's apparent victims seemed protected by the table and by the distance between them. A psychological protection perhaps, Harriet fancied, but it seemed to be giving them some kind of strength; long might it last, she hoped.

A flicker of movement from upstairs attracted her attention, a shadow right at the back of the minstrels' gallery. Harriet's long-distance sight, in her glasses, was excellent and she was astounded to recognize the thin dark boy she had seen with Gemma. He was gone almost before she could make sense of what she had seen but it had definitely been Gemma's boyfriend. But what of Gemma? Looking round anxiously Harriet could see Gemma standing at the kitchen doorway, actually looking a little more cheerful at last. Did she know the boy was there? And what exactly did he think he was he up to, upstairs where he certainly had no business to be?

A happier distraction gave Harriet a moment's satisfaction. It was the sight of Alice Marchant chatting comfortably with one of the guests while her mother, her wheelchair tucked right apart from the rest of the crowd, sat hunched and brooding like the bad fairy at the feast. Harriet smiled and sat down beside her cousin Sam, just in time.

"Right, peoples," shrieked the bandleader, with manic enthusiasm. "Now you vill do ze hand-klepping, *ja?*"

"Ja!" The thunderous reply rang out as the audience happily joined in and the bandleader started them off with a brisk nod of approval. The piece began with only the sound of Neil Slater on the clarinet along with a rousing virtuoso performance by the jolly-faced, tubby drummer, who sported a black mustache, while the other bandsmen demonstrated the hand-clapping.

The accordion player unhitched his instrument and pranced down to seize Matron as his partner, treating the audience to a spirited display of "Hands, Knees and Boompsadaisy." The euphonium player was about to follow suit, leaving his oversize horn where it had remained during the interval, precariously balanced on the wide, polished handrail that ran the length of the gallery, when there was a particularly loud roll on the drums, and the great brass instrument toppled over.

"Look out below!" The cry was accompanied by warning shrieks as those below tried to scatter. There was a sickening thud and a clang and clatter as the euphonium bounced once, twice, and settled on the polished oak floor.

The silence was…shocking. Harriet could almost feel the tension in the air.

"Oh my *God!*" It was Matron who cried out, a cry echoed in muted tones by all around when they realized exactly what it was that the euphonium had bounced off, before it clanged and clattered to the floor.

Christiane Marchant was still seated a little apart in her wheelchair, but now her body was slumped forward and she was hanging out of the chair, her shoulder and the side of her head a bloody, pulped mess. On the table beside her, in stark incongruity, were the smashed and broken remnants of the mince pies, shattered china plates and bloody tablecloth.

For a moment nobody moved, then there was pandemonium. Sam Hathaway looked to Matron but she had rushed straight to the woman in the wheelchair. No one else seemed to be taking charge, so, with a degree of diffidence, Sam stepped forward.

"Ladies and gentlemen," he said gravely, his voice shaken but clear and audible. "Please don't panic, there's obviously been a terrible accident and the best thing we can do is keep calm. Perhaps, Matron, it would be an idea if people went quietly into the drawing room?"

Pauline Winslow, kneeling beside the body, raised her head and nodded gratefully. "Oh yes, that would be best, I should think." She frowned, still looking at Sam. "Could somebody phone the doctor, please?"

At the same time Harriet half started to speak then thought better of it, and muttered, "Oh, what's the use?"

"What did you say, Harriet?" Sam queried. "Are you all right?"

"I don't know." She sighed. "It's just something that occurred to me, something ridiculous. I can't be sure so I'd be better off holding my tongue."

She looked over her shoulder to the cluster round the Breton woman's body. "Oh, for heaven's sake, be an angel and rescue Tim Armstrong, Sam, please. What on earth is he doing over there? It'll be enough to send him right over the edge."

In exasperation she turned away, to see what she could do to help, and spotted Alice Marchant still standing where only moments ago she had looked so comfortable. As Harriet steamed toward the younger woman, drawn by the frozen look of horror on her face, she was unceremoniously elbowed aside by Neil Slater, the clarinetist, as he came leaping down the stairs.

"Alice." He said no more but enfolded her so lovingly in his arms that Harriet slowed her approach until satisfied that Alice, who had collapsed in a torrent of tears, would be all right now.

"Is she dead?" The question came from Doreen Buchan, who had risen, white with shock. Her voice was harsh and her eyes wide and staring.

"Er—yes, I'm afraid she is," said Harriet. Surely it was obvious? It scarcely took a medical qualification to diagnose death considering the state of the woman's pitiful skull. Even though the heavy brass instrument had only caught the side of her head, there had been more than enough weight behind it to inflict a great deal of horrific damage.

"Good. She deserved to die." Doreen Buchan looked her fill at the dead woman's mangled body and smiled, a terrible, mirthless rictus. After a moment's silent contemplation she turned to her husband. "I think we ought to go home now, Vic."

"I don't know that we can, yet, Dor," he demurred from his seat beside his ashen-faced father. "They'll need to get the ambulance and inform the police first."

"The police?"

Curiously enough it was Ellen Ransom who spoke, a trace of hysteria in her voice, but old Fred Buchan and several other people jerked round to stare at Vic. "That's right, Miss Quigley, isn't it?" Why he appealed to Harriet, she had no idea; surely she was nobody's idea of an expert on sudden death?

"I believe so," she conceded. "I've an idea they have to be informed in any case of sudden death but it's purely routine."

The magic phrase calmed their jangled nerves until a sudden blast of cold air heralded the approach of the ambulance team, whose quiet, professional bearing soon reassured the anxious audience.

"Not much they can do, I'm afraid," murmured Sam as he came to stand beside Neil to watch the proceedings.

Arms still round Alice, Neil shrugged slightly then he gave Sam a measuring glance. "Do me a favor, Sam, will you?"

The tall clergyman nodded, head cocked, ready for further instructions.

"Go and have a word with Mike, the euphonium player, will you? He'll be feeling suicidal about this but you've got to reassure him that it was just a terrible accident."

"Will do." Sam made his way to the wide polished staircase and sat down beside the distraught middle-aged man who was sitting there, rocking himself in an agony of distress, hands clasped tightly round his bare knees, shivering in his brief lederhosen.

"Here." Sam put a comforting arm round the man's shoulders. "Come on, son, you mustn't blame yourself. It's ghastly but it's a ghastly *accident*. Not your fault at all."

"But it *must* be my fault," came the anguished reply. "I thought I'd balanced the horn safely, the coping on top of the railing is really wide, but I should have been more careful. Oh Christ! What am I going to do? I'll never be able to forgive myself."

Sam looked round, wondering if he could leave the poor tormented soul while he went in search of a jacket or something, for Mike was shivering. Suddenly a crocheted afghan was thrust into his hand and Harriet was there.

"Here, wrap this round the poor chap," she commanded briskly. "I just nipped into the small sun parlor for it. It usually stays there for anyone who needs a spot of extra comfort. It's sunny in there but you can get a draught whistling round your legs. And, here…" Her other hand offered a glass. "Get this inside him. I don't care what they say, I don't think you can beat a decent slug of malt for shock. Shouldn't do him any harm, it's not as though he's got concussion."

She clapped her hand to her mouth. "Oops, not a terribly tactful thing to say in the circumstances. Sorry."

Sam took the whiskey and held the glass to Mike's chattering teeth. "Here you are, get this down you, it'll dull the pain a bit."

TEA, COFFEE AND HOT, MILKY drinks were what Gemma was told to distribute among the rest of the audience

as a remedy for shock. She had been tidying up, in fits
and starts, averting her eyes from the ambulance team
and the surrounding mess, and she was glad of a diver-
sion. As she escaped thankfully to the kitchen a shape
loomed up out of the dark corner by the pantry.

"Shhh, don't make so much noise, you stupid cow."
Ryan made for the back door. "Let me out of here,
quick, before the pigs get here. Make sure you lock up
behind me."

Mute with distress she obeyed, fumbling at the door
catch with clumsy, shaking fingers, whimpering as he
glared savagely at her. "Right, you keep your bloody
mouth shut, you hear? I wasn't here, you never saw
me."

"Ryan…"

He shot a furious glance over his shoulder. "What
now?"

"You never…you never did anything, did you? I
mean, it wasn't you that—that pushed that thing over?"

"Are you out of your mind? I wasn't there, nowhere
near it. And no, I never had time to go round and nick
stuff, if that's what you're on about."

She winced as he slammed the door with an angry
bang. *No,* she vowed, *I won't tell the police he was here.*
He'd already had a first reprimand—for what the police
called "petty thieving" and which Ryan dismissed as a
setup. This had been followed by a final warning when
he'd been caught shoving some old woman around near
the chip shop and somehow her purse had fallen into
his pocket. Ryan had pleaded total astonishment at that,
but he turned eighteen in a few weeks and Gemma
knew the next time would be more serious, he'd be
considered an adult.

A uniformed police constable had turned up by now but he had little to do apart from recording the incident. "I expect somebody from the Coroner's Office will be along in due course," he told Matron. "There's not that much I can do, to be honest. Everyone seems to agree what happened and that it was just one of those unfortunate accidents, something nobody could have foreseen. I can't see anything untoward and the paramedic has pronounced life extinct so that's sorted. No need to hang around for an FME." At Matron's questioning glance, he explained, "Forensic Medical Examiner. Some forces call them in routinely for a sudden death but my guv'nor doesn't. Just as well, this is a busy time of year for them. I'll call for an undertaker—does the next of kin have any preference? No? Righty-ho, I'll fill in the sudden-death form and take another look round and after that I'll get in touch with my sergeant."

Sam Hathaway answered Matron's mute look of distress and joined the policeman as he toured the hall. "I suppose they should have left everything alone," he apologized. "But some of the residents are extremely frail and I think Matron Winslow was afraid there might be a few strokes or heart attacks!"

At the foot of the imposing staircase Neil Slater joined them and introduced the still-distraught euphonium player who was now being comforted by the band's drummer. The latter lifted his head and beckoned to the three men.

"Here, Neil, come and have a word with Mike. He still thinks it must have been his fault, but I've been telling him—I reckon if anyone's to blame it must be me."

"Really?" Sam and Neil clustered round, with the

policeman, eager to hear the reasoning behind this new theory.

"This is Tony Harris, the drummer," Neil said, by way of introduction.

"It's this way," said Tony. "Mike thinks it was because he stacked his horn on that ledge, yeah? But the thing is, he'd left it like that all through the interval and nothing happened to it then. Well, you check it out for yourselves, it's really wide. More like a shelf than a railing."

He indicated the gallery and they all craned their necks. Even from downstairs they could see the width of the coping rail. Tony Harris nodded as they noted it. "Not only that, but if you look there's that big speaker just there, comes right up level with the shelf and makes a kind of table. What I reckon happened is that my drum roll set up a load of vibrations and what with this being an old house, it upset the balance and over she went."

"That's plausible." Neil turned eagerly to the policeman and Sam. "It's a hell of a noise that he makes and the whole gallery was vibrating. I suppose the speaker could have been shifted off balance in any case, by all the earlier vibrations we set up, and the drum roll put the kibosh on it."

The horn player was beginning to look less devastated as the common sense of the drummer's claims sank in. Sam was glad to see a faint color in his cheeks and a more hopeful look in his eyes.

After further investigation the constable contacted his sergeant to report his findings so far. "Nothing anyone can do at this time of night," he told them. "You'd better shunt everyone off to bed and the guests can go home. Somebody will be here tomorrow, maybe, to take another look but it all looks pretty straightforward. Miss Winslow called her own doctor and he's agreed with the paramedic and is willing to sign the death certificate. It was an incredible stroke of good fortune that Mrs. Marchant was sitting there all by herself so nobody else was injured. We could have been dealing with a bloodbath!"

He missed the old-fashioned look that Sam Hathaway shot in his direction at this melodramatic statement, and stowed his notebook into his pocket. "It looks like you said, a load of vibrations, an old house and a bloody unlucky coincidence that had that poor woman just in the wrong place at the wrong time." He looked at his watch and sighed. "I'll stay here till the undertaker is finished, then I'll be off. There's been a big pileup on the motorway so it's all hands to the pump."

Sam looked round for Harriet as he was leaving and spotted her, wearing a preoccupied frown, as she watched Gemma and another member of staff replacing chairs and tables in their usual arrangements. He wondered what had caught his cousin's attention. Gemma looked shocked and upset, but so did everyone else, and no wonder. As he stared at Harriet she sighed and turned away, looking round the hall with a dissatisfied furrow between her brows.

"What's wrong, Harriet?" he asked quietly, buttoning his coat and winding his scarf round his throat.

"I wish I could put my finger on it." She sighed again as she walked him to the door. "I just don't like this coincidence idea. I heard what that policeman said and if it had been any of the other residents at Firstone

Grange I'd be inclined to agree. But Christiane March-ant was *hated,* Sam."

She turned anxious blue eyes on him as he bent to give her a cousinly peck on the cheek. "I'm finding it difficult to reconcile the fact that a woman who had so many people in her power, cringing with fear, should suddenly be—what did he say? *'In the wrong place at the wrong time.'"*

Sam heaved a sigh of his own. He knew Harriet wasn't going to let up on this. "I don't know, either, Hat," he placated her. "What I *do* know is that we're absolutely exhausted, and don't forget you're still not a hundred percent fit. Go on up to bed now, there's a good girl, we'll get together and have a brainstorming session in the morning."

The audience had straggled out, leaving Pauline Winslow and her helpers to round up their weary guests and coax them to bed. The band had packed up and left, once they had given their details to the police consta-ble. Now Neil was the only one left.

"Come on, Alice," he urged, wrapping her in her coat and towing her toward the door. "You're coming home with me tonight, or I'll stay with you, whatever. I don't care which but you're not going to be on your own, after all that's happened."

Grateful for his care and for the strong, loving arm round her shoulders, Alice managed a faint smile. "I think we'd better go back to my place," she said. "There'll be an awful lot to do tomorrow, starting early, I expect. I'd better be on the spot."

As Harriet trudged wearily toward the stairs she passed Mrs. Turner putting the finishing touches to her tidying up. The housekeeper nodded to her with a wry smile.

"I can't help thinking what a marvelous evening it was—up till *that* happened. It's ironic, isn't it? Such a successful concert."

Harriet's answering grin was equally rueful. "Yes, rather on the lines of 'But apart from that, Mrs. Lincoln, how did you enjoy the play?' wasn't it?"

"Oh, don't, Miss Quigley!" The other woman hastily stifled a sudden snort of laughter. "Oh well, that's about it for tonight, I think. Funny thing, you know—that reel of cotton I was searching for turned up on the mantelpiece, of all places. Somebody must have picked it up off the floor and not known what to do with it. Still, I'm glad to get it back. As I said, I'm rather mean about cotton reels, and button thread, being stronger and thicker, is more expensive."

Harriet carried on upstairs rather abstractedly. All thought of disappearing haberdashery vanished from her head, however, as she overheard a voice repeating the same thing, over and over.

"Ach mein Gott, mein Gott."

Fred Buchan was staring out of the front landing window into the starlit, frosty sky, desperate eyes raised to the pale gold sliver of a moon, his hands clenched and resting on the windowsill. As Harriet hesitated at the top of the stairs he turned and saw her, shooting her such a look of despair that she recoiled. He said nothing, however, swung abruptly round and stumped off toward his room.

EIGHT

SATURDAY MORNING DAWNED—if it could be called dawning, so comprehensively had the glitter and sparkle of the previous night vanished into a gray and frowsty murkiness—on the various participants in Friday's tragic happenings.

Alice Marchant woke early and discovered that she was wrapped in a strange man's arms. Not a stranger, she corrected herself, Neil had never been a stranger, though what was strange was this blossoming relationship, so unexpected, so swift, so wonderful.

With the thought of Neil came the memory of her mother and the horrors of the night before. Sick with revulsion she closed her eyes, trying to blot out the sight she feared would haunt her: the shattered skull, the blood, the grotesque puppet dangling over the arm of the wheelchair.

I won't think about that now. She bit her lip. *I've got other things to worry about.* Underneath it all, though, under the shock and the grief that was unexpectedly sharp, beside the happiness and surprise of Neil, ran a bubbling stream of excitement and relief.

I'm free! I'm free at last and she can never, ever hurt me again.

PAULINE WINSLOW WAS UP and about very early. She dressed quietly, checked on the silent house and then, with a word to the member of staff on night duty, slipped out of the back door and walked briskly over the road to the church. Kneeling alone and chilly in the gaunt Victorian building she nevertheless felt a warmth stealing into her bones as she laid her troubles before her God. Certainty filled her, an assurance that her dream would come through this trauma unscathed and that she and Firstone Grange would ride the storm and survive. Christiane Marchant, with her malicious, dangerous charisma and her messy, disturbing death, would not be allowed to destroy them. *I'm not alone,* she thought, looking up at the stained glass of her favorite window, showing the risen Christ.

"I'm not alone," she repeated aloud, comforted.

ELLEN RANSOM LAY IN BED racked with anxiety. So much anguish for such an old, old mistake. Was it worth it? Would Carol, or Jack, or the children really care if they knew? They'd be shocked of course and Carol might be upset, she'd been particularly close to her father, but old sins were just that—*old.*

Her sister, Mavis, would have a field day, that went without saying, if she were to find out, but again, so what? Mavis was an old woman, too, and maybe she had one or two things on her own conscience that might not bear too close a scrutiny.

No, Ellen decided that it would all be considered such small beer nowadays, hardly a sin at all, by modern reckoning. It had caused her so much torment, both in the past and particularly lately, since Christiane Marchant had made such an unwelcome reappearance, but at least, she thought, it could be explained away by apologists, considering the circumstances. The

paradox had been that what Ellen had considered a justifiable solution at the time, and had taken action to resolve with such a cool and steady nerve, had gradually
come, over the years, over the decades, to seem less
justifiable. Less allowable. Less bearable. Less forgiv-
able.

It all boiled down now to how Ellen perceived herself; it had been *her* problem, *her* solution, *her* guilt,
and however skillfully she had managed at the time—
for the most part—to suppress any qualms of conscience, now, as an old woman, she viewed her own
actions very darkly indeed. For that reason Christiane
Marchant had been Ellen's nemesis, always there with
her demands and a knowing smile in that long-ago time
of terror and lately propelling her inexorably toward
some drastic action.

Now the woman was gone but still Ellen writhed in
torment. Something more was needed, before this could
be laid to rest.

Along the landing Tim Armstrong lay awake, too,
quite still, only his eyes moving. He stared at the ceiling most of the time but now and then his gaze flickered toward the window where he could see a lighter
shade of gray struggling to break through the gloom.
He remembered the previous evening, first Christiane
Marchant's taunts and then her terrible death.

Oh Jane, he faltered. *Oh Janey, where are you? I
need you here with me now, I need you to be strong for
me, as I was strong for you that time.*

It was all too much to bear and he slipped gratefully
back into a sunlit past, walking in a long-ago summer
on a northern riverbank with dark-haired Jane, pretty

and happy in a flowered cotton dress, laughing up at him with love and promises in her eyes.

IN THE SNUG LITTLE VILLAGE of Locksley, nestling in the chalk hills over on the other side of the valley, Doreen Buchan slid noiselessly out of bed, careful not to disturb Vic. She shrugged on her toweling dressing gown and went downstairs, feeling drained and not at all rested after a night of broken, restless sleep. Putting the kettle on, she looked out of the window, seeking solace from the garden that normally gave her so much satisfaction. Handed round from relative to grudging relative, she had always craved roots, a proper house, a proper garden, so the White Lodge garden with its acre and a half of perfectly groomed lawns and borders and ornamental shrubs fulfilled her dream. The house, too, was a constant source of delight. Substantial, elegant, furnished and decorated in impeccably neutral tones by the interior designer who had soon taken her measure and played safe, it said everything about the lady of the house that she wished could have been the truth.

The village was another cause for celebration, with its mellow mix of cottages, some thatched, some slate-roofed, in the local brick and flint, together with houses of later periods. Some were small and elegant with Georgian sash windows and pedimented doorways, and one or two, like her own beloved White Lodge, were Victorian villas. In her own inarticulate fashion Doreen Buchan appreciated history, and the knowledge that just on the outskirts of the village ran the track of an old Roman road, trodden by countless thousands throughout the centuries, added to her feeling of having come home, having put down roots at last.

This morning she tried to summon up the warmth and comfort of those feelings but the memories and emotions that had been stirred up by the appearance of Christiane Marchant had deeply unsettled her. *What if Vic finds out,* she agonized, drinking her tea and staring blindly out at the cold gray garden. *What would the children say?*

She shuddered as she remembered her last sight of the tormentor, even as she felt again the flash of triumph that had elated her last night.

She deserved to die, Doreen thought. *Whatever happens to me now, I'll never be sorry that she died.*

DOREEN'S FATHER-IN-LAW was in his room at Firstone Grange, huddled into a high-seated, upright wing chair, trying to force heat from the radiator into bones that felt chilled right through with an ancient frost. So many memories, so many regrets. So much of the past buried, submerged, forcibly banished into limbo, all subordinate to the overriding need to survive.

Fred Buchan had made a success of his postwar life, working like a slave to establish himself, first as a good worker, then as a small businessman; still later as a major employer until he had built a modest empire which he had passed on to the willing and worthy hands of his only child. Yes, Vic was a son to be proud of, and Margaret had been a good and loyal wife. Not exciting, but who wanted excitement in a woman, when all he needed from her was a comforting security. Any excitement he craved came from his business life.

That woman, though, she had torn it all apart, destroying, with her hints and threats and whispers, the whole edifice he had put together, brick by painstaking brick, making a place of safety for himself, for his family. Making him remember.

On this Saturday morning Fred Buchan sat alone in his room, bowed down by the intolerable burden of his guilt.

Up in the attics of Firstone Grange, Gemma Sankey was asleep but she was dreaming. Nightmare creatures pursued her, dripping in blood and crawling with grayish-pink wriggly things that even in her troubled sleep she recognized as brains, spilled and writhing with a life of their own. As she had seen them spilling from Christiane Marchant's head last night.

Ryan. Her thoughts, sleeping and waking, spiraled around. Ryan, he had been there. He had been upstairs at the time of the "accident." It had been hours before troubled sleep overtook her last night as she fretted and tried to remember. She had told Ryan that Mrs. Marchant had seen them and that she was issuing veiled threats. Had Ryan seen the woman as an obstacle to his plan to milk Firstone Grange and its residents of a small but steady income? After all, if Gemma were sacked, bang went Ryan's chance of ingratiating himself into Matron's good graces; he had boasted to her about his plans the other night, and shrugged off her horror.

Surely it wasn't enough reason for murder? Was it?

AN HOUR OR SO LATER CANON Sam Hathaway was woken by the ringing of the telephone beside his bed. For a moment he waited, as he always did, hoping that Avril would answer it and let him sleep on, then, as he always did, he remembered that she was gone. The icy shock of memory never failed to distress him, even after four years, and of all his friends perhaps only his cousin Harriet was aware of his desolation. He had moved into a flat near the Cathedral close when she died, resigning his living near Bishop's Waltham for an administration job, trying to get away from the anguish of being in her house, her familiar surroundings—all hollow, all pointless.

Not a loss of faith exactly, more a suspension of belief. If Avril could die, with her joyous grasp of life, how could he reconcile that with his previous certainties? What kind of God could do that? Until he could answer his own bitter cry, how could he counsel others? *Time for me to retire,* he thought now, grim-faced, as he picked up the phone. It was Neil.

"Sam? Can you do me a favor, do you think?"

"Of course, my dear chap, name it."

Sam pulled himself together. He was still alive, he was still needed, he could still be useful, even if life had lost its color, its joy, its meaning.

"I wondered if you could spring Harriet for a few hours? I'm at Alice's house but I don't want to leave her here on her own." He gave Sam the address and went on. "I've got one meeting I simply can't get out of and another I really ought to make somehow, there's a really massive sale hanging on it. Alice insists she'll be perfectly all right but I'd rather she had somebody with her whom I can trust. Do you think Harriet's up to it? I don't want her to bust a gasket or something."

Sam let out a snort of laughter. "Better not let Harriet hear you, Neil. No, I'm sure she's quite up to it and in any case I can stick around and keep an eye on them both as well as provide extra backup, transport, protection, whatever."

He reached for his glasses and looked at the time. "Shall I go and pick Harriet up fairly early and then come on to you? You might ring Miss Winslow, perhaps, and give them a bit of warning. Say I'll be there for ten o'clock, that should give Harriet time to get her war paint on."

SAM WAS RELIEVED TO SEE that Alice, although pale and rather drawn, was quite composed and happy to see them. As she took them into the kitchen, saying that the rest of the house was too gloomy, she spoke frankly.

"It was a shock, of course it was," she said. "I wouldn't have wished that on anyone, it was…it was dreadful." Her voice faltered and she brushed away a tear. "But you probably know that Mother was—difficult and I can't pretend it's not a relief, in spite of everything."

Sam nodded kindly and was secretly amused to note that Harriet was firmly partisan, ranging herself on Alice's side against the late, unlamented Christiane, as she bustled round and made coffee. Still, he reflected, Harriet was aware that Neil had suffered from a dominant mother, too, though that had been the tyranny of love as his mother's long-drawn-out suffering had taken its toll on him and his marriage. *They both deserve a bit of happiness,* he concluded, as Harriet must also have done.

"We're just about to go through some of Alice's parents' legal papers," explained Neil as they surveyed the litter of yellowing documents at the end of the big pine table. "I've got to go in half an hour but I can help get things started."

"I didn't even know Daddy had a safe in his surgery," Alice admitted with slight smile. "But Neil says safes are sometimes disguised as paintings and when he spotted it, we tracked down the combination in an old notebook of Daddy's. I wonder if Mother knew about it? We'd only just brought this box in here when you arrived. Here, Sam, you must be used to this kind of thing, would you take a quick look, please?"

The others laughed away Sam's unconvincing noises about leaving them in private, so he picked up a document at random. "This is your mother's will, Alice. It's quite straightforward, everything goes to you." He handed it to her while Neil opened another brown envelope.

"This older one is your father's will, Alice." Neil was rapidly scanning the contents, and surprised them all by emitting a loud snort of astonishment. "Good God! He left everything in trust to you, Alice, apart from an allowance to your mother. That means the house is yours, it's been yours all along."

"No!" The bitter anguish of her cry shocked them all as she started up, her eyes grown huge and appalled. "That means it was all for nothing," she wailed. "I needn't have…"

She pulled herself up and pressed her hand to her mouth, pushing Neil away as he made a move toward her. "No, it's all right, don't worry. It's just… I can't believe she…"

She slumped down. Harriet quietly pulled the cafetière toward her and refilled Alice's mug. The younger woman, the earlier muted radiance drained from her face, leaving her olive skin sallow and uncannily like her mother, took the cup from Harriet and managed a tremulous but grateful smile. "Thanks, Harriet, I'm so sorry. I just— It was such a shock."

It might well be a shock, mused Sam gravely, watching her as she made an effort to recover. To discover that your mother had so little regard for you as to appropriate your inheritance for herself, to treat you as a slave, to keep you tied by your own timidity and strong sense of filial duty. All this might very well tip one over the edge for a moment. But beside this very reasonable explanation for her distress he was aware of an urgent query. What had she meant by saying: "it was all for nothing"? It might, understandably, refer to the years of drudgery, but might there be another, more sinister, inference?

At that moment a rattle and thump announced the arrival of the post and Alice, obviously glad of an excuse to be alone for a moment, retreated to the hall to collect it.

"Here, Neil." She held the solitary letter out to him. "You open it for me, it looks official and I don't think I can stand much more."

"It's from Egertons, the property developers." He spoke slowly after he had read the gist of the letter. "They want to buy this house and demolish it, and build a small, 'exclusive' group of luxury houses on the land."

Their eyes swiveled round to Alice, whose face wore an expression of blank astonishment, then Neil referred back to the letter in his hand. "It all looks kosher," he said, as he laid the letter down on the table. "They'll be talking big money here, Alice," he told her.

Again Sam wondered. Harriet's uncertainties and anxieties about Christiane Marchant's unpleasant but unfortunately only too welcome death had begun to infect him. Harriet was no fool and he respected her judgment. If she felt uneasy it was with good reason.

What if Alice Marchant had known beforehand about the property developers' forthcoming offer? What if they had approached her informally, holding out the lure of a gilt-edged freedom? Alice had not known until a few minutes ago that her mother was not the owner, or at least, part-owner of the house. He could swear her reaction had been genuine. What if she had seen her mother, that unhappy, difficult soul, as the only obstacle that could thwart her escape from drudgery?

What if Alice, somehow, had killed her own mother?

AN HOUR OR TWO LATER Neil, his meeting concluded unexpectedly early, knocked on the door to Pauline Winslow's office. Bidden to enter he greeted her politely, realizing that she had no idea who he was.

"I'm Neil Slater, Miss Winslow," he hastily introduced himself, shaking hands. "I was here last night, I'm the clarinetist in the Oompah Band."

Her face clouded at once and she looked distressed so he hastened to explain his visit.

"I'm here really on Alice Marchant's behalf, to act for her, if you like. She's very upset, of course."

Mollified by this she gestured to him to sit down, professing her willingness to be of assistance.

"I suppose I just felt we ought to keep each other abreast of developments," he suggested, disarming her very slight trace of hostility with his open, friendly smile. Not a handsome man, nor even a good-looking one, she found herself thinking, but there was something attractive about his angular face and crooked grin.

"I've been in touch with the police for Alice," he began. "There will obviously have to be an inquest, but my understanding is that it will be opened for evidence of identification, then immediately adjourned because of the Christmas break. I gather it's purely routine, happens in all cases of sudden death."

Pauline Winslow felt the tight band of pain round her skull begin to loosen. *Purely routine,* she reminded herself, *that's all it is.* "Yes, of course," she replied. "I've had a visit from a sergeant and he said much the same thing. I do understand, but from a purely selfish point of view I wish it didn't have to happen. There's bound to be adverse publicity, though I have to admit we seem to be escaping quite lightly so far, just the local papers and television. I just hope our luck holds and we don't get the tabloids descending on us."

She smiled at him, her rueful expression compounded with a touch of shame.

"I can't help feeling angry. I know that poor woman didn't deserve to die that way, nobody could, but she really was a most unpleasant person. I almost feel she did this to spite me, illogical as that sounds."

She flushed as he cast a look of mild surprise at her, and fiddled awkwardly with her pen. "She was a mistake. I don't know how I could have detected what a nuisance she'd turn out to be, probably not, but she seemed to attract unease, to cause trouble and unrest. She was a most unpleasant woman."

HARRIET WAS HELPING ALICE sort through her mother's clothes.

"You don't have to help me with this, Harriet." Alice looked gratefully at the older woman.

Harriet was putting underclothes into neat piles in an old leather suitcase that lay open on the bed and she raised her head at Alice's words.

"No, I realize that, my dear." She nodded. For a moment she concentrated on folding vests, smoothing the gossamer silk and woolen garments with a gentle hand, then she spoke again. "My own mother died last spring so I know how much there is to do. I'm very glad if I can be any help and besides…" She grinned suddenly, entirely mischievous. "As Sam and probably the entire population of Locksley Village would tell you, I don't think I could bear to pass up such an opportunity to meddle!"

"I don't think you're meddling." Alice smiled gratefully, aware that Harriet's calm, friendly company was exactly what she needed just now.

At that moment she heard footsteps and Sam appeared in the doorway looking slightly disheveled from his efforts in the garden. "Neil just rang," he announced. "He's got the go-ahead to arrange the funeral, so he suggests you have a think about what you want. He'll be back soon and you can get things rolling."

He turned to go. "Now, what else was there? Oh yes, I know. I've just made some more coffee, Alice, if that's all right, I'll go and pour it out, so don't let it get cold."

"You're an angel, Sam." Alice straightened up, rubbing her back. "Come on, Harriet, let's give ourselves a break. There's no real reason why we should do this now, I just have this urge to—oh, I don't know. Put all that part of my life behind me, I suppose. Does that sound quite dreadful to you?"

"Of course not." Harriet was brisk. "It's not good to

dwell on the past and action is always my panacea in times of trouble. You go and have a hot drink now and I'll do a bit more here. I'll join you in a minute or two."

Stretching and yawning Alice made her way into the kitchen to join Sam.

"Alice?" Sam handed her a mug of coffee, steam curling comfortingly upward. "Was your mother a Catholic?"

"Yes, I suppose so." She shot him a puzzled look and went on. "Yes, of course she was. I am, too, technically, though I'm afraid neither of us ever paid much attention to religion. Apart from the French service once a year."

Unlike Neil, Sam needed no clarification. He was acquainted with the little Huguenot church. "I just wondered about a priest for the ceremony," he explained and she gave a sharp exclamation.

"Oh no, couldn't you do it, Sam? I hate the thought of having to explain it all over again."

She was glad to see that after the first surprise he could see her point of view so she pressed him. "I just want a very quick cremation, no fuss at all," she urged. "I couldn't bear it, specially in the—in the circumstances. Will you do it, Sam? Please?"

Her eyes filled as he gave her a very kind smile and nodded. She thought for a moment. "Could we get it over and done with before Christmas?" Alice looked at him hopefully. "It'll just be hanging over us otherwise."

LATER, WHEN NEIL HAD reappeared and Alice seemed to be coping, Sam drove Harriet back to Firstone Grange.

"What about Christmas, Harriet?" he asked her. His cousin was very deep in thought and came to with a jolt.

"Mmm? Oh yes, Christmas. I haven't thought about it really. I'll be home, though—I can't call myself convalescent for much longer." She slid him a sidelong look, noting the suddenly bleak set to his not-unhandsome face. Avril, she remembered with a painful flip-flop of her heart. Avril and Christmas. "Sam?"

He had disappeared inside himself, forgetting that it was he who had raised the subject but now he came back, and cocked an inquiring eyebrow at her.

"Sam." She stumbled a little, choosing her words carefully. "I'd be really grateful, actually, if you'd consider coming to stay with me for a few days."

She was aware of his slight frown, that he was withdrawing proudly from her. As he opened his mouth, she hurried to forestall his protest. "My neighbor invited me but I wasn't entirely truthful with her, told her I'd be fine, but I'm not sure I'm really up to coping on my own at first. I didn't want to inflict myself on her—an invalid is such an imposition, specially when she'll have her family there."

Sam relaxed and gave her a malicious but affectionate grin. "I see. You don't mind being an imposition on me, I suppose?"

Pleased with the result of her cunning she composed her features into a semblance of shamefaced acknowledgment and his grin widened.

"It's actually rather convenient," he confessed. "Both the children invited me but I told them I'd be too busy looking after you. I just hadn't got round to telling you."

They bickered comfortably all the way back to Firstone Grange but as Sam gallantly helped Harriet out of the car she looked anxiously at him.

"I wish I didn't feel so uneasy about that woman's death," she persisted and was perplexed and a little troubled to see him frown.

"I wish I didn't feel like that, too, Harriet," he said.

NINE

THE HORRIFIC ACCIDENT spread ripples well outside Firstone Grange. Kieran was miserable. Ryan had told him about the old woman's death and now he was feeling upset, not that he'd known her, or even glimpsed her. No, it was something about the way Ryan had smiled when he described the shattered head and the gleeful relish in his voice as he spoke of brains and blood spilling out.

You didn't ought to be like that. Kieran frowned, astonished to find himself censuring his dominant friend, even here, in the safety of his imagination. *It's not funny, somebody dying, not like that, and it's not nice being glad about an old lady dying. It's not right.*

He thought about his own granny dying and, aghast, shied away from the image. The picture was so disturbing that it took him some time to conjure up a true picture of his granny, as a talisman: a small, cheerful woman who adored her lummox of a grandson. He decided to call in on her tonight rather than go down the pub with Ryan. *Wonder if Gemma would come out with me,* he pondered, shivering at the daring thought. He'd got the distinct impression that Gemma didn't actually like Ryan very much.

AS SHE MADE BEDS AND tidied rooms at Firstone Grange Gemma was thinking much the same thing. She had rung Ryan first thing in the morning and when his mobile failed to respond she rang his home, greatly daring, but his mother said she couldn't disturb him, he was asleep. *It's not right.* Gemma stood still, with a duster in her hand. *You didn't ought to be afraid of your own son, not when you're a grown woman.* A vision of the future flashed before her, herself with a son like Ryan, possibly Ryan's own son, and herself pussyfooting round him like Ryan's mother did, afraid of provoking one of his violent outbursts.

Kieran would have been greatly heartened by this and even more so had he known she couldn't help contrasting him with Ryan. *He's kind, Kieran is,* she said to herself. *He's nice to his mum and he loves his granny. You wouldn't need to be frightened of Kieran's son—he'd be like his father, slow and gentle, kind to women and animals.* Another picture rose up in her mind: Kieran's face and the way it lit up when he saw her, delight and desire mingling, but not in a scary way. Comforting, nice.

LUNCH WAS JUST BEING served as Harriet hurried into the dining room.

"Oh, there you are, Miss Quigley," Mrs. Turner greeted her. "Just in time. Another five minutes and you'd have been in the naughty corner!" Her smile belied the words and she indicated an empty chair. "Here's your place, come and sit beside Mrs. Ransom, she's certainly picked the best spot today, right next to the radiator."

Harriet smiled but was interested to see that Mrs. Turner's mild joke raised not a flicker on Ellen Ransom's somber face. Granted, Ellen was hardly noted for a sense of humor, except at other people's expense, but she usually tried to make an effort at the social graces. Today she looked very ill, so much so that Harriet's tender heart was touched; Ellen Ransom was far from her favorite person but no one should be this unhappy.

"Brrr!" She shivered, trying to establish a neutral topic. "Have you set foot outside today, Mrs. Ransom? It's absolutely freezing out there and not even bright and sunny like it was yesterday."

Ellen gave her a blank stare then shook her head, with a noncommittal murmur, but the old soldier, on Harriet's other side, was more forthcoming. He launched into a diatribe against the English weather and followed it up with a paean of praise in favor of wintering in Egypt, which, he informed them with some complacency, he had been fortunate enough to experience.

"How lucky." Harriet went with the flow. "I'd love to go to Egypt myself one day. I'll have to see if Sam would come with me. When were you there, Colonel?"

He gave a mischievous grin. "Well, it was 1945," he admitted. "I expect things have changed a bit now, but I bet the weather's pretty much the same." He joined in the laughter at this then turned to her again. "I noticed you drive up just now with your cousin, Canon Hathaway, isn't it? Been out on business, or just pleasure, dear lady?"

Really, he was just as nosy as she and Sam were, Harriet decided with a tolerant smile, though his hearty military persona could be a bit wearing. "I went to give poor Alice Marchant a hand," she replied, awarding him a crumb of gossip. "I gather she has no close relatives and it's rather a daunting business at the best of times, sorting out a parent's death, let alone in the circumstances."

Ellen Ransom made an indescribable sound, between a snort and a sob, blundered to her feet and rushed out of the room. Harriet half rose to follow her but was gently pushed back into her seat by Mrs. Turner.

"I'll see to her, Miss Quigley, don't you worry. We're all a bit on edge today, I'm sure there's nothing badly wrong."

I rather think you're mistaken. Harriet frowned to herself, but allowed herself to be overruled.

AFTER LUNCH HARRIET DRIFTED into the hall and perched uncomfortably on the oak settle, unable to relax. She ignored the ornately carved fireplace and the pitch pine paneling, staring instead at the minstrels' gallery with its wide handrail, as wide as a ledge. She thought of the fleeting glimpses she had caught, that brief momentary shadow that she had recognized as Gemma's dark and rather sinister boyfriend. If she could convince herself that he had somehow managed to push that heavy brass instrument off the balcony, she would feel more at ease, dreadful though it was to be suspecting anyone at all. *Ridiculous,* she scolded herself, *why is it better to think of a nasty little thug as a murderer than any of the other people here?* She sighed. *I didn't realize I was that bigoted.*

She took another look upward, conjuring up an image of the hall the previous night, mysterious, shadowed, with flickering candle bulbs. A perfect setting for an old-fashioned country house murder. Pity this wasn't actually an old-fashioned country house, with a parlor maid—and a butler whodunit. *Pity I can't knit.* She grinned, remembering Miss Marple and Miss Silver, with their incisive minds and their inevitable balls of fluffy pink or blue wool. *Maybe if I could whip up a matinée jacket I could whip up some inspiration along with it.*

Murder will out, she thought, then stopped short. *There,* she said to herself, *I've done it again. Murder!* In the teeth of all the evidence, in spite of knowing there was not the slightest shred of suspicion in anyone else's mind, she was suddenly quite sure it *was* murder. Except Sam, she reminded herself, there's more than a shred of suspicion in Sam's mind, too.

The enticing smell of freshly brewed coffee disturbed her concentration. Mrs. Turner was holding out a cup of coffee and, from her tolerant smile, had obviously been there for several moments. "My goodness, Miss Quigley," she said with a laugh. "You were miles away and no mistake. Here, perhaps this will aid the thought processes, you looked extremely puzzled."

Harriet reached for the cup with a grateful smile, then, after a glance up at the minstrels' gallery, she turned again to the housekeeper. "That reel of button thread," she said slowly. "You found it on the mantelpiece, didn't you? At the end of the evening?"

Mrs. Turner opened her eyes in surprise. "Yes." She nodded. "I can only surmise that it had rolled across the room somehow and some kind soul retrieved it."

"Mmm." Harriet tried not to let her doubts show. "Let me see, it went missing during the interval, didn't it? Or had you noticed it earlier?"

With an inward sigh she realized that the house-keeper was now wearing the patient look that accompanied her conversations with some of the dottier guests at Firstone Grange, but she persevered.

"It was certainly there just as the interval began." Mrs. Turner was definite. "I know that because I'd just tied up yet another strand of that wretched tinsel. Why do you ask?"

"Oh, nothing really." Harriet decided that vagueness was a good camouflage and took a sip of her coffee so Mrs. Turner whisked back to the kitchen, her curiosity unsatisfied.

"I wonder," thought Harriet, staring fixedly up at the gleaming polished wood of the gallery, remembering last night's cluster of residents and visitors chattering and inspecting the instruments. "I wonder."

"I'M SO SORRY TO TROUBLE you, Canon Hathaway." Pauline Winslow was uncharacteristically hesitant, sounding extremely apologetic. Sam was intrigued. "It's rather difficult but I'm afraid he insists that only you will do." She broke into Sam's startled query. "Of course, I haven't explained. It's Mr. Buchan. The one who is staying here, I mean, not his son." To Sam's ear Matron was sounding peculiarly unlike herself, with that note of uncertainty in her voice, where usually there was only supreme self-assurance.

"I rang your home, Canon, and you've got your mobile phone number on your message service, so I hope you don't mind— Oh dear, this is so irregular. It's just that Mr. Buchan Senior walked into my office just now and said he wishes to go to church. At once. Demanded it, really. Well, of course, there's no difficulty about that, our local church just down the road is very nice and I can easily understand anyone here feeling the need for comfort at such a time. But I'm afraid he's insisting he has to go to Winchester, to the Cathedral."

"Really?" Sam was curious. "It's a wonderful building, of course, but I hadn't gained the impression that Mr. Buchan was at all interested in architecture. Whenever I've tried to have a word, on my visits to Harriet, he's turned away with just a grunt."

"You must have made *some* impression on him," sighed Pauline Winslow. "Because he's insisting, not only that he must go to Winchester Cathedral, but that he has to go right now, and that furthermore, he wishes you, and *only* you, to take him there!"

"That *is* a surprise." Sam whistled softly. "I suppose I'd better come back to Firstone Grange straightaway. As it happens I'm luckily only just down the road. I looked into the nice little bookshop in Chambers Forge after I dropped Harriet back with you for lunch, then I nipped over the road to Waitrose. I needed some toothpaste so I thought I'd better buy it while I remembered, and the upshot is that the coffee shop here is very nice so I've just had soup and a roll. I'll be with you as soon as I can."

As Sam parked his old Volvo estate at the front door of Firstone Grange, Pauline Winslow came outside with Fred Buchan, who was looking shaky but resolute.

"Here we are, Mr. Buchan." She handed over her charge with a bright smile and a sprightly note in her voice that Mary Poppins might have envied. "Canon Hathaway has very kindly agreed to give you a lift in to Winchester." Without a word spoken, Fred slumped in the front seat while Sam fussed about with the seat belt. "Don't be too late," Matron said, sounding anxious as she exchanged a glance with Sam. For two pins, he thought, she would have rolled her eyes at him, but such behavior was well outside her code, so she merely gave a concerned nod of farewell as the two men drove off.

"What is it that you wanted to do in the Cathedral, Mr. Buchan?" Sam shot a look sideways at his passenger. "It's a wonderful building, of course, is that why you want to go there?" There was no response, so he turned to the more likely reason. "Or are you hoping to join in a service? I'm afraid you'll be unlucky, if that's the case, but I can easily arrange to pick you up tomorrow, if you like."

"Not a service." Fred shook his head.

Sam waited, then, as no further communication seemed forthcoming, he asked, "What denomination are you, Fred? I'd guess either Roman Catholic or Lutheran? Would I be right? Those are pretty widespread in Europe."

"Once I was—" The voice sounded harsh, in need of oiling. "Once I was a Catholic. But now I am nothing. *Nothing.*"

He said no more and Sam gave up, concentrating on making his way round the narrow backstreets and through the ancient gateway into the Cathedral close, which was thronged with people visiting the annual Christmas Market. Parking was always a nightmare at this time of year so Sam sighed with relief as he eased the car into a friend's conveniently empty parking space and helped the old man out of his seat.

"You are a priest? Yes?" The question took Sam by surprise and he stared for a moment.

"Well, I am," he admitted. "But not in the way I suspect you mean. I'm a priest of the Anglican church but that's not the same as being a Roman Catholic priest. What did you...?"

"No matter, but that was why I—" The old man stomped off toward the great gray building, head down against the chill wind and ignoring the crowds queuing at the open-air ice-rink, so Sam locked the car and set off in interested pursuit. They were nodded through by the guide at the door, who recognized Sam, and after a few tentative yards, Fred Buchan halted and gazed around. For a moment or two he stared up at the Perpendicular nave but there was no admiration in his eyes. He flicked a glance toward the black marble font but that, too, found no favor, so he headed toward the altar.

Bemused but curious, Sam followed him, close enough to assist if need be, but keeping enough distance so that the old man should not feel crowded. Did Fred know the Cathedral at all? Sam wondered. *There doesn't seem to be any rhyme or reason in all this, he's not following some predetermined plan, he's speeding up then slowing down and just looking right and left, as if he's searching for something.*

At the notice on the door to the crypt Fred stopped altogether, standing in front of it and peering at the wording. "I'm afraid we won't be able to visit the crypt today," Sam told him, concerned as he realized that the other man now seemed a bit panicky. What could be the matter? Had he forgotten what he was looking for? Had he perhaps never known, and merely burrowed like a frightened animal into the shadowy sanctuary of the Cathedral in search of safety?

"You know it's prone to flooding? After all that heavy rain we've had lately the water is knee deep down there." The old man's eyes flickered so Sam opened the door. "Look, even though we can't actually go in there, we can stand here on this step and see the statue."

Looking increasingly uncertain, and very frail, Fred Buchan allowed Sam to usher him into the entrance to the crypt. The old man took hold of the railing and leaned forward, staring in astonishment.

"What in God's name is that?" The question burst out in spite of his reserve, the hoarse croak echoing in the underground chamber. He indicated the life-size statue standing a few yards in front of them. It was the figure of a man, very simply made, with his head bent toward hands upheld in front of his chest.

Sam felt his throat constrict as the statue, as always, took him unawares. "It's by the sculptor Anthony Gormley," he explained. "It's wonderful, isn't it? And look, you can see the vaulting of the roof reflected in the water."

There was no reply, and as Fred seemed rooted to the spot, Sam leaned against the back wall and watched and waited. Five minutes, ten minutes; it was getting very cold and Sam was beginning to feel cramped. Had Fred, in this modern masterpiece in its medieval setting, found whatever it was he sought? Did the statue "speak" to him?

Just as Sam realized he could barely feel his feet, and decided that he really had to interrupt the old man's silent vigil, Fred sighed and straightened his shoulders. As he turned away from the light Sam was yet able to detect the trace of tears on the furrowed cheeks and his kind heart was wrung.

"We go now" was all the other man said but at the door he looked back at the metal man, a kind of longing engraved on his face.

Silently, Sam escorted his passenger back through the great, echoing building and out to the car. Whatever Fred Buchan had needed, Sam thought he had found *something,* though what it was, Sam had no idea.

"WHAT?" AT THE OTHER END of the line Neil sounded flabbergasted at Harriet's question, as well he might. She grinned wryly, picturing his expression. *He'll be calling for the men in white coats any day now.* She repeated her query with some acerbity to disguise her own qualms.

"It's simple enough, surely, Neil? All I want you to do is to find out, tactfully, from the euphonium player, whether there were any threads of black cotton attached to his instrument. I think he was the first one on the scene. I seem to remember the poor soul nearly tumbling out of the gallery after the horn, in what must have been a desperate, but forlorn, attempt to catch it."

"Well, I'll try," agreed Neil, sounding very doubtful. "But I really don't understand what you're on about. Care to explain, Harriet?"

"Certainly not," came the sharp reply. "But I'd be really grateful, Neil, if you'd do that for me as quickly as possible." She was about to switch off her mobile when a thought struck her. "Have you thought about Christmas, Neil? I mean, about what Alice is going to do?"

He grunted in surprise and she hastily explained,

"It's just that Sam is going to be staying with me. I'm going home on Monday and it occurred to me that Alice might like to come, too. Please tell her she'd be very welcome and you could easily see her there."

She thought he sounded amused as well as touched by her idea. "It's a kind thought, Harriet, but don't worry, I've got everything in hand. I rang the Coroner's Office and the postmortem's been done. It's as everyone expected, you might call it Death by Euphonium! Anyway, that being the case, and the insurance people seem disposed to be happy enough, the powers that be have okayed the cremation to go ahead on Monday morning at nine o'clock. That'll be the first one of the day, no publicity, no audience, no fuss, just us, which is what Alice wants, with Sam to conduct the service. Once that's over I've booked us both on a flight to Fiji."

He interrupted her exclamation with a chuckle. "I thought the sooner she was out of all this the better and Fiji was the nicest place the travel shop came up with at such short notice. We'll have a night in San Francisco, lose twenty-four hours crossing the International Date Line over the Pacific and bingo! South seas, palm trees, coral beaches, paradise."

She began to speak, then faltered, realizing that Neil had misinterpreted her silence as he laughed aloud. "It's all right, Harriet, my intentions are entirely honorable. It's very early days, I know, but I'm hoping that when all this is behind us Alice will be ready to think about maybe getting married. But just for now I want to take her right away from here. After all, it's been pretty grim just recently and from what I can gather, Alice hasn't had any fun since her father died. I think she deserves a treat."

Harriet summoned up the right amount of enthusiasm and congratulated him on his cleverness. He rang
off, leaving her to tuck her mobile into her bag with a
heavy heart. The knowledge that Sam, too, had been
visited by doubts about Alice somehow made everything so much worse. *If I prove to be right about how
it could have been done,* she thought drearily, *that puts
Alice right back there with all my other suspects.*

They're all back in the running now.

CHRISTIANE MARCHANT'S room at Firstone Grange had
been locked after the concert; nobody was quite sure
why but it seemed the right thing to do. When the news
had come from the Coroner's Office Gemma had been
sent upstairs to clean the room ready for the next guest.
She wasn't sure whether she was glad or sorry. On the
one hand it was a huge relief to know that she would
never again be caught unawares by that hated voice
with its faint trace of an accent, whispering in her ear.
Balancing that knowledge, though, was the fact that
death, horrible death at that, had loomed uncomfortably close.

I hated her. Gemma shuddered. *And I'm glad she's
dead, but I don't want to touch her things.* Was it her
imagination or was there a faint suggestion of perfume and sweat as she whipped the sheets off the bed?
Gemma didn't mind the usual smells; inevitably some
of the residents had a little problem, with one or two
of the men suffering agonies of embarrassment about
their prostate dribbles, while the women were more
stoic about their stress incontinence. That was nat-
ural enough, but this, this was a personal smell that
sent shivers down her spine and recalled the sly, smil-

ing menace, in spite of the bliss of knowing that Mrs. Marchant could never frighten her again.

But she could, couldn't she?

Gemma froze for a moment, bent double as she hooked out a slipper from under the bed. Ryan. Ryan had been there. Ryan might have done…something. The small, terrified idea that was hiding inside her mind reared its ugly head and looked out, didn't like what it saw and squirreled back into its hidey-hole.

I won't think about it. I won't.

Unbidden, the thought of her mother sprang to mind. Bossy old bag with a sharp, sometimes vicious tongue on her, much too interfering, but Mum nonetheless. And it had to be admitted that it was Mum who had seen through Ryan's glossy surface enamel and hadn't liked what she saw.

A whimper escaped Gemma. *I want Mum.*

"Gemma?"

The girl was so shocked at the sound that she really did jump, Harriet observed; if not out of her skin, then with a quite visible shudder. "What is it, Gemma?" Harriet was concerned; the girl's face looked greasy, greenish, the features slack with shock. "Did you think it was Mrs. Marchant come back?" She crossed the room rapidly and put an arm round the stricken girl. Gemma shuddered again but Harriet felt her relax, the fleeting prettiness visible again in the otherwise slightly vacant face.

"Here, sit down a minute and get your breath back." She pushed the girl gently down on the high-seated chair by the window, waiting while Gemma calmed down and some color came back into her cheeks. When

Harriet spoke, she chose her words carefully, anxious not to scare away her quarry.

"Tell me, Gemma," she said briskly, modifying her headmistress manner. "Tell me why Mrs. Marchant frightened you so. No—" She raised her hand as the girl gave a frightened exclamation. "I know she did, I saw that, and I also saw that she frightened a number of other people, too."

Gemma relaxed again as Harriet smiled at her. Miss Quigley was nice, she thought—very schoolmarmish, of course, but you could trust her. She made you feel safe.

"It was Ryan," she whispered, blushing and lowering her eyes.

"Ryan? Your boyfriend?"

Harriet tensed, remembering the dark shadow in the minstrels' gallery, minutes before the crash of the euphonium. Was this it? Was this to be the solution to the mystery?

Gemma nodded miserably. "Mum never liked him," she admitted and Harriet chalked up a point to the percipient Mum. "It was the cleaner, she talked to my aunty and then she told Mrs. Marchant about me. About me getting rid of the baby, I mean."

Harriet frowned slightly but gave Gemma a reassuring nod. "Well, that's a great pity, of course, and the cleaner should mind her own business, but I don't understand? What did Mrs Marchant say to upset you so much? After all, an abortion isn't exactly uncommon, is it?"

"It… She said, what would Matron think," came the stumbling reply.

Light dawned at once. Matron, with her strong, clear

beliefs, her single-minded faith, her own rigid adherence to right and wrong, what would Matron have made of a girl who had chosen to have an abortion? Harriet felt a frisson of sympathy with Gemma. Matron Winslow would be a difficult woman to face if you had something on your conscience, however sadly commonplace it would seem to the rest of the world. Harriet was sure, somehow, that Pauline Winslow would have strong and definite views on the subject.

"I see" was all she said, but she said it kindly and Gemma looked up eagerly.

"It wasn't *just* that," she urged, obviously desperate to confess now.

Harriet said nothing, just waited in attentive silence.

"It was one night last week. Ryan and Kieran, that's his friend, they came round late one night and I let them in the back scullery. Kieran stayed in the kitchen and Ryan and me—we went into the washhouse and we…we…"

As her voice tailed away in an agony of embarrassment Harriet took pity on her. "All right, Gemma, I get the picture. And Mrs. Marchant found out somehow and threatened to tell Matron?"

The girl nodded, still twisting her hands. "It was because…there's a skylight in the washhouse roof and you can see down from the landing window into it. We did it with the light on, you see."

"Oh, I see." Harriet was slightly nonplussed. Although she had made up for it later, her own teenage excursions into sex had been at a time when girls were still overshadowed by the threat of an unwanted, shameful pregnancy. The idea of asking the family doctor to put her on the pill would have been quite unthinkable; after all, he was a close friend of her father's. At seventeen, Gemma's age, Harriet's experience had consisted of a few desperately amateur fumbles and one dark, uncomfortable episode on a chilly spring evening out on the hills. *What had happened to that boy?* she wondered now with a wistful smile. *We'd certainly never have dared to "do" it with the light on.*

With an effort she wrenched herself back from more than forty years ago to the present and considered the girl beside her. The ingredients were all there, she sighed, sex and fear and blackmail. But murder? "And why was Ryan upstairs last night, just before the accident?" she asked, her tone severe.

"Oh!" The startled gasp confirmed her suspicions, the boy *had* been there after all, it wasn't just a figment of her imagination.

"Well?" Her voice remained a little stern, enough to jolt Gemma into obeying her but not intimidating enough to put her to flight.

"He said he…he had this idea, it was awful, I wouldn't have let him do it," Gemma pleaded, with a sob in her voice. "He said it was a good time to sneak upstairs and pinch some bits and pieces of jewelry from the old ladies when they were all downstairs. He said he'd do it really careful, not enough to notice, and he'd move their things around a bit so they'd think they were just getting muddled."

Harriet had to suppress a smile at the reference to "old ladies." Obviously she didn't fall into that category, but the cool nastiness of the boy's plan shocked her. It was clever, very clever, she conceded. *If I found my things shifted a little and something missing, would I be able to convince myself I hadn't just misplaced*

it? Several of the residents were indeed a little for-
getful and they strove manfully to conceal the fact.
Pride would have forbidden a hue and cry for a ring, a
brooch, while the short-stay nature of their visit would
ensure a rapid turnover of victims. Nobody would stay
very long so they could never be sure that their losses
were the result of theft rather than absence of mind.

"That's a wicked thing to do." She spoke sharply and
Gemma looked up at her, eager to placate her favorite
guest.

"I wouldn't have let him do it, Miss Quigley, honest.
It was just that last night he said he wanted to hear the
band and I was going to make sure he just stayed in the
kitchen, but I got called away. When I got back he'd
disappeared. I thought he'd got bored and gone home."
Her anxious face was a mirror for her emotions as she
stared at Harriet. "And he's not into drugs," she offered
in mitigation. "He's dead against them, ever since his
brother died three years ago, an overdose it was. Ryan,
he—he never did anything, not anything bad," she insisted.

As Harriet rose stiffly to her feet, aware of just how
tired she was feeling, she patted the girl's shoulder with
unfailing kindness.

"I hope he didn't, Gemma," she said quietly. "I certainly hope he didn't."

TEN

A SHORT NAP IN HER ROOM refreshed Harriet and after she splashed her face with cold water to wake herself up properly, she went downstairs with her book to sit in the sun parlor. The book failed to keep her interest, wrapped up as she was in this complex and unlikely puzzle at Firstone Grange.

Why can't I leave it alone? she wondered. After all, the coroner's officer was satisfied that Christiane Marchant's sudden death was nothing more than what everyone else had all assumed, a gruesome accident. Why get involved? Why should she interfere? Was it to serve the ends of a noble cause like Miss Silver, Patricia Wentworth's governess sleuth, or perhaps Miss Marple with her passion for justice? A grin flitted across her face. It was, she admitted, much more the case that she, like Hercule Poirot, was full of overweening conceit. In the long-ago world of her childhood, she had overheard a much-tried babysitter complain, "Young Harriet's a real little madam sometimes, she simply won't be told!"

She was right. Harriet sighed now with an air of nostalgic complacency. *I simply* won't *be told*.

THOSE OTHER OCCUPANTS of Firstone Grange whose slumbers had been troubled on earlier nights by the malevolent presence of Christiane Marchant and her nasty little ways now found themselves equally troubled by her malevolent absence. No peace for the wicked, the saying goes. Or for the very slightly wicked, for that matter; or even the not-so-much-wicked-as-just-plain-stupid. Whatever the heinousness of their misdeeds, those who had found themselves involved, to their cost, with the woman when she was alive, now found themselves unable to be rid of her lingering animus.

PAULINE WINSLOW, SECURE in the certainty of her faith and the support of her church, sat in her office looking at her Bible. There was no further cause for concern, she told herself firmly. That woman was gone, tidied away with as little fuss as possible given the circumstances, and the police were only too willing to be accommodating. That was the advantage of working with the "old folks," especially at this time of year; nobody wanted to spoil Christmas for them. Even the press were no longer breathing down her neck, eager for gory details. They had been distracted by a heady cocktail of motorway madness, a parliamentary scandal that threatened to be deliciously deplorable and an alleged monster spotted in the Peak District which might, just possibly, be an escaped puma, or, more likely, might turn out to be just a wild boar. The papers were too engrossed in pursuing these snippets of news to spare time for a nasty but admittedly comic-sounding accident.

Matron turned a page and tried to read, to gain peace and refreshment from the beauty of the King James Bible—no modern rubbish for Pauline Winslow—but

the small print jiggled hectically in front of her eyes and
the well of quietness she sought failed to materialize.

"Damn that woman," she swore aloud. "God damn
her," and she was horrified as much by the vehemence
that rang in her voice, as by the unaccustomed blas-
phemy.

ELLEN RANSOM HUDDLED in her room, escaping from the
slightly overexcited festive cheer that some of the residents were trying to whip up. She had ignored a cry
of "Life goes on, dear" from one woman and retreated
to the safety of an armchair by her window to brood.
What should she do? What *could* she do? The memories crowded in on her, making their presence felt more
strongly even though they had been buried for more
than sixty years. Buried until Christiane Marchant had
greeted her with that knowing smile and she, Ellen, had
felt the years melt away till she was young, and ill, and
frightened, and it was 1945 once more.

Nineteen forty-five. Douglas was still in the Far East
after three years, a reluctant hero, caught up in something he'd wanted no part of, shipped over to the East
and wounded during the Burma campaign. He had been
sent back to his unit afterward, where he kept his head
down, made no complaint and got on with the grim
business of survival.

Survival. That had also been uppermost in Ellen's
mind at that time. She had survived the war, certainly,
but that had been the least of her worries that spring
and early summer of 1945. In those days she had been
working in the munitions factory at Holton Heath on
the south coast of Dorset, between the busy working
port of Poole and the walled Saxon market town of

Wareham. She had lodged with her elder sister, who, with three small children and a husband in the navy, had been glad both of Ellen's company and her contribution to household finances. Production was winding down a bit at work with the imminent cessation of hostilities in Europe, and Ellen had been out and about enjoying herself. *Well, I was entitled to, wasn't I?* Even now she felt aggrieved, as though someone had just scolded her.

There was even a bomb; dropped right into the munitions factory, it had been. She clapped her hand to her mouth as she recalled the terror that had transfixed them all when they realized they were sitting ducks. And the silence. She had never forgotten that moment of silence as they realized the bomb had not exploded. Then one or two women fell down in faints, several screamed or sobbed, a couple had soiled themselves, but she, Ellen, had pulled herself together and poked her nose in. "Rags, it was," she had told her daughter years later. "Them slave laborers in the camps had packed it with rags so it wouldn't detonate. It was the bravest thing I ever heard."

It had been at a friend's house, or rather a friend of a friend, that she met the vivacious young French woman who dazzled them all with the exotic story of her escape, in a fishing boat, from occupied western Brittany, and of her tribulations as a refugee before she had ended up working in a small private hotel in Bournemouth. She and Ellen had struck up an unlikely friendship, the one so small and typically French; not at all pretty but unforgettably vivid. And the other, a big, fair, chocolate-box pretty English girl, a trifle slow and missing her husband. Even at the time of that fateful meeting there had been a worm of panic gnawing at Ellen's heart as she resolutely ignored a problem that was shortly set to become both self-evident and a complete disaster.

Ellen ground her teeth in an agony of pity for the foolish girl she had been, and of rage at her so-called friend. What had happened that long-ago summer had soured her for the rest of her life, and now, when old anxieties should have been long at rest, back she had come into Ellen's life, that small, vivacious Breton woman with her only too excellent memory.

I'll have to confess, she thought suddenly. The idea manifested itself entirely unexpectedly, but the more she tried to dismiss it as both foolish and dangerous, the more attractive it became as an option. The only option, for her peace of mind.

Yes. She felt a sudden surge of hope, uplifting her. *I'll have to confess it, what I did. But how? Who would listen?*

DOWNSTAIRS IN THE DRAWING room Tim Armstrong's son was trying to broach the subject that occupied his mind to the exclusion of any other. He fidgeted uneasily as he watched his father fiddle with the button on the cuff of his tweed sports jacket. How would Tim take the news? Would he understand what was going on anyway?

"You might as well get it off your chest, son." Tim was sitting up, looking suddenly alert. "What's bothering you?"

Tony stared at him, aware of a sudden sharp pang of memory as his father fixed him with a keen, intelligent eye, just as he had always done. "Is it Pam? Doesn't she want me back after this visit? I can understand that, you know. It's hard for her with her job and the children to manage, and now me to cope with, too. If I could stay on top of things I could…I could give her a hand now and then, but I can't guarantee that things won't get scrambled anytime."

His son's eyes filled with hot, unbidden tears as his father put out an awkward but kindly hand and patted his shoulder. "It's not that, Dad," he mumbled, pulling out his handkerchief and loudly blowing his nose. "It isn't that, Pam loves you, she knows you can't help it. No—" He stared round the room seeking inspiration, relieved and appalled at the same time that the moment had come. No help for it, better just to spit it out.

"It's something different, Dad. I've been offered a promotion and a hefty pay rise but it means moving. The company's relocating to Cheshire, been in the pipeline for quite a while, but we only got the official say-so yesterday."

He cast an anxious glance at his father but Tim's face was hard to read. "I spoke to your doctor about it, Dad," he ventured diffidently. "He wasn't very keen on the idea, said it could do more harm than good if you had to uproot. He said…he said you'd be better off staying down here, where everything's familiar."

To his surprise his father greeted this stammered verdict with a genuine smile. "Of course I would, son," he agreed heartily. "Don't worry about me, I'll be all right, something will turn up."

The smiling hazel eyes that were so unusually alert suddenly underwent one of those disconcerting shifts of focus, and Tim Armstrong was gone. With a very different smile on his face, he looked inward. "In any case, I couldn't go away from your mother," he said reproachfully. "She's here, waiting for me. I couldn't leave her alone."

For a moment Tony Armstrong fought a bitter urge to wail aloud, to burst into sour and bitter tears. *Oh God,* he thought, surreptitiously wiping his eyes. That Dad of all people should have come to this. Dead for twenty years or so, Tony's mother was no longer a factor in his own life. Oh, he had loved her, he had loved her dearly, and it had been dreadful when she died so suddenly like that, but his dad had been the one who had held him together. *Well, we held each other together.* His mouth twisted in a smile as he remembered their awkward, English attempts to make a semblance of a life, to make things bearable somehow.

He was pierced by a sudden memory. Three weeks ago Pam had rung him at the office in a panic. "It's your dad," she had cried. "I can't find him anywhere. I thought he was asleep but he's disappeared, he's not in the house."

Loath to call the police yet, Tony had driven around while Pam waited anxiously at home. He tried to picture his father's movements; his old home perhaps? Then inspiration struck and he took an illegal right turn at the T-junction so that he could head back toward their local cemetery. *Mum,* he thought, *he'll have gone to find Mum.*

As he drove slowly, looking from side to side of the road in case his father was walking there, Tony screwed up his face in an effort to keep the emotions at bay. *I love Pam,* he thought, *well, of course I do. But if it happened to us, if she died, would the grief still be so raw? After all these years? Sometimes it's as though Dad has only just lost her, he's so engulfed in sorrow.* He swung into the graveled parking circle and leaped out of the car, scanning the avenues. Yes, Tim was there, just standing by Jane's grave a couple of hundred yards away. It was pouring with rain and he was bareheaded and not wearing a coat.

Now, staring at his father, Tony Armstrong could scarcely believe they were one and the same, the quiet old man in this peaceful room, smiling his inward smile, and the distraught figure he had caught up with a few weeks previously. In his head he could still hear the sound that had rung round the gravestones: the difficult, anguished sobs of a man who had never been known to shed a tear.

I never once saw my father cry. Tony bit his lip. *Not until that day.*

DRIVING OUT OF THE WHITE Lodge gates Vic and Doreen Buchan slowed down when Harriet's neighbor hurried up to them, dragging her old retriever.

"Sorry to stop you," she panted. "I was just wondering if you'd be popping over to Firstone Grange tonight?"

"Yes, we will be." Doreen looked doubtfully at the dog. "Did you want a lift?"

"Oh no, thank you, it's not that. I just wondered if you'd let Harriet know that I'll make sure her cottage is aired for Monday, with the heating turned on. Sam told me that's when she'll be home. And I'll make sure there's bread and milk in, and put a casserole in the oven so she doesn't have to bother about cooking."

With a wave she was off, towed homeward by the dog, leaving Doreen to lean back in her seat as Vic headed the Mercedes toward Chambers Forge. *I could tell Miss Quigley all about it,* she thought suddenly.

The idea was so shocking that a gasp of surprise escaped her, causing Vic to grunt and half turn his head. "Nothing," she murmured dismissively but the thought persisted, comforting her. *Yes, I could tell Miss Quigley.*

GEMMA SANKEY WAS FEELING comforted, too, relaxed and safe at home, letting Mum's scolding flow over her, aware that her mother was actually pleased to see her. With one last caution against Ryan, Mrs. Sankey disappeared upstairs for the Saturday night bath that was part of her ritual as she looked forward to watching *Casualty* in her dressing gown.

The front doorbell rang. Gemma sighed, put down the magazine she'd been reading and pottered out to the hall. The chill blast of air made her recoil so that for a moment she failed to recognize the two figures on the threshold, huddling under the small tiled porch.

"Hullo, Gem." Ryan was slightly at a loss, an unusual situation for him when it came to girls. He'd tried ringing and texting Gemma's mobile but she had turned it off, and a couple of tentative calls to Firstone Grange had only produced a snotty voice that told him Gemma was not allowed to take personal calls while she was at work. "You coming out, then?"

Her resolution wavered for a moment as she registered his ingratiating smile. She had loved him for so long, been his adoring slave, proud to be seen with him, then she caught sight of Kieran in the background. There was a small frown creasing Kieran's kind moon-face as he regarded Ryan's back and as she looked at him she saw him give a tiny shake of his head. Kieran, who was kind to his granny, was warning her about Ryan—who was not kind to anyone.

"No," she said calmly, preparing to close the front door. "I'm staying in tonight, Ryan, and I won't be going out with you again. You'd better go now, before my mum catches you."

"What?" She was almost amused at his astonishment at this unexpected rejection, and she pressed it home. "I mean it, Ryan, I'm dumping you. I don't like the way you act—my mum was right about you."

She swiftly shut the door before he could pull himself together, but not before she spotted Kieran's broad beam of approval, hastily wiped off his face when Ryan turned round in a fury and kicked off down the path toward the pub.

Gemma leaned against the door, her breathing steadying, her pounding heart slowing its beat. *I did it,* she triumphed. *I really did it. I dumped him.* Somewhere deep inside she felt a tiny warm glow, the spark lit when she had spoken earlier to Miss Quigley. Kieran had been pleased with her, glad she'd done it. Kieran liked her, she knew, and maybe now he might say something to her, ask her out or something. *I'd like that,* she realized, with a hopeful lift of her spirits.

At eight o'clock that night Neil yawned and looked at the remains of the takeaway he had picked up earlier. "Let's call it a day, Alice," he suggested. "We've been sorting out this house all day, d'you fancy a quick drink? I could do with a breath of air and it's stopped drizzling now." He swept the foil containers into the kitchen bin and looked at her. "What do you think? Are you game for a gentle stagger up to the pub?"

As she shrugged herself into the coat he held out for her, she turned to him with anxious eyes. "You don't think people will think I'm awful, do you?" she wondered. "I mean, going out for a drink when my mother's only just…"

Her voice, which had started to tail off as she fretted, was suddenly stifled completely as he took her in his arms and kissed her soundly. "Don't be daft" was all he said but she was comforted.

The brisk walk did her good, blowing the cobwebs away, and when they reached the brow of the hill and the beginnings of the village, she felt almost human again. To reach the White Boar they had to walk past Firstone Grange and as they did so they spotted Sam Hathaway just parking his Volvo estate. He waved at them but made no attempt to join them until Alice, who had grown fond of the rangy clergyman, called out to him.

"Sam! Sam?" When he came up to them, greeting them with beaming pleasure, Alice held out her hand on a friendly impulse. "We're going to the pub for a drink," she explained. "Why don't you spring Harriet again, if you think she'd like it, and come and join us for a drink?"

She glanced quickly at Neil for confirmation and was glad to see him smile and nod. Sam, too, looked delighted and agreed to pick up Harriet and meet them shortly in the White Boar.

HARRIET SMILED WHEN SHE saw the pair of them tucked in beside the inglenook, already presenting a united front to the world, a couple, a twosome. There was a flurry of greeting, including a warm kiss from Harriet on Alice's cheek which clearly surprised but touched the younger woman, followed by desultory chitchat while the men made a business out of ordering a round of drinks, arguing over payment and eventually settling at a larger table in the corner.

While the others talked Harriet fell silent, gazing steadfastly at her hands.

"Harriet?" asked Alice, who looked surprised at Harriet's air of distraction.

"What? Oh, I'm sorry, my dear." Harriet stopped studying her hands and looked gravely at Alice. "I'm really sorry but I have to ask you about this, I think it might be important. Why was it that your mother was so—so difficult? So much disliked by so many people?"

Neil made a movement of protest, which was brushed aside by Alice with an impatient gesture. Sam sat waiting, pint in hand, his eyes flicking from Alice to Harriet and back again, watching and waiting.

"It's hard to say," Alice began slowly, almost speaking to herself as she looked down the years. "I suppose it all goes back to her youth in Brittany. I don't know what happened—she would never speak of it, but Daddy told me the bare bones, to make sure I didn't put my foot in it."

She took a reflective sip at her gin and tonic. "It's really odd, you know. I'd completely forgotten until now what it was that Daddy told me. I wasn't very old at the time and he didn't dwell on it. He was just concerned that Mother mustn't be reminded." Her eyes darkened at the memory. "She always made him pay, you see, if anything upset her, and that was her weapon, reminding him of her terrible ordeal. They were in Occupied France, you know, and it was very hard. The Bretons have a reputation as fierce fighters—they were strongly royalist during and after the French revolution and there's a tradition of fighting hard and dying hard. I don't know, I told you, I've never known exactly what it was that happened, what it was that was so terrible, but I know, because my father told me, that there was some dreadful, unimaginable tragedy. It was the Germans, of course, in retaliation for some Resistance exploit."

She looked at them sadly. "It all seems such a long time ago to us, ancient history." She turned to Harriet and Sam, who were listening intently, Sam looking sympathetic, but Harriet wore an unreadable expression. "You two can only have been small babies then," she said reflectively, then she continued. "The village where Mother lived was right out at the back of beyond, on a little peninsula, nowhere important, just a skinny granite neck sticking out into the Atlantic on the wild west coast of Brittany. By the time the outside world found out what had happened it was all too late."

She flicked her fingers in exasperation. "The trouble is I've absolutely no idea what it was that actually happened. Anyway, whatever it was, all of her family were killed—the men, that is. I think her mother was already dead but she had four brothers aged between twelve and about twenty-five. Mother was the only girl and she came somewhere in the middle of the boys but she was always cagey about her age. Said it was a woman's prerogative to lie about such things."

Alice's smile, through sudden tears, touched Harriet's heart. "I did try to love Mother, you know," she said simply. "But she was so difficult. I—I feel awful saying that I just didn't *like* her at all. If I could only have believed she loved me, even just a little, in her own peculiar way, but it was only Daddy who... And after he died Mother and I had nothing in common." She paused, running her tongue over dry lips. "I've tried and tried to work out why she was like she was and all I can think is that if the worst has happened to you—as it did to her—nothing else can touch you very much. I've an idea she might have been raped at that time, too, from something she once said, about my arrival being a shock, something she'd thought could never happen."

Her voice died away and she took another sip from her glass in the silence, smiling faintly when Neil reached out for her hand and tucked it between his own warm ones. "I know that doesn't excuse the way she was, but she did like to have power over people. I think it all went back to the war when you used whatever weapons came to hand."

Harriet's eyes narrowed and she gave a thoughtful nod; Alice shot her a quick look of inquiry. "Why did you want to know, Harriet?" she asked, with a sharply intelligent gaze. "Do you think there could be something—irregular, perhaps, about Mother's death?"

Sam interrupted abruptly. "Time for another drink, everyone? My round this time." His breezy smile earned him a troubled frown from Alice but a surreptitious nod of thanks from his cousin.

In the ensuing activity Alice's question was allowed to drop but Harriet was uneasily conscious of that level, measuring look and that Alice was, now and then, pre-occupied with some sort of internal appraisal.

"Oh, by the way, Harriet." It was Neil, looking up from his pint of Ringwood bitter. "I rang Mike, you know, the horn player?"

Harriet was all attention. "Did you indeed? And…?"

Neil wore a puzzled frown. "Yes, how did you know, Harriet? That there might be some black thread tied on to the euphonium?"

Harriet gave a little sigh and Sam paused, his beer glass in mid journey to his lips, his eyes eager and acute, waiting for Harriet's reply.

She disappointed him by shrugging her shoulders and making a noncommittal sound.

"You were quite right," continued Neil. "Mike said he assumed it was left over from where they were all decorating the horns with tinsel. Did you notice? I even had a little bit on my clarinet, though of course it doesn't lend itself to fancy trimming, not like the bigger horns."

"Think carefully, Neil." Harriet was leaning forward now, very earnest. "Did your friend say whether he himself had used thread to tie the tinsel on to the euphonium?"

"No." Neil was quite definite. "He just twisted it round but when he spotted the thread it was actually tied, but as it was when he was cleaning up…" Their eyes all swiveled toward Alice but she seemed lost in thought and hadn't picked up the reference. Neil went on. "Anyway, he just assumed one of the others had decided to make it more secure. However, when he put the horn away the black thread was gone and now he's not even sure it was there in the first place."

Harriet jerked her head up and stared at him, not speaking. Neil looked across at her, a frown creasing his brow. "What is this, Harriet? I checked with the rest of the band—I thought that would be the next job you set me. Nobody had done anything at all with any black thread."

"Ahhh." It was a sigh of pure content, then Harriet hastily pulled herself together with an appalled shiver. For a moment she had actually reveled in her own brilliant deduction, forgetting completely the horrific circumstances. This wasn't an academic puzzle.

Aloud she said, "I don't know. It's odd that he thought he saw it but then it was gone. I just don't know."

To herself she added, *if I'm correct,* and she shivered in the warmth of the pub—*if I've got it right we could definitely be talking murder.*

HALF AN HOUR OR SO LATER Harriet poured herself and Sam a snort of Laphroaig and sat back cradling her glass.

"Do you think they bought it?" she asked, giving Sam a worried look as she sat on the bed.

"What, your explanation that you had been afraid the tinsel could have caught in the railing somehow and brought the euphonium tumbling down?" He wrinkled his nose in thought. "I think they did, actually, it's a daft idea but it seemed to fit well with your sudden impersonation of a frail old lady who needed to go to bed right then. Besides, somebody could be keeping quiet about decorating it, because they feel guilty. And the same person could have nipped in a little later on after the initial fuss and cut off the thread, again because they felt guilty. You have to admit it would be a difficult thing to own up to and as there's been no mention of any thread, it would be easier to keep your mouth shut."

She grinned and raised her glass in a toast. "Very true. And as for the 'poor old Harriet' act, well, I had to get out of there some way or other, and I really did feel tired. It seemed as good an excuse as any." She sobered quickly. "You're right, of course. It *could* be the way you describe or it could have been quite deliberate. But still, I think they bought it."

"Yes." He sniffed the malt appreciatively. "I, on the other hand, am not taken in by the daft-old-biddy syndrome, so let's have the truth, Harriet."

"It's hard to know where to start." She made no pretense of not understanding him, and then, as he shifted restlessly in the room's sole armchair, she told him about Mrs. Turner and her missing reel of thread.

He listened carefully, nodding once or twice; then, when she stopped speaking, he thought it over. "Let me get this right," he mused. "Your theory is that somebody picked up the reel of black thread during the interval, sneaked upstairs to the minstrels' gallery and, inspired by the tinsel, tied the thread to the euphonium?" He gave her an old-fashioned look but she said nothing, merely nodding, so he went on. "Then, you believe, the perpetrator snuck back downstairs, carrying the cotton reel concealed about his or her person, still quite undetected and, at the appropriate moment, whatever that might have been, gave the thread a tug and down came the euphonium. And then he, or she, skipped back and disposed of the thread?"

He snorted with scorn. "Bollocks!"

"Really, Canon Hathaway," she countered swiftly. "Such unbecoming language from a man of the cloth." She subsided and shot him a look of resignation; she had expected no less. This was yet another reason why she had insisted on coming back to her room at Firstone Grange, though she had also preferred not to air her theories in Alice's hearing. Any such discussion would be bound to be upsetting.

Harriet topped up her modest nightcap from the flask Sam had donated earlier. There was only one glass so she sipped her whiskey from her coffee mug, knowing that her continued silence would infuriate Sam.

Sure enough, here he was, rising to the bait. "Well, honestly, Harriet. You have to admit it's a bit rich, as theories go. I mean, look at the facts. For a start you'd have to be completely round the twist to take that kind of risk. The thread could be spotted or it could have snapped earlier and rendered the whole exercise pointless, or the damned euphonium could have killed half a dozen people at the same time as Christiane Marchant. It could even have killed other people and missed her completely."

He looked down his nose with a dismissive shake of his head, then came up with another objection. "And what about the actual thread, if that's really the way it happened? I mean, a long trailing thread leading to the killer, standing there with the reel in his or her hand?"

She maintained her irritating silence and his kindly, patronizing air began to dissipate.

"For God's sake, Harriet, say something. Don't just sit there with that smug Sphinx smile on your face.

You've obviously thought about this. What makes you so sure?"

"I don't know that I *am* sure." She ducked her head in apology and waved her flask at him with a grin. At his nod she topped up his drink with a very small dollop of Scotch, then rummaged in her bedside table and brought out some stem ginger cookies. "Here, nibble on his and see if it brings any inspiration."

She took a sip of her own whiskey and thought about it for a moment. "Your most valid objection to my theory is that it put other people at risk. Well, I agree, but perhaps you didn't realize that during the interval Matron insisted that Christiane Marchant had to be parked away over to one side. The excuse given was that the tires on the wheelchair were damaging the parquet floor but I think myself that was just quick thinking on Matron's part. She must have noticed how uneasy Mrs. Marchant was making some of the others. But it means the wretched woman was there all alone, tucked in a corner beside the table, and it seemed to me then—and I don't believe this is purely hindsight—that they had all rejected her somehow, pushed her away from them with Matron's help. They had sent her to Coventry in a way."

She looked backward at the events of the previous evening, trying to summon up an accurate image. "I'm right, you know, Sam. She was really out in the cold. They were all there, the people she had dancing and twitching as she pulled their strings—Ellen Ransom and Doreen Buchan. Tim Armstrong and old Fred Buchan with Alice Marchant and young Gemma in the doorway. Even Pauline Winslow was close enough to tug at an invisible thread, bearing in mind just how dark it was then, with the candle bulbs dimmed."

"Haven't you shot yourself in the foot, rather, if you suspect Alice?" he inquired, making no comment on the theory so far.

"You mean by talking about the threads of cotton? Just now in the pub?" She shrugged. "Could be, I suppose, but equally one could argue that I'd merely fired a warning shot across her bows. To let her know that she couldn't get away with it."

He nodded and waited patiently.

"Oh, I don't know, Sam. I think she was getting a bit worried until I babbled on about the tinsel on the musical instruments but I'm pretty certain my explanation satisfied her. I don't really think she had anything to do with it, but the trouble is, I don't *want* it to be Alice and once you start having favorites you might as well give up."

She put her glass down, glad of the opportunity to turn away from Sam's scrutiny. She knew she was looking her age, and more, tonight, and that Sam was remembering that she was, after all, recovering from a fairly major operation.

"Look, Harriet," he ventured, making no comment on her weariness. "I'm not so sure I was right to dismiss the whole idea straightaway, but I do see that as a plan for a murder it's about as foolproof as a leaky sieve. I'll take your word for it about Mrs. Marchant being set apart—I was talking and didn't take much notice of her—and I'll concede that it could have happened that way. But to my mind the black thread is the weak link, literally."

"But it was *button* thread," she interrupted him eagerly. "I certainly wasn't the only person Mrs. Turner mentioned it to—that it was the extra-strong thread, I mean, rather than the usual weight and thickness. You're right, ordinary cotton would have been useless." She clenched her fists for a moment and turned to him. "I think Christiane Marchant said something more than usually dreadful to somebody just before the concert began and that this was a spur-of-the-moment, opportunistic effort, using whatever came to hand."

"Mmm." He sounded unconvinced. "Could be, I suppose, but that's a two-edged argument. I mean, yes, if you like, it would probably ensure that the thread was strong enough to take the weight of that huge instrument for a short time, but equally, unless it was arranged somehow over a fulcrum—a fixed point like the keys, perhaps, or even twisted round one of them—you couldn't be sure it would break after the event, which would leave a long trailing pointer to the cotton reel in your guilty hand."

"Unless you had a pair of nail scissors in your handbag or a penknife in your pocket, all ready for a quick snip at the incriminating thread, under cover of the inevitable hysteria and confusion that such an accident would bring about."

He let out a tuneless whistle and stared at her, obviously intrigued against his better judgment. "They were all underfoot as soon as it happened, even Tim Armstrong," he admitted slowly as he thought back to the horror, the noise and the mess of the aftermath. "Both the Buchans, Fred and Doreen, and Vic, too, were there as far as I recall. They were on the spot at once and Mrs. Ransom was hovering around there, too. I remember thinking what a ghoul she was and scolding myself for lack of charity."

She nodded encouragement. Just so had she regarded a particularly bright pupil in her teaching days, when a knotty problem was being untangled by use of logic and applied intelligence.

"Did they all go up to the gallery?" He answered his own question with a nod. "I remember Ellen Ransom's face," he went on, speaking slowly, thoughtfully. "It really did look like a case of 'if looks could kill.'" He looked at her. "I remember something else. Tim Armstrong, did you hear what he said? He said, 'That woman deserves to die.' I remember his very words."

Harriet gave him a startled look. "But that's exactly what Doreen Buchan said, her very words, too, I'm quite sure of it."

They stared at each other, not knowing what to think.

"I don't think Alice moved." He was squinting back in time again and she nodded.

"No, you're right, she didn't," Harriet admitted. "I was about to go to her but Neil was there. She certainly didn't move toward her mother's body, but it's possible, remotely, I agree, that she could have done it and left it to chance about the thread."

He gave her another of his old-fashioned looks and she conceded defeat. "Oh all right, it's far-fetched in the extreme and highly unlikely. That's why, besides partiality, that I don't really believe Alice killed her own mother, though I must admit that property development business this morning gave me a bit of a jolt."

She frowned then remembered the snatched five minutes earlier on when he had managed to fill her in on his unexpected trip to Winchester on Matron's errand. "What was all that business with Fred Buchan, do you think, Sam? I mean, why the Cathedral? I could understand if he'd gone there to pray but from what you say, all he did was stand and look at the statue in the crypt."

"Oh no," Sam corrected her gently but firmly. "I'm pretty certain that Fred was praying while he stood there. In his own way. For some reason he'd decided that the Cathedral was the place he had to be, though I soon realized he didn't know what to do when he got there. He had no coherent plan. I think it was just some blind instinct that took him there, but the crypt attracted him and when he saw the statue he was transfixed. He'd picked me for the job because I'm a priest—though he didn't seem confused about that, as I'd initially suspected. He seemed to know the difference between Roman Catholic and Anglican priests, all right. However, even after asking for my help, he wouldn't open up to me however gently I probed, so God only knows what he was looking for—or what he found. But it was certainly some kind of prayer, Harriet."

Saying nothing, she shot him a smile that mingled deep affection with considerable respect, then she looked at her watch and stood up, brushing biscuit crumbs off her plaid woolen skirt and tut-tutting as a drop of whiskey spilt on her lambswool sweater as she drained her mug.

"Lick it off, Old Hat," suggested Sam absently then raised his head in surprise at her sudden giggle. "*What?* What did I say? What are you laughing at?"

"You." She grinned as they emerged from her room

and set off downstairs. "Is that what you do, you old soak, reduced to sucking drips off your jumper? Thank God I'm not so dependent on alcohol, you old villain."

He gave her one of his rueful schoolboy grins, looking a little abashed. "Can't keep anything a secret from you, can I? Still, the price of whiskey nowadays, you have to take it where you can get it."

She saw him to the door, their problem unresolved, but as he said good-night he frowned suddenly. "Be careful, love," he urged, with an anxious look round the entrance hall. "I don't know that I like the idea of you trapped here with a you-know-what on the loose. If you're right, that is."

"A what?" Startled at first by his unaccustomed endearment, she suddenly interpreted his cautious euphemism and swept a comprehensive glance round the hall. There were still a few visitors, Saturday being the only day when relatives and friends were welcome after dinner. Not everyone was allowed to entertain guests in their rooms but Matron had been happy to make an exception of Sam, who traded shamelessly on his cloth when it was politic. Before Avril's death he had pandered happily to his legion of adoring female parishioners, keeping them all from squabbling by the exercise of his charm, but nowadays he tended to steer clear of women who could be described as fancy-free and might be suspected of having designs on him.

"Don't be silly." She gave him a kiss and a little push to send him on his way. "I'll be all right, don't worry."

His words haunted her however, as she made her way toward the drawing room, passing the Buchans as she did so and encountering Fred Buchan's pale, frozen stare. Doreen Buchan started to rise from her nervous perch on the edge of her seat when she saw Harriet, but just at that moment the colonel made a beeline for them.

"Ah, there you are, Miss Quigley. How about a game of Scrabble, eh? Just a quick one. I've wiped the floor with the girls over there." He pointed to a smiling quartet of women clustered round a small table. "I'm thirsting for new blood."

Doreen Buchan subsided unnoticed as Harriet smiled and accepted, glad of a challenge to use her brain in a mental exercise not connected with death or disaster. *Thank goodness he didn't suggest we play Cluedo,* she thought, *that might be a bit too close to home.*

THERE WAS A HAND OVER Harriet's mouth, holding her down, stopping her breathing.

"Urgghh!" She struggled to free herself, her arms flailing wildly as she struck at her attacker. As the grip on her jaw slackened a little Harriet managed to sink her teeth into the other's flesh.

There was a shocked, half-smothered scream and the other person fell back with a whimper. Even at such a time Harriet had a fleeting moment of complacency that she had all her own teeth. Gums, in such a situation, she reflected, would hardly have been so effective.

Shaking with fright and with a righteous indignation, Harriet reached out and snapped on the bedside light.

"What the hell is going on here?" she demanded, glaring ferociously at Ellen Ransom, an incongruous assailant in her pink brushed-nylon dressing gown and her hair screwed into curlers and tied up in a chiffon scarf. She was nursing her injured hand and examining the marks of Harriet's teeth, clearly visible in the fleshy mound at the base of her thumb.

"What did you do that for?" she asked, sounding unreasonably aggrieved.

The affronted tone penetrated Harriet's red mist of anger and shock and she hauled herself up to a sitting position. She scrabbled for her glasses then reached out for her watch.

Midnight.

"How did you get into my room?" Harriet demanded and saw that the other woman looked suddenly shifty.

"There's a spare key to each room." She shrugged, not meeting Harriet's angry stare. "I just borrowed it for a while. I'll put it back tomorrow morning. Nobody will notice."

"So—you stole the key. But why were you trying to kill me?" Harriet snapped, still shaking. She was savagely glad, though startled, to see the color drain from the other woman's sunken cheeks as she recoiled as though Harriet had smacked her. Then the color rushed back until she was scarlet-faced with indignation.

"Kill you? Don't talk such nonsense. What on earth are you talking about? I just wanted to talk to you in private. All I did was put my hand over your mouth so you wouldn't scream and wake up the whole house. There's no harm in that, is there? And you didn't have to bite me like that, it was a stupid thing to do, it really hurts."

She managed a flounce even though she was actually standing still, rather too close to the bedside, and she examined her injured hand with a sulky ill grace.

"So get a tetanus jab." Harriet had no sympathy for

her. "Why on earth couldn't you have told me earlier that you wanted to talk to me? We could have got together downstairs sometime, at a civilized hour. No need for all this ridiculous cloak-and-dagger stuff." She was speaking in a reasoned tone now as she began to calm down, feeling her thumping heart slow to a more acceptable rate.

She got a sniff and a sneer in reply.

"What? And let that load of busybodies get an earful? No, thank you, I haven't discovered a single spot in this place where you can be completely private, not during the day."

Harriet's experience of Firstone Grange differed considerably from Ellen's in that respect. The house had plenty of semiprivate corners where the chairs were arranged into comfortable conversation spots, but she let it pass. After all, Ellen Ransom had spent most of her time here in the toils of Christiane Marchant, never knowing when that hateful presence would manifest itself over her shoulder. She might well have had difficulty finding a place of private sanctuary.

"Oh all right." Harriet heaved a grudging sigh. "You're here now." She indicated the light but comfortable armchair by the window. "Pull that up if you want to and then you'd better get it off your chest if you must. Are you warm enough? Want a blanket or something?"

Ellen shook her head and pulled the chair up close beside the bed. Harriet retreated a little. It was no good: try as she might she really could *not* like Ellen Ransom, no matter how distressed the woman might be; no matter what it was she was about to confide to her.

"Are you comfortable?" Harriet sat up in bed feeling quite magisterial, wrapped in her own warm red dressing gown, bought from John Lewis in Southampton expressly for the period in hospital and the subsequent convalescence. "Well, Ellen, get on with it." She took a deep breath and plunged in. "Tell me what it was that Christiane Marchant was holding over your head? What it was that made you want to kill her?"

"Ohhh!" It was a long-drawn-out sigh and Ellen cast a glance of astonishment mixed with awe at Harriet. Years of practice, Harriet reflected complacently, had made her an artist in her ability to appear superhuman, with paranormal powers of deduction. *There's not a lot of difference between little girls and very much older ones,* she decided, disguising a slight smirk as the old magic worked yet again.

"I never thought I'd see her again," whispered Ellen, twisting her hands in nervous anguish. "It was at the end of the war. I never thought…" She raised haunted eyes to Harriet, as if pleading with the other woman for understanding, for mercy.

Harriet managed a kindly nod, but said nothing, waiting for Ellen to continue.

Ellen bent her head and went on. She explained about the munitions factory near Poole and how she had lived with her sister. She told Harriet about Douglas being sent out to the Far East, about his injury, about her first casual meeting with Christiane in the spring of 1945.

"Douglas and me only had the one night together when we got married in 1942, then he had to go. He was on embarkation leave when we met and he only plucked up courage to pop the question right near the end of his time." She had a nostalgic look in her eye as she described the wedding. "I was only eighteen, poor silly little cow, but I did look nice. My sister borrowed a dress for me from her neighbor, a rose-pink crêpe it was, with a lovely draped bodice, and somebody else lent me a really classy fur stole. What with that and a pale gray hat I already had, with a pink rose pinned to it, I looked the bees' knees."

Harriet waited quietly, a reluctant pity wrung from her as she, too, contemplated that young bride and her shy bridegroom, about to go off to possible death and even more possible injury.

"I did love him," Ellen said abruptly, almost to herself. She sounded resentful as she remembered her younger self. "But he was away for three years, the war didn't end in the Far East till the August of 1945, and then he had to wait for ages till they were sent home in the transport ships.

"I had three years of having to live like a nun. I was married but not married, not really. You could only go out with a crowd if you wanted some fun but you couldn't really go out with a crowd because they all paired up and there you were, like a lemon, all on your own. So—I ended up having some fun of my own."

Decades later the defiance was still there. Harriet could hear it quite clearly in the other woman's voice. *Would I have felt like that?* she wondered. *In the same circumstances. If—what was his name? David, that's it—if David had been about to go abroad, perhaps to die, would I have married him when we were only eighteen, just to have a moment's happiness? To give him a taste of a normal life, knowing—both of us knowing— that a taste might be all he would ever have?*

Harriet had always been singularly clear-sighted and logical, even as a teenager, but given Ellen's circumstances, with a war raging round the world, she knew that however much her head might have recognized the inevitable pitfalls, she would have done just the same. *But if I had married David,* she thought, *I don't think I would have gone out looking for* fun. *Still, not everyone felt like that,* she conceded, trying to recapture the fleeting moment of sympathy she had felt.

Ellen went on talking, more confident now, her words tumbling over themselves sometimes; at others, halting and faltering.

"There was this bloke," she admitted at last. Harriet waited, concealing a sigh, for the inevitable corollary. Was this what it was all about? Guilt about an illegitimate baby still so shameful that it could cause that amount of pain more than sixty years later?

"I got caught." Ellen spoke bluntly. "In the family way," she elaborated and Harriet nodded.

"Somehow or other, *she,* Christiane, spotted it. I don't know how she knew. I didn't show and I'd managed to hide it from everybody, even our Mavis and I was actually living with her. Still, one day Chris said to me that she knew lots of old country ways of getting rid of my little problem so that nobody would ever find out."

Harriet pricked up her ears. Not a baby then, whose existence had been concealed from Douglas Ransom, but an abortion. It had been illegal in those days, of course, but still…even allowing for the change in attitudes, was it so heinous a crime? Enough to contemplate murder?

Ellen was still spilling it all out, speaking quietly, almost to herself.

"We went down to the beach, near Canford Cliffs it was, between Poole and Bournemouth," she explained. "You couldn't actually get onto the beach itself because they still had the barbed wire and concrete blocks all across but they weren't so strict about keeping watch at that time. I suppose they thought the Japs were unlikely to be invading up the English Channel."

She bit her lip, clearly shocked at her own temerity in actually making a joke, at such a time. "It was really early on a Sunday morning, about the middle of May, I suppose it would have been. I'd stayed the night with Chris, who worked as a live-in chambermaid in a hotel just outside Bournemouth. We picked that night because we knew she had the whole day off. We hitched a lift in a lorry with some bloke she had met locally— he was driving to Poole, down to the Quay, and he did a bit of a detour and dropped us off in the village. He made some crack about wishing he could see us in our bathing costumes and we just played along, joshing him, you know. It was all very light and jokey. If only he'd known.

"Chris had brewed up this drink and she made me swallow it when we woke up, long before we went out. Horrible stuff it was, herbs and so forth. I don't know what it was—she said she learnt all sorts of things like that, herbal remedies and medicines, from her grandmother. She came from somewhere quite primitive, I always reckoned, for all her airs and graces and the little hints she used to drop about being landed gentry. Mind you, I never believed that, not for a minute, though she fooled the rest of them. She never said, but

I got the idea that she'd used it herself and that's how she knew it worked.

"Anyway, it was pretty powerful stuff, whatever was in it, and I'd already started having some contractions by the time the bloke put us down near the top of the hill. It was horrible, I could hardly walk down toward the shelter for the pains, and then the waters broke. It made an awful mess."

Her eyes closed briefly on the memory of that ancient pain and the shame of it all.

"I didn't dare scream out loud, even when we stumbled into the shelter, so Chris broke off a branch of a tree and gave it to me. I bit right through it, even though it was quite thick. It was a dreadful labor, even though it was very fast. When it was nearly over, and the head and shoulders were out, Chris made a funny noise, a sort of shocked gasp. 'I thought you said you were only about four months gone?' she said to me."

Harriet scarcely drew breath, not wanting to distract Ellen from her narrative but she watched her narrowly through half-closed eyes.

"I had no idea what she was talking about but at that moment I gave another great push and the rest of the baby came out. Then there was another contraction and the afterbirth followed almost straight afterward. I just lay back, completely exhausted and gasping and crying, just relieved it was all over. The only thing I wanted to do was have a rest then get away and forget all about it.

"That was when I heard her."

Ellen's eyes darkened at the memory of the long-ago horror.

"Christiane said…she said, 'This baby is alive!

You lied to me, you stupid bitch, you were at least six months gone. What on earth are we going to do now?'"

Harriet jerked upright, staring at Ellen, her attention entirely focused now. What had happened? Was this what had given the Breton woman such a hold over her English friend?

"She started to scream at me, but then she hushed up in a hurry. We hadn't seen anyone but it was too risky to draw attention to ourselves." Ellen's tone was resentful, even at this distance in time, clearly aggrieved at the way her companion had spoken to her. "She was a hard, unfeeling cow of a girl, even then, Christiane, but she really went right over the top when she heard that baby cry. I think it was the only time I ever saw her look almost mad, she was usually so controlled, but her eyes looked all fiery and she reached out, went to pick it up, but I grabbed at it first. 'What are you going to do with it?' she asked again. I didn't say anything at first, I was trying to think what to do, thinking about Douglas and what he'd say, all the scandal. I knew I couldn't face it.

"I was in a mess so she went off to look for some water, to see if there was a standpipe anywhere near by. There was a café there, though, of course, it was shut at the time. 'You'd better start thinking *fast*,' she snapped at me. She had found the tap and managed to spot an old jam jar half buried in the sand. I think she had a bit of a hunt round but that was all she could find, and then when she came back she was still in a black temper. I was almost frightened of her but I'd been thinking hard while she was gone.

"I'd decided by then and I knew what to do."

Something in her tone sent a chill right through Harriet. There was a manic gleam in the other woman's eyes as she recalled that long-ago desperation. In the end, however, she spoke in the most matter-of-fact voice imaginable as she told Harriet what she had done, what her solution to her little problem had been.

"I realized I couldn't rely on Christiane to do another hand's turn to help me," she said calmly. "She told me straight that I was on my own now. The baby was barely breathing so I took out my handkerchief and wadded it into a pad, then I pressed it over the baby's nose and mouth until it stopped breathing. I remember I was surprised—it didn't take much doing. Like I said it was only very little and very weak. Then when it was definitely dead I got another stick and scratched out a hole in the sand and buried it."

ELEVEN

AROUND SIX O'CLOCK THE next morning Harriet reluctantly opened heavy, swollen eyelids knowing that once she was properly awake she would have to allow the previous night's revelations and horrors to come flooding back.

She had managed to get rid of Ellen Ransom quite easily. The other woman had obviously felt a great weight fall from her shoulders as she confessed to her actions and she explained volubly that from the moment Christiane Marchant had arrived at Firstone Grange, she had been blackmailing her erstwhile friend. Apparently, Ellen explained, Christiane had recognized Ellen's name and photograph from the article in the local paper, when a carefully posed picture had appeared, of Matron Winslow welcoming her first guest to Firstone Grange. This had been the circumstance that had reconciled Christiane to Alice's desperate venture and made her decide to stay.

No, there had been no suggestion that she wanted any money, that wasn't it at all, Ellen said, as Harriet had pulled herself together and thrust her out of the room. It had been power that was Christiane's heady brew. "Mind you—" Ellen had glowered with anger as she recalled the circumstances "—she made the most of it at the time. The stuff I had to hand over to that bitch. Silk stockings that I got from some of the boys

in the American Army, extra clothing coupons, any
treats I got from friends. I had to hand them all over
to her, because she threatened to tell the police. She
said I'd made her an accessory to murder and it was a
small price for me to pay, coughing up all those luxury
items. Specially—she used to smirk at me as she said
it—when a word from her could have got me arrested."

Closing the door on the woman had been the last
thing Harriet had managed to do before she collapsed
on the edge of her bed in a storm of tears. *Why was I
so upset?* she wondered now, still glue-eyed from that
breakdown.

After some difficult introspection she came up with
a painful diagnosis. If *I had been in Ellen's situation,
left alone, married yet not married, and* if *I had taken
the same course and had what Ellen had referred to
as* fun—*what would I have done, faced with the same
terrifying outcome?* For terrifying it must have been,
she acknowledged, for a young wife to be faced with
the prospect of living, breathing evidence that she had
betrayed one of the country's heroes.

She gazed down the years and remembered David,
that long-ago first love, with his floppy dark hair and
his gangling arms and legs, smiling as she recalled that
he had courted her with talk of the geography degree
he planned to do at Oxford and by enthusing about a
coming school field trip where he would be let loose
with theodolites and other exciting equipment. *Well,*
she thought, *if I had married David then become preg-
nant by another man while he was away fighting, would
I have got rid of the baby?*

It would have been difficult, to say the least. When
Harriet had been seventeen, abortion was still illegal

and dangerous, but what if the situation *had* been similar to that long-ago hypothetical wartime emergency? *I wouldn't have done what Ellen did,* she told herself fiercely. *It would have broken my parents' hearts but they would never have rejected me. We'd have managed somehow. They'd have stiffened their already upright spines, held their noses and their heads in the air and brooked no malicious remarks from family, friends or neighbors.*

That was one reason why she had felt so upset at Ellen's confession. The other had to be dredged up from a much deeper, darker place of secrets. There *had* been a man, there had been a baby, but no drastic action had been necessary; nature had taken its course and at the time her overriding emotion had been one of relief. The man was married and she had just been appointed to her first deputy headship. It would all have been extremely messy, but now she realized that part of her bitterly regretted that loss. That she had never grieved, never felt a need to grieve. Now Ellen's story had unlocked that secret door.

Last night's harsh and painful tears had been some kind of release, she acknowledged; a final admission of grief for the children she had never had, never before recognized that she had wanted. She was dismayed now to find that her dislike of Ellen Ransom had hardened perceptibly and that the momentary sympathy and fellow feeling she had experienced during the previous night's confession had completely vanished.

Wiping a stray tear away and blowing her nose, she considered those two other women, the young girls on the beach, long ago. Christiane Marchant, for so long now appearing in Harriet's imagination like the Bad

Fairy at the feast, was confirmed in her role now. It's possible, Harriet supposed, that there's an argument that the woman had just escaped from a terrifying situation and was afraid of landing in something just as bad. Harriet pursed her lips. Reasons, she thought—but not an excuse. People have survived worse ordeals and stayed humane.

Not my place to judge, though, she concluded. *It's so far outside my own experience, so how can I say what I would have done?* But what about the other one, Ellen Ransom, who saw herself so completely as the innocent victim, caught in the toils of a cold, scheming blackmailer? Ellen resented the fact that she had been, in her own eyes, treated badly both by life and the circumstances that had let her to stray in the first place, and now, recently, by the terrifying reappearance of her nemesis. Suddenly Ellen didn't look so much like a victim after all.

Among the many sensible and sensitive innovations that Pauline Winslow had introduced at Firstone Grange, one of the most appreciated was the provision of an electric kettle and tea- and coffee-making facilities. Every evening Gemma flitted from room to room, turning down the bedclothes, checking on the radiators and placing a small covered jug of fresh milk on the tea tray, along with a small Tupperware box of homemade biscuits. Firstone Grange might well be expensive, but, Harriet thought, you certainly got your money's worth.

She clambered stiffly out of bed and switched on the kettle, thoughtfully refilled last night by Gemma as part of her routine. Cuddling into her holly-red dressing gown and thrusting her feet into sensible fleecy-lined moccasins, Harriet went to stand by the window, managing, in spite of her misery, to find some kind of uplift in her spirits as she made out a lighter streak to the east breaking through the early-morning gloom.

"Morning has broken, like the first morning," she sang, then sniffled at her own eternal optimism. *You corny old Pollyanna,* she scolded herself but she knew she was already feeling better; had turned the corner from the ordeal of the previous night.

And even then, she clicked her tongue in annoyance, *I still didn't find out if Ellen Ransom actually killed her old friend and enemy.* After all that emotion, Harriet realized, so urgent had been her need to get rid of the woman, to be alone, that she had forgotten to probe further. *She's poisonous,* she reflected, *just as bad as the other one was.*

She sipped her coffee, still standing at the window, wondering what the day would bring. With a slight shrug she turned back into the room and spotted the blanket tossed casually across the armchair. Ellen had changed her mind, once into her narrative, and without comment had reached for the soft woolen blanket and draped it over her knees as she sat there, leaning forward to justify her actions. Harriet shrank at the memory of that self-righteous face, with those unpleasant eyes, and the slight flecking of spittle at the lips. Ellen had thrust her face too close to Harriet, invading her personal space, and Harriet, intimidated, had recoiled, leaning back into her banked-up pillows.

Harriet stared now in distaste at the blanket then quite deliberately she took it between her thumb and forefinger and threw it onto the floor. With an equally deliberate motion she emptied the dregs of her coffee mug over it, the brown stain spreading shockingly over the blue fine-woven wool.

Sorry, Mrs. Turner, she apologized, *but I don't want that in my room, not with her smell and her touch and her slime on it.* She scanned the rest of the room, her eyes dissatisfied, wondering if she should spray the place with deodorant in a vain attempt to rid the room of all traces of Ellen Ransom. *I want the whole place fumigated,* she thought.

Foolishness. She looked at her watch and calculated that it would be another forty minutes or so until the early-morning tea arrived. Not worth going back to bed for, so she had a quick bath and put on a comfortable gray skirt with a heather-colored cashmere sweater, clasping a string of rough-cut amethyst beads round her throat.

Now what? What to do till the early tea arrived? She sat down on her bed, shrinking from the thought of the armchair with its recollection of Ellen Ransom pouring out her story. No use trying to concentrate on the book that lay open on her bedside table, and early-morning television held no attraction. However, she really needed to rid her room of the forbidding silence, so she turned to the radio to seek distraction with the local BBC breakfast show. In the cheerful, friendly company of her favorite early-morning presenter, Harriet found herself calming down a bit.

There would be time enough to think about this latest development when she could get hold of Sam and discuss things with him, to mull it over and offer it up for his consideration. In spite of her siblinglike relationship with him—which meant, by definition, that like most male relatives, he was useless—Harriet knew very well that when it came to a crisis Sam was rock steady.

Besides, he was quite simply her oldest and best friend. A rueful grin lightened her face as she recalled his anxious warning of the night before. He wasn't very far wrong, she conceded, harking back to the suffocating terror of that first waking, with Ellen's hand clamped tightly over her mouth. Well, now she knew. If she and Sam were looking for a suspect who could be capable of murder, Ellen fitted the bill only too well. She was a physically strong woman, in spite of her years, and she had killed once. She had also, by her own admission, felt a murderous hatred for the Breton woman, the cuckoo in the nest at Firstone Grange.

But, and it was a fairly big but, she had not been alone in feeling that particular emotion. There had been others in that little group in the hall, so conveniently situated to do murder, if indeed murder had been done. There had been several people clustered near that table, others who could have pulled the fatal thread, and yet others who had been well positioned to give a quick snip with nail scissors or with a penknife. Most important of all, there had been other people there who had hated and feared Christiane Marchant.

DRRING! DRRING! FOR ONCE, when the alarm went off, Sam Hathaway woke straightaway, eager and alert for the challenges of the day. There was the inevitable stabbing at his heart as he thought of Avril, but he scrambled out of bed and into the bathroom without that dreadful hiatus between hope and despair, that momentary belief that it had all been a nightmare, that she was there beside him. This morning Sam knew it had all been a nightmare all right, and that it was a nightmare that was never going to leave him, but today he had things to do, people to see, a sense of purpose. Avril would have understood, he knew that; she would have been pushing him out of the house, encouraging him to get on with life.

Showered and shaved he set out briskly for early Communion in the Cathedral and in the glorious frosty peace he was more aware than ever of Avril's loving presence. *Don't leave me,* he pleaded silently and knew a moment of comfort, knew that she would always be in his heart. Refreshed spiritually he was ready for the fray, bursting to get over to Chambers Forge to sort out Harriet's problem. A glance at his watch made the decision for him. Matron Winslow would be impervious to his charm at such an early hour so he might as well go home and refresh the body, now that the soul had received its top-up. His administrative duties and his work in the Diocesan Office were none too onerous; in a sense he knew that he had been winding down ever since Avril's death and he determined now that his next birthday would be the clincher. Not that he intended to sit back, certainly not. There was always locum work, particularly when it came to services conducted at the crematorium, which, unlike some of his colleagues who disliked them, he quite enjoyed in an odd way—he was often meeting people who had no other contact with the church and so he tried to make the encounter both meaningful and comforting. Beside this there must be other people who had need of his energy and his experience. Financially comfortable, Sam was trusting to Providence that something would turn up soon.

In the meantime here was Harriet and the conun-

drum she had set him; not a three-pipe problem *à la*
Sherlock Holmes, he decided, but definitely a full English breakfast with all the trimmings. Replete after
egg, bacon, mushroom, fried bread and black pudding,
Sam lingered over his third cup of coffee and reflected
on the situation at Firstone Grange. His first inclination had been to laugh at Harriet's far-fetched theory.
Murder? It was absurd, particularly when considered
in the light of the slightly stifling gentility of Pauline
Winslow and her creation. But much as he had pooh-poohed the idea, especially her suggestion as to the
method, he was gradually coming round to the notion
that she might indeed have a point. He was sensitive
to atmosphere and right from his first visit he had felt
the general unease amongst the residents at Firstone
Grange. It had been there then and it was still there
now and it could not be explained away by the events
of Friday evening.

He applied logic to the "accident." Of course it
could be explained away as an entirely unfortunate sequence of occurrences which had culminated in such
a distressing result. That in itself would be enough to
establish some bad vibes but he, like Harriet, was now
almost convinced that there was something else.

The phone interrupted his train of thought. It was
Harriet.

"I wondered if you'd be free to come to lunch with
me, Sam?"

Her voice sounded slightly odd, carefully neutral,
as though she was afraid to say too much. It was very
unlike Harriet. He tested the water.

"That would be very pleasant," he replied. "Any particular reason or just the pleasure of my company?"

For a moment he thought the sound she made, and hastily disguised, had been a sob, but it was ridiculous, Harriet never cried, so he dismissed the idea and she went on.

"Matron just buttonholed me," she said, her voice still sounding flat. "Apparently the colonel has ordered a taxi and two of the ladies are going out to lunch with him, meeting up with his son and daughter-in-law somewhere. It was an unexpected, spur-of-the-moment treat, and that being the case, a favored few of us are allowed to invite guests. I'm one of teacher's pets, you see."

It had occurred to him that Harriet might be speaking so formally because Matron was there, but apparently not. He set aside the slight anxiety her tone had aroused and welcomed the livelier note in her voice, accepting her invitation with pleasure.

"Come quite early, Sam." It was back again, he could detect that odd, slight unhappiness. "We can have a sherry before lunch and a good long talk."

She rang off and Sam was left staring at the phone in his hand. Wondering.

GEMMA WAS WASHING UP the breakfast things at Firstone Grange. She had arrived back at work on the dot of eight-thirty this morning, and she sang as she scrubbed out pans, emptied the dishwasher and scrubbed down the kitchen work surfaces. A night at home under her mother's powerful but benign influence had gone a long way toward settling her mind. Her surprise rout of the hitherto sacred figure of Ryan had also given her a boost, though she was starting to feel slightly apprehensive.

What if he won't take no for an answer? she fretted. *What if he gets, well—funny?* It took very little to make Ryan "funny," she knew from past experience, and it wasn't good when that happened. As she scrubbed and sang and daydreamed there came a knock at the back scullery door and she gave a little scream as she saw a large shape outlined against the frosted glass panel. A large, *male* shape.

"Hullo, Gemma." It was Kieran, bashful moon-face beaming, big clumsy hands fidgeting, great clodhopping size thirteens shifting from side to side.

"Oh! You didn't half give me a fright. I thought it might be Ryan." She shrank back a little, giving him a nervous, sidelong glance. "He isn't—he isn't out there, is he, Kieran?"

"No, I'm on me own." He hastened to reassure her, breathing hard in his earnestness. "I just wanted to come and tell you I'm glad you dumped him, Gemma. He's not good enough for you, never was."

They stood in the doorway, smiling foolishly at each other, then she shot him a look of apology. "I can't ask you in, Kieran, I'm ever so sorry, but we're not supposed to have personal calls or visitors. But I'm ever so glad you came round, it was really nice of you."

He beamed even more widely and she realized that he was shifting around on the spot, obviously trying to pluck up courage to say something. He opened his mouth and burst out: "I wish, I mean—will you come out with me, Gemma? We could go to the pictures in Southampton if you like. I could borrow my brother's car—you know I passed my test in the summer. I'd look after you, I promise. I wouldn't drive too fast or nothing."

She felt a warmth spreading through her, a genuine feeling of pleasure and her eyes shone. "I'd really like that, Kieran. But what about Ryan? What if he gets, you know—what if he gets all funny about it, about us?"

For a moment Kieran's shoulders drooped, then he rallied and puffed out his chest. "What can he do? I'm twice as big as him and I'm the one that always has to get him out of trouble whenever he picks a fight. He's all talk and trousers."

THE VILLAGE CHURCH AT Locksley was not Doreen Buchan's usual haunt on a Sunday morning but today her mind was restless and sought any solace, any distraction that it could find. The exterior of the church always disappointed her a little, her taste running to imposing Gothic with spires and gargoyles. The small village church, with its squat, square brick-built tower, red tile-hung roof and walls of the local dressed flint, render and stone, was undoubtedly ancient, but to Doreen it looked scruffy and run-down. The only bit she really liked was the addition the locals all regarded as a joke, the spindly late-Victorian spire added by a Gothic enthusiast in the mid-nineteenth century, a vicar with private means. Doreen admired the iron-framed monstrosity while deploring the ominous tilt to starboard that the rest of the village regarded with tolerant amusement.

The inside of the church was much better, closer to her expectations. With its stark white-washed walls, uneven floors paved in ancient terracotta quarry tiles and rush-seated chairs instead of pews, it lacked the glamour Doreen felt a church should provide, but the atmosphere soothed her. It was so old, there were even gas brackets carrying mantles on the walls. Doreen had once been about to ask the vicar if they were as old as the church when a chance remark from Harriet Quigley, about the Edwardian parishioner who had donated them to the church, had set Doreen right and prevented an embarrassing faux pas. There was a stillness, a peace that transcended the bustle of outside life, but the church was also alive with a kind of energy and power, and the light that streamed through the colored glass in the east window threw a delicate rainbow pattern across the transept.

The service was strictly traditional in accordance with village inclination, held there once a month as part of the vicar's rounds. Doreen always found comfort in the majestic language of the King James Bible and the Book of Common Prayer as well as the well-known hymn tunes, strictly Ancient and Modern. But calmed and refreshed as she undoubtedly was, Doreen Buchan knew that today it had not been enough, that there would be no rest for her troubled spirit until she had sought the confessional.

"Good morning, Doreen." It was Neil Slater, waving to her as he drove past. It looked as if he had just nipped home to pick up something, she thought. He wasn't there last night—Vic had remarked on the unlighted flat when he came in from a swift half at the pub; he had made some joke about Neil getting his oats, something like that. Vic could be very coarse sometimes. He had whistled loudly, a real builder's wolf whistle, when he saw what she was wearing this morning.

"Blimey, Dor," he had said, opening his eyes as he took in her new look. "You're all done up like a Christmas tree! What's this in aid of then? It's not like you to go for bright colors like that."

"Don't you like it, Vic?" she had faltered, but he soon put her right.

"I certainly do, you look smashing, Dor," he told her. "Ten years younger and good enough to eat. Here, what on earth has brought this on?"

"Oh." She shrugged and fobbed him off. "Time for a change, I suppose."

The explanation had satisfied him, and somewhere inside she felt a tiny glow of pleasure as she caught him looking at her now and then during the morning, admiration—and yes, mounting desire—written clearly on his face.

So what *had* brought it on? she wondered, as she walked slowly along the lane. Vic was right, it was completely out of character for her to buy any clothes that drew attention to herself. Sensible navy blue, plain black, beige—oh yes, plenty of beige—that was what Doreen Buchan usually wore. Beige was safest of all. But yesterday morning something had snapped and while Vic was busy out on a site visit, Doreen had jumped into her car and headed for Southampton and the huge West Quay shopping center.

As she queued to park she had felt her courage begin to fail. *What possessed me,* she wondered, *to decide to go shopping this close to Christmas and on a Saturday, too?* Whatever it was that drove her, had made her go on. *John Lewis,* she thought, *they're bound to have what I want.* So she had found herself on an escalator to the women's fashion department. The place was packed with heaving bodies and she was jostled at almost every step, people everywhere chasing their tails in a desperate attempt to finish their present-buying. As she stood irresolute, diffidently fingering a soft woolen dress in a light, glowing turquoise, an elderly woman shopper beside her, elegantly kilted out in a classic style, turned to her with a friendly smile.

"Go on," she urged. "Try it on! That color would look beautiful on you—your eyes are almost the same color."

As Doreen hesitated, looking surprised, the other woman nodded toward the dress. "Do it," she said in an encouraging tone. "If you like, I'll wait outside the fitting rooms and you can show me, if you'd like a second opinion. Yes, honestly, I'm not in a hurry."

Now, on Sunday morning, Doreen paused to look up at the sky. No, it wasn't going to rain, thank goodness. Oh, but it had been such fun, she recalled, shopping with her new friend. Together they had collected skirts and tops and jackets in colors and styles that the aloof, awkward Doreen Buchan had never dreamed of trying, and time and again, the other woman's taste proved spot-on. She had been in fashion all through her working life, she had confided, and adored clothes, so it was a pleasure to help Doreen find things that suited her so well. The two of them had exchanged telephone numbers over coffee in the panoramic restaurant and Doreen had driven home with her new friend's promise to meet up again soon ringing in her ears.

Whatever got into me? Why did I do that? She struggled to understand the impulse that had shaken her out of her lifelong caution. After much heart searching, something, some kind of explanation finally occurred to her. *I used to wear all those dark colors so nobody could see me,* she realized, remembering how, at school, she had hidden in the girls' lavatories every day at playtime, lest her tormentors find her and start their chanting and bullying again. Later, when she was safely married to Vic and they were making their way up the ladder, the habit of concealment had remained with her. *Be discreet, be a good wife, be a good mother. Don't draw attention to yourself, don't behave in a common way, don't let them see you. If nobody can see you, nobody will ever know. They'll never find out about...that.*

She squared her shoulders and walked quite briskly past the part of the churchyard that she found distressingly untidy. She had to keep quiet about that, though, when discussing it with the locals. Visiting the village some months earlier, during the negotiations about the purchase of White Lodge, she had been surprised and perturbed to notice that a section of the churchyard had been left apparently untended, the grass long and strewn with weeds.

When she had remarked, rather acidly, on this to Neil, he had explained that the parish was involved with the Living Churchyard scheme, whereby the growth of grasses and other plants was encouraged in the hope that it would provide a habitat for birds, wild flowers, insects and small animals. Doreen supposed it was a good idea, but it had certainly looked a mess at that time and she dreaded to think how high the weeds would be in the middle of summer. She soon realized she dare not comment adversely when she discovered that the rest of the village thought it was a wonderful scheme and took every opportunity to boast about it like anything.

She and Vic had a light lunch together in the kitchen,

and as she cleared away, she inquired casually what he planned for the afternoon.

"What? Oh, sorry, Dor." He looked very sheepish and waved a hand at a pile of correspondence on the side table. "I've got to get on top of this paperwork before it gets on top of me."

Unusually this feeble pun drew a correspondingly feeble smile from her instead of a moan and she fidgeted around for a few moments before making her tentative suggestion.

"Shall I... Would you like me to drive over to Chambers Forge, then? To spend an hour or so with your dad? I'm not that busy today, I can spare the time."

He looked surprised but touched and grateful. "That's really good of you, Doreen. I know you find the old man heavy going, and to tell you the truth, so do I. If only Mum hadn't gone first, she was the glue that kept us all together, and without her, well—you know what it's like, trying to talk to him." He pushed back his chair and lumbered to his feet. "That's my girl." He planted a smacking kiss on her cheek. "You're looking lovely today—that blue suits you a treat. I did all right when I married you, didn't I, Dor? Never a bit of bother, eh? And no secrets between us, either."

She could see that he was puzzled, wondering what he could have said to set the color draining from her cheeks, but she knew how he would settle the question in his mind. Women's troubles, that's what Vic would decide. He always did and he always shied away in case she pressed any details upon him.

SAM AND HARRIET ESTABLISHED themselves in comfortable wicker basket-chairs in the bay window of the sun parlor, each with a glass of sherry pressed on them by Matron, who liked them both. They had been secretly amused to realize that Miss Winslow thought they added to the cachet of Firstone Grange. Harriet had taken great delight in telling Sam about the conversation she had accidentally overheard a day or so earlier, when Pauline Winslow had described the pair of them to Mrs. Turner, as an asset, "a very well-known family, of course, and both so tall and distinguished in their looks and bearing."

Harriet recognized that he was humoring her today, letting her play it her way, in her own time, by his response to her welcome. He gave her a pleasantly expectant smile but said nothing while she fussed over settling the chairs. At last, with the chairs arranged rather forbiddingly with their backs to the empty room, Sam looked at her and waited for her to open up, so she took a deep breath.

"Ellen Ransom regaled me with a surprising story last night," she began, then she gave him a concise rundown of what, exactly, Ellen had told her.

At his shocked indrawn breath when she recounted the dreadful conclusion of Ellen's tale, she gave a slight nod, pursing her lips. "I didn't get round to asking her about Christiane's death. As you can imagine, it was all a bit much to take in at one go." She shifted a little in her seat and avoided his eyes. Best, oldest and dearest of companions that Sam might be, there were still some topics too private for discussion, even with him. Suddenly she felt a sharp pang of regret that Avril was no longer there to share the burden. Harriet, too, had her times of desolation without the beloved friend she had met on their first day at their Swiss boarding school, when they were both age eleven.

She eyed him narrowly. "You'd better make sure you don't start giving her one of your 'hard stares,'" she advised. He responded with a faint grin. It was a family joke. A small parishioner had once accused him, not to his face but via Avril, of being like Paddington Bear in his employment of the "hard stare" as a weapon. He took pride in the accomplishment; otherwise the gentlest of men, he could make someone with a guilty conscience tremble at thirty paces, with that clear, impartial, blue-eyed stare.

The gong boomed out for lunch and they dropped the subject, both relieved to discover that they were seated some distance away from Ellen Ransom. Even without employing Sam's secret weapon they felt they would find it difficult to engage in social chitchat with the woman. They were both fair-minded, intelligent people, accustomed by training and by inclination to giving the benefit of the doubt and looking for the best in everyone, but ultimately they were upright, law-abiding citizens and they were privately appalled by the woman's confession.

After lunch they retreated with their coffee to their sanctuary and were sitting there in companionable silence, enjoying the sudden burst of pale but valiant sunshine, when a slight cough disturbed them and a diffident voice broke into their peace.

"Excuse me, Miss Quigley?" It was Doreen Buchan, nervously clutching her tan leather shoulder bag in both hands, twirling the strap into a spiral, her face looking drawn and gray against the pretty light blue dress that showed under her open dark coat. "Could I… Do you think I could possibly have a word with you?"

"Do sit down, Mrs. Buchan." Sam rose, offering her his seat as he prepared to leave, but she gestured to him to sit down again. "No, please stay, Canon Hathaway." She spoke with a quiet dignity but her eyes were dark with despair. "I'd like to talk to both of you, if you don't mind. There's something I have to say, to tell somebody before I go mad, and I thought you might agree to help me. To listen to me."

Sam pulled up another chair for her and she sat between them, primly upright, the bag lying on her lap, her hands resting on it, folded tightly.

"Go ahead, Doreen," suggested Harriet quietly. "I think you want to tell us just why you were so afraid of Mrs. Marchant, don't you? What was it that she threatened to tell your husband?"

Doreen's gasp of astonishment was followed by a ragged sigh as she visibly relaxed the rigid control of her body. Harriet knew the phenomenon, recognizing it from a thousand guilty children who had come to the conclusion that Miss Quigley would know what to do. Sam, too, had seen this before, when someone let go and handed their conscience over to a person in authority, a clergyman, for example.

"It was my mother," Doreen Buchan began in a quiet, unemotional voice. "She was always a bit moody and one day she got very upset about something so she took the coal hammer and battered my father to death while he was dozing beside the fire. Then when my baby brother woke up and cried, she hit him, too."

"Oh my dear!" Harriet put out a swift hand to

Doreen's arm, desperate to comfort her, but Doreen just went on speaking in that quiet, frozen voice.

"I wasn't there at the time because she'd sent me down to the shops to buy some bread. I was about six at the time. I found her when I got home—she was sitting there amid all that blood, cradling the coal hammer in her arms and singing to it like a baby. With her real baby dead in the hearth and my dad making terrible, gurgling sounds as he died."

She raised her eyes and looked at Harriet. "It turned out that my grandmother had ended up in an asylum and her mother had jumped overboard off the Isle of Wight ferry. They put my mother away for the rest of her life and I was passed round all the aunts on my dad's side of the family."

Her listeners had no idea that her head was filled now with the sound of children chanting, holding hands in a circle, hemming her in so that there was no escape from their words. "Loony kid." "Murdering bitch's brat," and the chorus of shrill young voices singing, "Dippy, dippy Doreen, your mother is a moron."

"I worked and worked and I got out. I got away. Nobody knew, I could have sworn it. I was sure there was no way they could find out, but it turned out she knew… I changed my name and moved to Portsmouth, away from Bournemouth where it all happened. Maybe I should have been braver, gone to London, or to Scotland, or even abroad, but I would have felt too strange. Anyway, in the end Portsmouth was far enough and it worked out well, all those years, it worked like a dream. I met Vic and we got married and had the children and we got on, moving up in the world and now we're really well-off. I've got everything I ever dreamed of.

"And then Vic's mother went and died and his father started to go downhill quite fast, so we got him to try out this place."

Her eyes were tragic as she stared bleakly out of the window.

"And then I came here. And saw *her*."

"But how did she know?" asked Sam in a gentle voice.

"She knew one of my aunts," began Doreen, her face twisted in anguish, so Harriet interrupted to spare her the difficult story.

"Of course, Christiane Marchant worked in Bournemouth when she first came over to England. I expect she kept up with some of her acquaintances and must have seen you, heard about you, or rather your mother, sometime when she was visiting them. Your aunt must have let something slip and Christiane seems to have had a taste for scandal." She patted Doreen's hand with great kindness and sympathy. "It sounds more like postnatal depression, you know, than some kind of hereditary insanity. That can certainly run in families, too. You haven't told your husband and children about your family history, I suppose, have you?"

"Of course I haven't." The younger woman looked appalled and ignored Harriet's suggested diagnosis. "How could I do that? What could I say? How can you tell a man that your mother was locked up in an asylum for murder and that your grandmother was mad and your great-grandmother must have been, too, except that she killed herself before she could be locked up?"

A harsh sob broke from her. "I'd have lost him if he'd known, he's so proud of us, so proud of what we've achieved, this would kill him. He's very set on things being done properly, everything has to be normal. And what about my son and daughter? What kind of an inheritance is that to wish on your children? I can't tell you how I've watched them, panicking when they had tantrums, wondering if it was coming out in them."

Her lips were pressed tightly together to stop them trembling. "When that woman started to taunt me about it, something seemed to snap inside me," she volunteered. "I knew then that I was just like my mother after all. I wanted to see her suffer. I wanted to *kill* her."

TWELVE

THE WORDS HUNG IN THE AIR. Harriet looked at Sam, schooling her face to be absolutely blank, then she turned back to look at Doreen Buchan. She had seen her cousin stiffen with shock, as she had felt herself do also, during that confession of an old and dreadful anguish. As they took on board the horror of it all, so, she realized, did Doreen begin to relax. She seemed quite composed now, her burden laid on other shoulders, much of the coiled spring tension eased, and as she rose to her feet with unhurried movements, she held out a hand to Harriet, with a grateful smile.

"I can't tell you how much better I feel now," she said quietly. "Thank you so much for listening."

"I… We haven't done anything to help," protested Harriet rather feebly, while Sam held his tongue, but Doreen waved the disclaimer aside.

"Yes, you have," she insisted. "You let me talk and it's helped me to sort out things in my head. I've decided to tell Vic." For a moment the anxious look was back, doubt lurking in her eyes, then her face cleared and she gave a brisk nod.

"I don't suppose I'll tell him all of it, not about my grandmother and *her* mother perhaps, but I could sort of gloss over what my mother did. I could say something like—she had a breakdown, something of that kind. He needn't know about my little brother, he's never heard that I even had one. I told him I was an only child. And he already knows that my father died when I was little. I don't have to go into detail about how he actually died."

She pulled on her suede gloves and hitched the shoulder bag up over her left shoulder. Giving them a bright social smile, she prepared to leave, with just a parting comment at the door.

"Of course, everything I've told you today is in the strictest confidence," she said.

"Naturally," Sam assured her, speaking for both of them.

Doreen nodded graciously. "As long as you understand that," she said and walked out of the room with a spring in her step, leaving them thoughtful and silent.

At last Harriet let out a long, sighing whistle. "Am I alone in sensing the tiniest hint of a threat in that parting thrust?" she queried, regarding Sam with an intelligent interest.

"No, I should say you weren't" was the response. Sam's piercing blue eyes were alive with eager calculation. "Good God! What on earth are we to make of that little lot? Did she do it, Harriet, do you think? On balance I'd say she had the strength of resolve, not to mention the inherited talent."

"Ouch, that's hardly fair," protested Harriet. "That's exactly the kind of crack she must have lived with all through her childhood and dreaded encountering again since she made her escape. She must have been living on a knife edge all through her married life, in case Vic should discover her secret. No wonder she's such an awkward creature. Still—" she frowned at a fingernail that needed filing "—did you notice how she was dressed? I've never seen her wearing anything other than dull beige or brown, or navy, but today she had on a dress that looked brand-new, and in a lovely glowing light blue. I wonder why? Perhaps something has just snapped? I have to admit you could be right. I'm beginning to wish we hadn't started this burrowing into the past, Sam. God only knows what we're going to dig up next."

"Poor old Harriet." His grin was sympathetic. "I'm not sure, though, that we actually did any digging for that latest effort. Doreen Buchan wished it on us of her own free will. But you do have a point. Here we are, both of us quite convinced we witnessed a murder, and all of a sudden we're confronted with two perfectly plausible suspects."

He took a surreptitious look round the sun parlor, lowering his voice as a couple more residents entered, and scanned the section of the entrance hall that was just visible through the open door. He shot her another look, with a slight frown and still speaking in a quiet voice.

"I remember you told me right at the beginning of this, even before the concert, that there were one or two other possible contenders, as well. What are we going to do about it all, Harriet?"

He was destined not to hear whatever solution Harriet had in mind at that moment, as they were interrupted by Neil and Alice, both trying manfully to disguise their glowing happiness in view of their surroundings, with all the distressing connotations.

"Hi, guys. Having fun?"

Neil was clearly having real trouble trying to suppress his high spirits, and Harriet, who had known him since his babyhood, took great delight in witnessing his happiness after the years of loneliness and heartache. Alice was, not surprisingly, taking it much more quietly but she had a glow of radiant contentment that warmed Harriet's sentimental heart. Alice was beginning to look like an attractive woman.

"What are you doing here?" Sam got up to pull some more chairs forward so they could look out and enjoy the sunshine that was now pulling out all the stops and making an effort to impress. The other occupants of the room got up and departed, looking a bit sniffy at the cheerful buzz of greeting.

Alice answered after a glance at Neil, who nodded encouragement. "We just dropped by to tell Miss Winslow that I don't want any of Mother's things back," she told them quietly. "I said she could give them to charity or chuck them out, I don't really care, as long as I don't have to do anything with them."

Harriet's approving nod seemed to reassure her and she hesitated, then spoke again.

"Sam," she began, turning to the tall man who was regarding her kindly and shrewdly. "Are you sure you don't mind coming to the crematorium tomorrow? I've said all along I don't want a fuss, just the quietest affair possible, in the circumstances, but it will be a real comfort to have you taking the service."

As Sam smiled and started to reassure her, she turned to Harriet with a pleading look. "And you'll come, too, won't you, Harriet? There's nobody I'd rather have as support." She drew in a sharp breath and the anxious look was back on her face. "But will you be up to it? It's a bit of an imposition, asking you to stand around in the cold, not long after your operation."

"Of course I'll be all right." Harriet's answer was brisk; she was determined to forestall any discussion of her health. "Sam can drive me and there's no standing around at the crematorium, it's not like a burial. I'll be fine and only too glad to help out."

"Excuse me?"

For a second time that afternoon Harriet and Sam found themselves being interrupted by a member of the Buchan family. This time it was old Fred Buchan himself, looking painfully formal, standing upright with a military bearing, an expression of bleak despair clouding his face.

"I wish to speak with you, if you please." His voice, still so strongly accented, was heavy and dead, and the younger pair rose to leave, clearly glad of the chance of escaping this haunted old man with his echoes of a past they could never share. "No, if you please." He held up a peremptory hand. "You, too, please, if you will. I want that you should stay and hear what I have to say. It concerns the young lady. And you, Mr.—that is— Canon Hathaway, you were kind to me. That helped. And now I know that I must make my confession to you all."

Alice and Neil took their seats with very obvious reluctance, clearly puzzled and in Alice's case beginning to look distressed. Harriet sneaked a look at her cousin Sam. What now? He gave a tiny shake of his head and looked back at Fred Buchan. A shiver of dread seized Harriet. There was something about the old man that told of long-ago torments and present despair. Whatever he was about to tell them was going to be unpleasant at the very least. At worst it would be unbearable.

She braced herself. "Well, Mr. Buchan?" Her voice was cool and, she was relieved to note, unfaltering. "I suppose you're going to tell us about Christiane Marchant and what happened to the men in her family? On that godforsaken little neck of granite that sticks out into the Atlantic, over in the far west of Brittany."

"Hexe!" Unbelievably, the man made the sign of the horns as he shrank back in his chair. "You must be— *aber vas*—a witch, yes? How else could you know that? Nobody could possibly know—there is nobody left."

Alice and Neil had jerked upright in their wicker chairs, both staring at him, open-mouthed. Sam Hathaway's face wore only an expression of grave interest while Harriet's face looked remote.

"I know" was all she said at first. Then, as the old man sat there with the light shining on his bald head, his tongue flicking around his dry lips and his frozen, fearful light blue eyes fixed on her, she turned to the other people in the group. "We all know the story," she said quietly. "You told us the other day, Alice, remember? Your mother lived in a tiny village, remote from any big towns, remote even from the bigger villages and other communities. For much of the time I imagine the Germans left them to their own devices. I don't suppose it could have been worth much to them."

A flicker from Fred Buchan caught her eye and alerted her.

"Or perhaps..." She thought it over. "Perhaps it *was* useful? Would there have been some strategic value, I wonder? Anyway, something went wrong, a Resistance attack on the local Germans maybe? Who knows, but whatever it was it went wrong and the Germans rounded up all the men, or rather all *males,* in the village." She bit her lip and fell silent for a moment then continued, "What happened next, Mr. Buchan?" She fixed him with an accusing stare. "Did you shoot them all, even the little boys?"

"If only we had," came the shocking reply. "If only we had."

There was an appalled silence, broken by Alice, who was looking puzzled.

"But…but I understood Mr. Buchan was a Czech, or a Hungarian, or something like that? Eastern European anyhow. Are you telling us that he's a German? That he was a Nazi soldier?"

"That's *precisely* what I'm telling you," agreed Harriet. "Because that's what he is, and what he was."

They all turned to look at the old man seated quietly with them in the sunny bay window. Bald, broken, in his eighties, a harmless old man. Somebody's husband, somebody's father, even somebody's grandfather. But not, surely not, a murderer?

"Well, Mr. Buchan?" Her clear voice was inexorable, jabbing at him, stirring him to sit up, forcing him to answer. "What did you mean when you said that? *If only you had shot them?* What did you do to them that would have made death by shooting a merciful release?"

Alice looked green and nauseated and as she clapped a hand over her mouth, Neil pulled his chair close to hers and put a comforting arm round her.

"There was a tunnel in the granite," he said, still in that flat, dead tone. "There had been a small fort, more of a lookout post, I understood, during the Napoleonic times, and they blasted a narrow ammunition store out of the solid rock and sealed it with a stout door. In the Second World War also, there was only a small guard, when I was posted there. Just an observation crew, mostly boys, that was all."

He glanced at Alice, a kind of pleading in his eyes.

"I don't expect you to believe this, but they did not hate us, not the small crew of us, just boys and young men. We kept our noses out of their business and they made no trouble for us. They were mostly fishermen, of course, and sometimes we turned a blind eye to their smuggling. It all worked out smoothly, even some joking, a little bit of harmless flirting. Then they sent us a new officer." A frown creased his pink, innocent old face. "There was a rumor that he had been in some trouble with his previous unit. *Ach,* he had a hasty temper, that man. There was some bad trouble, it is too long ago to dig it all over now. But the *Herr Oberst*, he... How do you say it? He overreacted and said that they must all die."

There was a long, long silence, when even the temperature seemed to drop. Fred Buchan appeared unwilling, or perhaps unable, to break it. A slight movement from Sam, who shifted his chair out of the direct path of the weak sunlight, recalled the old man to his surroundings.

"All of those men—there were about a dozen grown men and some lads in their late teens and then...then there were the three young ones. We had to herd them into the tunnel, it had been emptied earlier, all the ammunition carted away into the storerooms. Those of us who had been there for quite a long time, we had no quarrel, we liked the people and they got on with us, but he just laughed at our protests. He stood there and laughed and threatened us, he said he would shoot us. We were ordered to club them to death. He said… the officer said it would be a crime to waste bullets on such. He told us to collect up stones from a derelict house and…he made us build a wall."

The dead voice faltered and died away into an appalled silence that went on, and on, and on. At last Harriet let out a shaky little sigh and whispered the question that was uppermost in all their minds.

"Did you kill them first? Did you make sure that they were all dead? Before you walled them up?"

He made no reply. There was no need.

"I ran away that night," he whispered. "I stole some clothes off a washing line and I stole a rowing boat also, then I just set off down the coast, not caring about what happened to me. I had some luck, though. The rowing boat capsized and I was knocked out, but a passing Spanish fishing boat picked me up just in time." He shrugged. "I think I knew nothing for a long time, I had severe head injuries, you see." In spite of themselves they all looked at the scar crossing his scalp. "The rest of it? *Ach,* at first I could not speak, then I *would* not speak, so they thought I must be a refugee. And so I got out of France. They put me off the fishing smack in Spain and from there I fell in with a lot of other displaced people and ended up in England."

"And Christiane Marchant recognized you?"

Fred Buchan nodded in answer to Sam's quiet question. "After all those years…" He shook his head in disbelief. "I did not think it could be possible at first. Oh yes, she knew me from the time I was part of the guard and so she knew I had been there when it happened.

She knew that I was part of it. And the other day she told me the things that happened after I had escaped."

His tongue darted out, licking dry lips. "The *Herr Oberst,* he kept the girls and the women locked up in the church for six or seven days, and he allowed them just enough food to keep them from starving. Then he let them out. She said that they tore that stone wall down with their bare hands but of course it was too late, they were all dead—by then. But they had not all been dead to start with. A few lay huddled up against the wall, their fingers worn to bloody shreds, even the little boys. There were two young ones among those who died…last. They were very, very young, the little one was only twelve. They were both her little brothers."

The words hung in the silence, then Neil pulled Alice into his arms, rocking her as, her face twisted in an agony of shock, she wept harsh, wrenching, difficult sobs that racked her slight frame.

"Oh God," she whispered when she could speak. "No wonder she was like she was. How could you be normal, how could you ever recover from something like that?"

Harriet's face had been buried in her handkerchief but now she raised tear-filled eyes to look at Fred Buchan. Sam was staring fixedly out of the window and she caught the words he whispered, *"Man's inhumanity to man,"* before he turned back to look into the haunted eyes of the man sitting beside him. Neil was too preoccupied with Alice, with her shock and grief, to have fully taken on board the implications of the old man's story.

Fred Buchan hauled himself awkwardly out of his

chair and pulled himself erect with a slight bow. "I must thank you for allowing me this time and for listening to my…confession," he said. He turned on his heel and headed heavily toward the door to the hall.

"Sam?" It was just a shred of a whisper but Harriet knew Sam would understand. She watched with approval as Sam stood up hastily and hurried after the other man.

"Wait a moment, Mr. Buchan," he called softly. The older man halted and hesitated with an apprehensive look on his face. "I'll just walk along with you, if I may?"

Harriet relaxed with a nod of approval. Sam's compassion had kicked into action and he was going to give the man what comfort he could, drawing on the wells of humanity deep within his own nature, and on his years of training. That was good, she sighed. It would make him feel less impotent, less strapped by their total inability to accept that any one human being could do such a thing to another, still less to a child. Sam would be gentle with the old soldier, recognizing the anguished conscience that had tormented him for a lifetime. And what could he have done anyway? He would have been just another dead guard and the villagers would still have been massacred.

For herself there was nothing she could do to help Fred Buchan. By inclination and by upbringing he was not the type to accept help from a woman. *Kinder, Kirche, Küche* were probably still his watchwords. But Sam might get through to him.

And what about Christiane Marchant? Harriet wondered, and went over the terrible story again. *Yes. Alice is right, something so dreadful* would *poison you, could destroy you.* And yet…and yet…people had suffered even worse tragedies, in the concentration camps for instance, and survived with their spirits whole and un-sullied. *It's as I thought before,* she realized. *A reason is not an excuse.* Christiane had suffered horribly, there could be no question of that, but it was still no excuse for seeking out weakness and preying on other people. No excuse for tormenting those other human beings for sins committed a lifetime ago. No, in spite of her un-doubted ordeal, Christiane Marchant had been a first-class bitch and that was all there was to it.

She turned her attention to Alice, leaning brokenly against Neil's shoulder. They'd be all right, too, no need for any of Harriet's ministrations there. "I think you ought to take Alice home, Neil," she suggested gently but firmly. "She's had a nasty shock. You run her a hot bath and once she's soaking in it, get her a nice cup of tea." As he raised an eyebrow, she grinned. "Well, I always find it a great comfort," she said defensively.

"Me, too." Alice struggled into an upright position and managed a watery smile. "I like to have a good book to read as well, but this time I think I'd settle for Neil to come in and talk to me instead."

As they prepared to leave, Neil gave Harriet a searching look. "You look pretty exhausted yourself, Old Hat," he suggested. "Why don't you take your own advice for once?"

"Go away, Neil, I'm as tough as old boots, I'll be fine." She shooed him away, flapping her hand at him, and when she found herself alone at last in the now empty room, she sank back in her chair, intending to apply her mind to the various puzzles perplexing her. Instead she dropped asleep almost at once and never stirred when, an hour later, Sam looked in on her. He tiptoed out, holding a finger to his lips as he encountered Matron Winslow.

Pauline Winslow was always glad to see her clients enjoying themselves in whatever they chose to do, and Harriet, when Matron looked in on her, certainly looked pretty blissful, snoozing away to the tune of a gentle buzzing that was far too ladylike to be called a snore. Matron nodded gaily to Sam and hung a Do Not Disturb notice on the door of the sun parlor as she gently drew it to a close.

"That ought to do the trick." She smiled up at Sam.

"Thank you, Miss Winslow," he told her gratefully. "That's a very kind thought. Harriet could do with a decent long sleep." As she turned away he called out to her again. "I wonder, do you think I could leave a note for Harriet? And borrow a sheet of paper to write it on?"

"Of course you may, Canon Hathaway." She nodded immediate agreement, trying a little joke. "And would you also like a pen to write it with?" She was all smiles and eager to help. Harriet had proved to be a model guest and Pauline Winslow was well aware that between them, Harriet and Sam knew a surprising number of what she thought of as the *right* people, the kind of people who could afford, and would appreciate, a short stay at Firstone Grange. Especially if it was endorsed by a personal recommendation.

With a grateful smile Sam accepted the offer of pen, paper, envelope and a desk, together with a chair to sit on while he wrote. He scribbled a note, then put the sealed envelope on the table in the entrance hall.

"I'll see Miss Quigley gets it the moment she wakes up," promised Matron as Sam picked up his scarf and gloves and departed.

MORE THAN AN HOUR LATER Harriet emerged from the sun parlor, slightly embarrassed but considerably refreshed, yawning and stretching as she met Matron's eyes with a bashful grin.

"Heavens, isn't it shocking? I must watch myself—it's only old people who can't get through the day without a nap. I must be slipping."

"Not you, Miss Quigley." Pauline Winslow gave her a reassuring smile. "Oh, by the way, Canon Hathaway left you a note. He had to get home, he said, but he'll be in touch."

She watched curiously as Harriet picked up the envelope addressed to her in Sam's tall, pointed handwriting, a sudden frown creasing her brow at a recollection.

"Canon Hathaway said I was to tell you to be careful," said Pauline Winslow, looking puzzled.

Harriet smiled and shrugged it off, but she knew what Sam meant. Perhaps Doreen Buchan might not be on the premises and therefore not an immediate threat to Harriet's safety. However, at Firstone Grange there were at least two self-confessed murderers, both of whom had entrusted Harriet with their secrets. Secrets that had proved a deadly burden for more than sixty years.

Might they not find themselves regretting such a confidence?

Her frown deepened as she read Sam's hasty note.

Just a line to let you know I had a word with Tim Armstrong. He obviously wanted to get something off his chest. (Seems to be the "in" thing round here today.) I let him get on with it as it was one of his clear spells.

It seems he moved down to Hampshire more than thirty years ago, after applying for a transfer from a branch of Lloyds Bank in Yorkshire, because of a scandal that involved his wife. He said she was suffering from "female troubles," so I assume he was talking about the menopause. Anyway, she got herself had up for shoplifting. It's a common enough story but in those days the courts weren't so likely to accept hormonal deficiencies as a plea, so they threw the book at the poor woman and gave her a short custodial sentence. Apparently the magistrate was a real "hanger and flogger" and he said he was making an example of her. When she came out of jail she tried to kill herself but Tim managed to get her to the hospital in time, then he spoke to the bank about a transfer, which was arranged and put through in half the usual time. He reckoned they were glad to be rid of the embarrassment: it had been plastered all over the local papers, of course.

That was all he told me, then he suddenly did one of those shifts of his, drifted away, you know how he does. And that was that. But I thought you'd better know, as he was there in your little group of suspects.

Wonder how Christiane Marchant found out about Tim's wife? Perhaps her husband knew—I suppose he'd have been Jane Armstrong's family doctor once they moved down here.

Anyway, keep your head down below the parapet. I'll be in touch after dinner tonight.

Harriet read the letter a second time then folded it and slipped it into her pocket as she went thoughtfully up to her room. She splashed her face with cold water to freshen up and went to look out of the window at the garden below. The feeble burst of sunshine had long since fizzled out and the shadows were closing in as the midwinter darkness fell.

Well, Miss Harriet Quigley, she spoke sternly to herself. *This is another fine mess you've got yourself into and no mistake. What with Tim Armstrong desperate to keep his wife's shame a secret—or at least, I assume that's what it was all about, poor old devil. Then there's Doreen Buchan with her unfortunate family history, terrified that Vic and the children would find out. And as if that wasn't enough, we've now got Ellen Ransom and Fred Buchan to add to the list. They say it's easy to kill, after the first time.*

"I wonder," she spoke aloud, dragging the words out. "I wonder if one of those two found it so?"

THIRTEEN

"ARE YOU SURE, HARRIET?" Sam sounded extremely worried when his cousin, after some profound thought, telephoned him and asked him not to call round after dinner.

"Of course I'm sure." Harriet made an effort to sound her usual competent, no-nonsense self. "I don't think I can possibly be in any danger but if it makes you feel better I'll lock my bedroom door and locate a blunt instrument to tuck under my pillow."

She laughed out loud at his snort of indignation. "Oh, come on, Sam. I'll be perfectly safe. Besides, what could you do? Matron would scarcely let you sleep in my room, after all." She allowed her voice to falter slightly, which in any case wasn't difficult and needed scarcely any acting ability. "If you must know, Sam, I'm completely worn-out. I want to get a decent night's rest so I can cope with going home tomorrow. To tell you the truth I could really do without this early start for the funeral tomorrow but I do feel I ought to be there to provide extra support for Alice."

His silence spoke volumes and she conceded the point with a tired laugh. "Yes, I know, I know. I could have got out of it so I've only myself to blame. But the fact remains that I'll be up and about rather early in the morning and I'm terrified the powers that be, in the shape of Pauline Winslow or, perish the thought, the doctor, might spot that I'm dead tired and say I can't go home tomorrow."

He grunted but she detected a weakening in his determination, and carried on. "Well, I'm going home and that's that, but I'd rather be relatively fit and able, hence the early turn-in tonight. All right?"

She took his irritable mutter for an assent and wound up the conversation. "You'll pick me up at about quarter to nine tomorrow then? Lovely, see you then. Good night, Sam."

She flicked her mobile shut but not before she had heard him burst out with: "Damn!" A grin flickered across her face as she pictured him standing irresolute, probably chewing at his bottom lip as he always did when perplexed. She shrugged. He'd get over it; he knew, none better, that she was no fool and she had promised to take sensible precautions.

Harriet ate sparingly at dinner that night, then took her coffee into the drawing room, reluctant, in spite of her genuine weariness, to be on her own with her increasingly uneasy thoughts.

"Come and join us, dear lady," boomed the colonel, with a welcoming smile. With a feeling of relief, she sauntered over to his corner while he fussed about, rearranging his harem of ladies to make room for her.

"How was your day out, Colonel?" she inquired politely.

It turned out to be the perfect conversational opening gambit. A gentle stream of inconsequential chatter ebbed and flowed around her as the colonel, a relative newcomer to Hampshire, bubbled over with enthusiasm about his day's sightseeing trip, accompanied by his lady friends. He proceeded to give her a lecture, a rundown on the day's excitements.

"We took a little drive into the New Forest," he told her, beaming at the memory. "I simply had to have a look at the Rufus Stone, of course. Did you know that it marks the spot where King William Rufus met his death by an arrow?"

He pressed the question and she gave in. "Er, yes, I had heard that," she said, managing not to roll her eyes. You couldn't live in Hampshire, she thought, and not know about the New Forest, surely?

"Oh, yes." He nodded with a smile. "Well, I bet you didn't know that there's a connection with that event, right here in Chambers Forge, did you, dear lady?"

She swallowed and pretended ignorance. He meant no harm and getting irritated with the old bore was a million times better than sitting alone in her room and brooding about murder, or worse—the possibility of a murderer on the prowl.

"Yes, indeed." He grew expansive, happy to be instructing the weaker sex. "They brought Rufus's body right through Chambers Forge on the way to the Cathedral at Winchester. That's where King's Road gets its name, they say."

She let his voice wash over her, as he waxed lyrical about the cream tea he and his ladies had enjoyed in Lyndhurst on the way home. She opened her eyes at that, admiring his cast-iron digestive system; she had been slightly awed, sitting opposite him at dinner, to see the amount of food he tucked away, and that on top of scones and jam and cream and almost certainly cake, as well.

"People talk to you," a friend had once told her, and

she knew it was true. She was a good listener and other people brought her their troubles in the hope that Miss Quigley would make it all better. *Even the colonel,* she thought, *he's maundering on because he's got a new audience, and then there are those wretched life histories that have been forced on me in the last twenty-four hours. No,* she thought with a frown. *That's not strictly true, nobody forced me to hear them and I wasn't reluctant to listen—until I heard them, that is. I suppose you can't pick and choose what to let people tell you, if you practically invite their confidences.*

Tim Armstrong was nowhere to be seen but Ellen Ransom was sitting alone in a corner, her forbidding silence as eloquent as a sign hanging round her neck. Matron tended not to encourage visitors on Sunday evenings, though it was not uncommon to see the occasional son or daughter exhibiting the customary mixture of guilt and gratitude, but tonight the residents were alone. Fred Buchan was glued to the television, though what he made of the nostalgic comedy drama set in the 1960s was hard to detect.

Weariness got the better of Harriet in the end and she rose, offering the colonel an apologetic smile. "Time for bed, I believe," she murmured, nodding pleasantly to her companions. "No, Colonel, don't get up, please. Good night, everyone, pleasant dreams."

Pleasant dreams? Now what on earth made me say that? She sighed. *Must have been trying for the power of positive thinking, I suppose.* Her feet dragged a little, in spite of herself, as she made her way along the landing to her room. The last time, she thought, a small surge of excitement reminding her that this time tomorrow she would be in her own home, able to relax in her own way and not obliged to maintain her bright, social smile whenever she encountered anyone. *I can sulk and slob, shout and cry, and be thoroughly miserable if I want,* she thought, her face brightening.

A sudden footstep close behind her gave her a hideous shock, the jolt causing her spine to judder painfully.

"Ohh! Tim! You made me jump," she panted accusingly, putting out a hand to steady herself against the wall. "I nearly had a heart attack."

"I'm sorry, Harriet." His voice sounded grave. "I didn't mean to frighten you. Are you all right now?"

She nodded, swallowing and letting her panic subside when, to her astonishment, he gave her a tiny awkward bow. "Can I escort you to your room, *madame?*"

Still extremely shaken, Harriet suppressed an insane desire to quote her late, much-loved headmistress and reprove Tim with the words, "You can, but the question is, *may* you." Sam's wife—dear Avril—would have shrieked with laughter at the memory, the pair of them having had that particular rule of grammar dinned into their heads at school, but no…it was scarcely appropriate here. So Harriet nodded silently and he walked her to the end of the landing. At her door she paused in the act of reaching out for the handle. The door was very slightly ajar.

"Tim?" It was the faintest thread of a whisper, accompanied by a frantic pointing. The two of them advanced cautiously, listening with all ears. There were faint sounds of movement inside the room. They stared anxiously at each other.

Tim, who for some strange reason actually seemed to be enjoying himself, showing no sign of one of his increasingly common lapses, put a finger to his lips and looked round the landing, obviously searching for something. On a small polished side table stood a tall, rather ugly vase, glazed in shiny reds and blues and containing a bunch of dried bulrushes and pampas grass. With a dapper flourish Tim removed the grasses and presented them to Harriet with another, more practiced bow and a grin of genuine mischief on his frequently bewildered, careworn face.

For a moment Harriet's heart sank. *Oh no, don't let Tim go doolally, not now when I need him,* but she realized that he was alert and excited by the situation. Astonished but amused, Harriet accepted the improvised bouquet with a graceful curtsy. *Maybe I can tickle the intruder into submission,* she decided, making a face, then her wry amusement disappeared as she realized that Tim had hefted the heavy stoneware vase in his right hand and was slipping noiselessly into her dark bedroom.

The next few moments passed in total confusion as Harriet brought up the rear, armed with her dusty bouquet and pausing only to shut the door behind her and turn the key. Snapping on the light she was stunned to find that Tim had taken the intruder completely by surprise and had brained him with the big vase. It was a tribute to the ingenuity and workmanship of Victorian pottery workers, Harriet decided, feeling slightly hysterical, that the ugly great thing had bounced back unscathed.

That was more than could be said, however, of the intruder who had proved less fortunate and lay groaning on the floor, his head cradled tenderly in his hands.

"Here, let's get a look at him." Harriet surged forward, dropping her grasses onto the dressing table while wondering how on earth she and Tim were going to restrain the young thug. *I wonder why the average convalescent home for the elderly isn't equipped with handcuffs and rope,* she thought, still on that slight note of hysteria. *I suppose retired bondage freaks would make that a number-one requirement.* She felt a bubble of laughter begin to rise and bit her lip. *Get a grip, you daft old biddy,* she gave herself a stern scolding. *This isn't a game.*

"Good God!" She had by now managed to get a good look at the skinny boy, clad in black leather, writhing on the floor. "It's Ryan, Gemma's ex-boyfriend."

"Gemma?" Tim peered short-sightedly at his groaning victim.

"You know Gemma." Harriet tugged at her dressing gown cord. "The little dark girl who helps Mrs. Turner in the kitchen and around the house. Here…" She bent to whip the cord neatly round Ryan's wrists, giving him a brisk shove onto his front with the aid of her foot— no heavy lifting, she grinned to herself—and yanking the cord up round his ankles, as well. "There we are, trussed up like the Christmas turkey."

"Gemma?" Tim was still one or two steps behind, then, to her surprise, a slow smile of pure, red-blooded masculine lust spread over his face. "Oh, I know, you mean the one with the enormous—"

"She's certainly a well-built girl," Harriet interrupted in reproof, frowning primly. For God's sake. Did men never, ever stop thinking about sex? Even when they were over eighty?

She unlocked her bedroom door and looked out, casting a swift glance up and down the corridor. "Nobody about, thank goodness. Let's take a look at what we've caught."

They stood there silently gazing down at him, watching the expressions chase themselves across Ryan's face. He was easy to read. Uppermost was incredulity, that two stupid old buggers should have caught him so easily. There was also a tiny germ of fear. Harriet could see that he was worried, and that Tim's fierce onslaught with the heavy vase had set him off balance. He was probably wondering whether they were quite sane. *After all,* she thought with a philosophical shrug, *he's only a kid. I wouldn't be surprised if he thinks this is some kind of asylum.*

She felt a slightly shamefaced delight in his unease. *Let the little scrote be afraid of someone else for once,* she thought, while she took a comprehensive look round her room. No sign of anything missing, no obvious damage, either.

"Let's have a look at you, Ryan," she announced briskly. "Turn out his pockets, Tim."

They netted quite a haul. Ryan had so far only been in one room but it had been the room occupied by the colonel's chief lady friend, who was a great one for flaunting what she called her bits and bobs. Although guests were asked to deposit valuables in Miss Winslow's safe, the colonel's lady tended to forget and wore her jewelry in rotation. *God only knows,* thought Harriet in despair, *why the woman brought real stuff with her. It's quite unsuitable.* But although tonight had been an outing for the impressive sapphires, Ryan's pockets still yielded a glittering collection: a diamond ring and brooch, a pair of ruby earrings and an emerald bracelet. *More money than sense,* sniffed Harriet, *and not a shred of taste, either.*

"Were you just in the one room, boy?" Tim asked sternly, brandishing the lethal pot with a casual flourish when Ryan hesitated. An urgent nod was the reply, accompanied by a groan as the movement made his headache smart.

"How on earth did you think you were going to get away with it?" Harriet wondered out loud. Jumpy as a cat in case anyone spotted her, she had stealthily crept into the next room, left unlocked as casually as it had been strewn with precious stones. She had scattered the jewelry onto the untidy dressing table, taking the precaution of giving the pieces a rub with her handkerchief. *I don't know much about fingerprints,* her face creased in a frown, *but a quick wipe won't hurt. I don't really want the brat arrested.* "You know Gemma and Kieran would give you away. They'd crumble as soon as a policeman spoke sternly to them. What did you hope to gain?"

"I wasn't going to stick around," he muttered sulkily. "I was going to pinch a car and go to London. I'm pissed off with Gemma and my mum's always nagging at me. I thought I'd be able to trade the stuff when I got there."

"No doubt you would." Harriet sighed, looking at his dark, thin face. There was no question, she admitted, he was a sexy-looking little runt, in spite of a slight ferrety look about the eyes. *I wonder why that is?* As always she was happily sidetracked by trivia once more. *You always get spivs and villains portrayed in fiction with their eyes set too close together, or having a weak mouth.* She found herself sneaking a peek at

Ryan's mouth. *Hmm, no sign of weakness about that one,* she sighed, *only a tight, mean little trap.*

"All right," she decided. "We'll make a deal with you. I'll let you go free now provided you go away and leave Gemma and Kieran and Firstone Grange alone. In fact, you've got to leave Chambers Forge altogether. Have you got an aunt or a grandmother or somebody, somewhere in another part of the country?"

He looked hopefully at her, through narrowed eyes, measuring her. *Surely the stupid old bat wasn't that gullible?*

She watched him with amusement as she read his expression, though his mental description of her was probably a lot less ladylike than "bat." Or "stupid," come to that.

A happy thought struck her and she went to her suitcase, packed and almost ready for tomorrow's departure. She rummaged inside it. "Photos, of course. Now where…? Ah, here we are." In her hand she held her mobile phone, which she switched on as she walked back to where he lay trussed on the rug. "Let's see now. Smile. Ryan! Lovely. And again?" She took half a dozen photographs of him from different angles, smiling as she showed Tim her favorite, which clearly illustrated Ryan and his predicament.

"Well, Ryan?" She grinned maliciously at him. "I'm sure Kieran and Gemma would have a good laugh if they saw these pictures, don't you think? And I imagine the police would think it was even more amusing. Come to think of it, I could post it on YouTube for the whole world to see—that'd give everyone a laugh. So be a good little thug and stay away. Now, where will you go?"

Sulkily, he gave the matter some thought.

"My mum's sister lives in Taunton," he offered. "My aunty Maureen. I could go and stay with her, I expect. She hasn't got any kids of her own so she always used to like buying me sweets and treats and stuff like that."

"Poor misguided woman," Harriet said dispassionately. "Still, that ought to get you out of the way for a while. You can say you thought it would be nice to go and see her at Christmas. Now, what about your mum?"

"She always goes to stay with Aunty Maureen anyway, every Christmas." He was still sulking but Harriet paid no attention.

"There you are then." She gave a triumphant little laugh. "You go home, right now, and tell your mum you've decided you want a proper family Christmas, I'm sure she'll be thrilled—once she gets over the shock. You're to get going tomorrow, all right?"

The look he gave her was pure vitriol but he was defeated and resigned to his fate. He nodded reluctantly.

"Very well, let me have your aunty Maureen's phone number." She took a pen out of her bag and picked up a notepad from the bedside table. "That's good. Ryan, just be thankful that you've made the right decision." Her expression was forbidding and the boy squirmed, clearly wondering what the wrong decision would have merited. Harriet looked down her nose at him. "Don't think about coming back here yet awhile, will you? I shall be mentioning this little episode to the police in a day or so and I'm sure they'll keep a lookout for you. Ever been in trouble before?"

His sullen silence was eloquent.

"I thought so. This time it would mean jail, I should think. Didn't Gemma mention that it's your eighteenth birthday anytime now? Dear me, that means you're a Capricorn and they're usually such solid, upright citizens. I wonder what went wrong in your stars? Anyway, I doubt if you'd really enjoy prison. For one thing there are lots of lonely men there and you're quite pretty in a weasel-faced kind of way."

It took a moment for her meaning to sink in, he really wasn't very bright, she reflected; then he recoiled in horror, staring at her wide-eyed.

She stooped to untie his bonds. "Just you bear that in mind whenever you think about coming back to this neck of the woods," she cooed as he staggered to his feet, rubbing his ankles and wrists. "Now get out. You can climb out of my window and down the drainpipe, it should just about hold you. It's quite nasty out there, getting icy, but if I don't mind, I don't see why you should."

The logic of her last remark puzzled him, she could tell, but the threat implicit in her attitude was unmistakable. He departed, climbing awkwardly but rapidly, out of the window, and to Harriet's intense pleasure they heard a ripping, a hastily smothered howl and the noise of a body slithering downwards at great speed.

"Goodness, but you're a hard-hearted, intrepid woman, Harriet," offered Tim with a nod of admiration.

"Maybe," she said, gesturing toward the armchair. "Take a seat, Tim. I'll put the kettle on. I don't know about you but I'm quite desperate for a cup of tea after that little adventure."

He sat down and stretched his legs. "Do you think he'll go straight?" he wondered.

"I shouldn't think it's at all likely," she said with a cynical grin as she boiled the water. The idea at the back of her mind was somehow beginning to crystallize into a certainty and she was only too glad of a distraction. "As far as I'm concerned it doesn't matter, to be honest, whether he goes straight or not—apart from the general principle of the thing, I should say. I was just concerned to get him away from here just now and particularly to give young Gemma a chance to recover from him. I gather the lumpy henchman, Kieran, is making overtures of a romantic nature and he's much more suitable as a long-term romantic prospect. I don't altogether care what young Ryan does as long as he does it somewhere a long way away from here."

Harriet handed Tim a mug of tea and sat down on her bed, watching as he fished a couple of pills from his jacket pocket and washed them down with his drink. "Sleeping pills," he answered her raised eyebrow. "An old prescription but they still work. Had 'em for years, since Jane…" He said the beloved name with only a slight twitch of an eyelid. "I only take them when I get wound up. I reckon I'll need them after all this excitement."

She nodded and took a deep breath that was half a sigh. "Tell me about Christiane Marchant, Tim," she suggested gently.

His eyes flickered and for a moment she thought he was going to shut down the system and deliberately retreat into his other world, but he straightened his shoulders and made a slight face at her.

"I told your cousin, Canon Hathaway, about her. I expect he told you?"

She nodded.

"Well, then, what more do you want me to tell you? I told him everything."

"No, you didn't." She put her mug down on the bed-side cabinet, carefully positioning it on a mat so that the polished surface wasn't marked. *Melamine would be a lot more practical,* she thought inconsequentially, *but the wood is much nicer.* "Not everything. You could try telling me why you killed her?"

She gazed straight into his eyes and saw that her hunch was right. She wondered whether he would try the vanishing trick with her, either real or assumed, if she confronted him with her suspicions. There would be nothing she could do if he did, she knew that, but no, he blinked rapidly once or twice, then heaved a sigh of what sounded very like relief.

"Why? Because she filled me with an all-consuming blind hatred, that's why."

It was Harriet's turn to blink and she stared at him in astonishment.

"Because of your wife, Tim?" she prompted.

"Because of Jane." He nodded wearily. "And because of Tony, my son, and his wife and the grandchildren."

"She threatened to tell them about Jane?" Harriet's eyes showed only sympathy when she looked at him.

"Of course she did, but it wasn't only that. It was the way she…she somehow smirched my memories of Jane, she left a trail of slime so that I couldn't remem-ber her clearly."

His eyes were tragic as he looked across at Harriet. "It's hard enough for me to remember what she looked like at the best of times," he confessed, with a tremor of distress in his voice.

"Oh, Tim." Her voice held warmth and understand-ing but sadness, too.

"I can't begin to tell you how dreadfully Jane felt

the shame. Nowadays I don't suppose the case would even have gone to court, she was suffering very badly from…with, with the…change."

He muttered the word awkwardly, eyes averted, and Harriet heaved a sigh of exasperation mingled with pity. *Poor Jane,* she thought, *trapped in a body full of rogue hormones at war, at a time when few enough doctors, let alone lay people, were sympathetic to the idea of a hormonal deficiency. And stuck with a husband like Tim, loving and kind but unbearably squeamish. I bet he never told her he loved her, either,* she thought suddenly. *Not after they were married. Why would he? He's a typical Englishman of his generation—said it once, when he proposed, why should he say it again? Of course he loved her, he'd married her, hadn't he?*

A sudden vision of her cousin Sam flashed into her mind. Sam with his passionate and enduring love for his beloved Avril. Sam had often told his wife that he loved her and Harriet remembered Avril, managing to summon up a faint smile, that last evening at the hospice as she whispered, "Take care of him for me, please, darling Harriet. He'll be so dreadfully lonely without me, and you've always been his next dearest love."

Remembering Avril, Harriet swallowed once or twice and waited for Tim to go on.

"I saw the reel of button thread on the table," he was saying. "And I overheard Mrs. Turner mention it to somebody—that old army chap, I believe—could have been him, I don't remember. That woman, you know the one…she had been simpering and hinting at me just before the concert started. She said how

handsome Tony was and what did he think about his
mother and—and what she had done. Like a fool I said
he didn't know, that he'd been at college when it happened and just took the move down south in his stride,
assumed it was promotion for me, that kind of thing."
He shrugged. "Played right into her hands, of course.
She smiled at me and said, oh dear, what a pity, and
I'd have to be so careful that he didn't find out. Boys
always put their mothers on a pedestal, she said."

"What did you do with the button thread, Tim?"
Harriet nudged him gently back on track, picturing
with reluctant clarity Tim, the last one down from the
gallery. Tim hovering close to the body.

"I still can't believe nobody noticed me," he said. His
voice was beginning to falter and the look of exhaustion aged his face but he kept going, still surprisingly
alert. "Nor that it actually worked. It was when Matron
stuck her away in that corner that I had the idea. I
looked up and there was the horn balanced above her
like the sword of Damocles, the light from the candle
bulbs glinting off it. At first I just wished it would fall
down on her and smash her to pieces. Then when you
went to see about some drinks, I remembered the tinsel
I'd seen on the euphonium and it gave me the idea. I
simply picked up the cotton reel and wandered across
the room and up the stairs, tying a loop in the end of
the thread as I went. There were several other people
who had gone up for a look so there was nothing out
of the ordinary about me being there.

"I saw the euphonium balanced on the rail and
thought again that it looked like—what do they say?—
an accident waiting to happen, so I slipped the loop
of thread that I'd already tied over those brass things,

keys, or whatever they're called, and shoved it even closer to the edge. It was quite dark up there so nobody noticed what I was up to in the crowd, then I went back downstairs, carefully paying out the black cotton behind me, making sure I kept it loose."

He took a sip of tea, swallowed it and drew a deep breath. Harriet remained quiet, waiting. She thought he looked as if he had gone beyond exhaustion.

"I'd left it very late." It was clearly an effort but he managed to go on. "The interval was almost over. In fact I passed a couple of musicians on their way back to their places." He rubbed a hand across his eyes. "I don't know if I was really planning to do it, it was just a kind of game at that stage. A kind of, 'I know something you don't know,' directed at Christiane Marchant, the kind of thing she specialized in on her own account. It was only when the band started up again and she gave me such a malicious, knowing smirk across the table that I knew what I had to do. It was as though everyone else was in a conspiracy with me, to force her out into the open where she would be vulnerable. Where I could take my revenge."

Tim leaned back in his chair, his eyelids drooping, and Harriet held her breath. *Please,* she prayed silently, *please let him tell me, don't let him lose the plot completely. I have to know.*

"If the euphonium player had picked up his instrument I would simply have dropped the reel of cotton and abandoned it and it would just have been a puzzle for them later on. But he didn't, he left it balanced there and I felt like the Angel of Death then, that it was up to me, that I had a kind of duty to preserve the rest of humanity from such evil. I did a rough calculation of the trajectory of the horn if I tugged it from where I was standing and then there was that terrific roll of drums and she was grinning at me again, she even gave me a little wink. Something must have snapped in my head because the next thing I knew, all hell had broken loose and there was this bloody awful mess everywhere."

Harriet moistened her lips, feeling her way carefully. "But what about the black thread?" she asked. "Weren't you afraid someone would notice it? And cry foul?" she added.

"I don't think I cared two hoots at that moment, not when I pulled the thread," he replied simply. "I remember trying to pull the thread tightly across and round the stops, or keys, or whatever those knobs are, so that there'd be something for the cotton to tighten against and snap in midair, but I had my pocketknife in my hand just to make sure. It's my old Scout knife," he said casually. "I've carried it on me for more than seventy years. Anyway, I simply surged forward with the throng after the euphonium fell, rubbernecking with the rest of them, and under cover of all the fuss and panic, I bent down and snipped the thread off short. I'd have cut through the lot if you hadn't sent Sam over to rescue me but I managed to do that a little later and rolled up the loose thread and chucked it on the fire. Then when no one was looking I tucked the cotton reel away on the mantelpiece, behind a sprig of holly."

He set his cup down and rose stiffly, looking at her very kindly.

"Well, there you are, Harriet. The murderer's confession. What would you like me to do about it? I suppose I ought to tell someone in authority about it, but do you think anyone would believe me?"

She was startled. It was an aspect of the situation that had not occurred to her, but she could see his point.

"Don't worry." His smile held warmth and affection and a measure of resolution. "They won't do much to me, should you think? After all, what can they possibly do to me that is worse than what nature is doing already?"

Harriet had forgotten for a while just how prone he was to slip into his lost worlds. He had remained lucid for a long time tonight, empowered by triumph perhaps. Or more likely by desolation, she reconsidered, looking at his ravaged face.

"Years ago," he told her, in a conversational tone, "I remember reading that there was some old fellow in an old folks' home, who put a pillow over an old woman's face and smothered her. His defense, such as it was, turned out to be that he believed she was in pain so he thought he ought to put her out of her misery."

In spite of the exhaustion that by now had him hanging on to the back of the chair to keep upright, he shot a glance of pure mischief at her, then his face slid into an exaggerated version of the lost look and he began to mumble.

"Poor creature, I thought she was in pain, you see, having to spend her entire time in a wheelchair. I couldn't bear to see her suffer."

The ancient leer he directed at her was perfect, just over the edge of vacancy. He was quite right; a plea of insanity would be a cinch, if it even came to that.

"All right, Tim," she told him, her voice dry. "You can snap out of it now. I believe you."

"It's all for the best, really," he urged. "Tony's been offered a promotion and relocation to somewhere in

Cheshire, so they'll be a fair distance away. The shame won't be so acute with a journey of a couple of hundred miles or so from there back down here, and their new friends won't ever need to know. Besides, a secure unit, or wherever they send me, won't be any worse than some old people's homes that you read about. There's no way we could afford a place like this for more than my fortnight, so it's quite convenient, really."

She put out a tentative hand as he opened her door. "Tim?"

He looked down at her, his face sweating, the skin a greenish-gray with strain, but with a slight smile twisting his mouth. "Don't, Harriet. There's nothing more to say, except, thank you for everything."

He bent to kiss her swiftly on the cheek and gave her a kind of salute, then he was gone and she was quite alone in her room.

FOURTEEN

Christmas Day

"Pass the port, Harriet, there's a good girl." Sam reached out a lazy hand and took the bottle from his cousin. It was nine o'clock on Christmas evening and they were both sprawled out on the comfortable sofas by the fire in Harriet's cottage parlor.

"It's been a good day, hasn't it?" Sam nodded with satisfaction. He had driven over to pick her up the evening before and later they had gone to the midnight service at the Cathedral in Winchester, stamping their feet and rubbing their hands in the frosty air when they came out. Christmas morning had begun with Sam's culinary speciality, the full English breakfast which they had eaten in Harriet's kitchen because the dining table was decorated and laid ready for the turkey.

"I know it seems a bit silly, doing all this just for the two of us," Harriet had confessed as she opened a box of crackers, "but I'd already decided to go to town this year, even before all the shenanigans at Firstone Grange. That made me even more determined to put on a bit of glitz to put all the horrors out of our minds, if we can."

"Don't apologize, Hat," Sam assured her. "I like a bit of glitz myself and you're quite right. After what

we've recently been through we could do with thinking of something else."

When it came to opening presents they ended up
almost in tears of laughter. Harriet had earnestly
assured Sam that she really didn't want anything this
year and he had agreed, equally solemnly, that there
was nothing he wanted, either. It came as a surprise to
Harriet therefore to find Sam offering her a parcel, but
she merely grinned and reached behind the sofa, to give
him his present, too.

"Talk about great minds…" Sam was almost speech-
less when he unwrapped the blue cashmere sweater
Harriet had chosen for him. She looked surprised but
started to laugh as she unwrapped her own gift; also a
cashmere sweater, though in a slightly lighter shade of
blue. "Bet you haven't done the same thing *this* time,"
she said, handing him a smaller parcel, with a flourish.

He opened a boxed set of Joan Baez CDs and went
straight over and put one on. "No, I didn't get you Joan
Baez," he said, with a suggestive twinkle. She pursed
her lips and felt all round the packet he handed her. It
felt like…well, she knew what it felt like. The wrapping
fell away and she was looking at a set of CDs. Elgar,
her favorite.

"Yes," she agreed, with an answering smile. "Great
minds. Definitely."

Calls from both of Sam's children followed and Harriet found herself agreeing that she and Sam would
spend next Christmas in Australia with Sam's son and
his family. Then it was time for a drink with the people
in the cottage next door, but they managed to escape
before the noise levels generated by the neighbors' six
small grandchildren reached pain level.

"You're right, Sam," Harriet said suddenly, agreeing with his earlier remark. "It's been a really good day. Church on Christmas morning is always special and the new vicar is rather dishy, much more decorative than our previous incumbent. And we did all right with the turkey, too, didn't we?"

He raised his glass of port to her with a grin, just as the phone rang. Harriet searched under cushions and books, then, just as she was getting exasperated, she unearthed it by the Christmas tree.

"Hullo? Who? *What?*" She beamed at him delightedly. "It's Neil and Alice," she told him.

He grabbed the phone from her to add his greetings.

"Happy Christmas, Sam." It was Neil. "Congratulate me—she's agreed to make an honest man out of me at last. We got engaged yesterday on a deserted beach, with white sand, turquoise sea, sapphire sky and all bathed in tropical sunshine. It was magic."

"Congratulations indeed." Sam was delighted. "That's terrific news, when—"

Harriet snatched the phone back from him. "Here, let me… Neil? You're not married? Oh, engaged? How wonderful. Where are you, are you still in Fiji? Tell us all about it."

"Yes, we're still in Fiji," he said, the happiness in his voice bubbling over into a spontaneous peal of laughter. "It's magic," he said again. "Here, Alice wants to tell you all about it."

"Harriet?" Though she was nearly 12,000 miles away, Alice sounded near at hand and so happy that Harriet had to wipe away a tear. "It's Boxing Day morning here, Harriet. We got engaged at midday yesterday, Christmas Day. It was so romantic, we went for a walk along this wonderful empty beach and Neil suddenly went down on one knee and asked me to marry him. Of course I said yes!" Harriet smiled at the excitement in her voice. "There's a jeweler's here and I've got the most beautiful ring, rubies and diamonds, and when we get home we'll start thinking about planning a wedding. We'll wait till we've sorted everything out with getting rid of the house first." Harriet heard the catch in the younger woman's voice but Alice took a deep breath and continued in a lighter tone.

"We're staying at an island resort. It's like a hotel but with cabins, they call them 'bures,' instead of rooms, all scattered round. We can lie in bed and look straight out at the Pacific—the sea is only a few yards away down the beach. Oh, Harriet, I do love him so!"

The news seemed to put an extra gloss on their happy, comfortable day. While Sam went back to slouch in front of the roaring log fire, Harriet gave a sudden exclamation and went out to the kitchen. She reappeared holding a couple of tall flute glasses and a bottle of Moët she had been hiding in the fridge and which she handed to Sam to open.

"I suppose I had a sort of inkling that something like this might happen," she admitted, accepting her glass from him and raising it in a toast to the happy couple. "If they hadn't rung, it wouldn't have been wasted. I was going to get it out anyway, to drink to ourselves. Neil did the right thing, getting Alice away so quickly. It was pretty grim once the tabloids did a double take and decided the story was worth pursuing after all. Still, Matron was wonderfully starchy with those reporters and they soon went haring after another victim."

"It's odd how it all worked out, isn't it?" Sam leaned back and stretched out his long legs again, kicking off his shoes to warm his toes at the fire.

"You thought it was Tim, didn't you?" she asked him suddenly. "When you left me that note, telling me about his wife. That's why you were so cross with me when I wouldn't let you come over to Chambers Forge that night. You were afraid he might do something to me."

"Something like that," he admitted. "I wasn't sure, not really, any more than you were, that it *was* him. It was just, when you weighed it all up, the haphazard nature of the enterprise, the whole thing seemed completely mad." He shifted into a more comfortable slouch and nodded to her over the rim of his glass. "That's what alerted *you,* I imagine. The fact that the other two, or three, I suppose, if you include Doreen Buchan—though I was never really convinced that she was a player—no, the other two were more or less in full possession of their marbles.

"I mean, Tim's plan was downright crazy. It was only by sheer chance that the whole thing came together. So many things could have stopped it in its tracks. The thread could have been spotted by the horn player or it could have snapped harmlessly. Somebody else could have been hurt and in any case it was a miracle nobody else was even touched, no matter what he said about calculating the trajectory. There were too many things left to chance and Ellen Ransom and Fred Buchan had shown themselves to be capable of cunning." His eyes clouded for a moment. "I know Fred was a victim of circumstances, just as much as Christiane was in her way, but once he'd got away and when he came to this country, he certainly showed plenty of guile. Though who can blame him. I doubt if I would have done anything else, given the circumstances."

Harriet nodded. "That's more or less how I reasoned it, too," she said. "Everything you've said about Fred, being a victim of sorts, applies to Ellen, too, though I can't get that picture out of my head, of her calmly killing her own baby down on the beach one early summer's morning. It's almost as bad as the other one... I've been having horrible dreams about Fred and his terrible story. Here, pour me some more champagne, Sam. I might sleep better tonight."

He topped up their glasses then cast a considering look at her. "It was surprisingly fortuitous," he ventured diffidently. "Tim having a fatal heart attack that last night, wasn't it? A very peaceful death, Matron told me, and not unexpected according to the doctor, not with Tim already having a heart condition. After all, Matron had organized a medical check on all of you, on the Sunday, hadn't she, to make sure everyone was coping after such a trauma. It was much less distressing for Tim's family, the fact that they didn't have to go through all the palaver of an autopsy, seeing that the doctor had only just examined him."

She gave him an innocent smile and a very slight nod of agreement but his forehead creased in a thoughtful frown.

"It must have given you a bit of a shock," he said, watching her. "Finding him like that with his heart tablets on the floor where he must have dropped them before he could open the bottle. What made you go and check up on him?"

She shrugged. "Well, you can't deny that his late-night discussion with me was pretty stressful," she said. "It seemed a good idea to make sure he was feeling better. After all, he'd looked dreadful when he said good-night."

No need, she thought, to mention Tim's sleeping pills to anyone: an old prescription, he'd said, dating back to the time of his wife's death. There had been no autopsy, no worrying revelations and no empty bottle left inconveniently on his bedside table. She felt no qualms of conscience about any of her actions, so she resolutely kept her own counsel. She knew however, none better, that her cousin Sam was nobody's fool.

"There didn't seem much point telling anyone about what he had told me," she said casually. "After all, everyone, including Alice and the police, accepted Christiane Marchant's death as an accident. The musicians were completely exonerated and Neil had told me only that morning that the euphonium player was now beginning to feel very much better about the whole sorry affair. Why stir up a hornet's nest? It might well have been an accident after all. Who's to know Tim wasn't talking nonsense? He sounded logical enough, I grant you, but he might have completely flipped. Besides—" she reached for the bottle again "—I was the only person who heard him and who knows? I might have dreamed the whole thing. After all, I was completely exhausted that night."

"Quite right, Old Hat." Sam smiled affectionately at her and she knew that whatever suspicions he might harbor, the matter was now closed. "As for our other two prime suspects, I gather poetic justice has befallen them?"

"It certainly has." She roused herself to pass a plate

of mince pies. "Here, take one, you're quite safe, I
didn't make them. I bought them in Waitrose yesterday morning. Yes indeed." There was a gleam of triumph in her eyes. "Fred Buchan had a massive stroke
that night so Doreen and Vic have fixed up to move
him next door into Hiltingbury House on a permanent
basis once he's out of hospital." She munched reflectively. "I suppose we were right not to report him as a
war criminal? He was a Nazi, after all."

Sam shook his head. "No, he suffered divine retribution, I'm quite convinced of that. No human agency
could touch him. But it was retribution tempered with
mercy." He was wearing his inward look. "As divine
retribution always is." He sat up straight and smiled
affectionately at her. "I do truly believe that he found
some kind of peace down in the crypt of Winchester
Cathedral that day, staring at the statue. That, and con-
fessing his tragic tale to Alice and the rest of us. Besides, there's a time and place for a spot of mercy from
the likes of us, too."

"I suppose you're right." She pursed her lips and
nodded. "After all, Alice was so anxious to be rid of all
the horrors, all the past anguish and the recent misery.
What would be the point of raking it all up? Fred
Buchan had suffered years of the most dreadful guilt,
which is retribution after all, a life sentence, in fact. I
understand he's severely paralyzed down his right side
and can't speak, but Doreen says it's quite obvious that
he can understand all they say to him."

Sam winced. "Oh Lord, that's the cruelest punishment of all."

Harriet nodded in sympathy then recalled the other

resident at Firstone Grange whom they had thought deserving of punishment.

"Did I tell you...?" She sounded slightly gleeful, and then looked abashed. "Matron had a word with Ellen Ransom's son-in-law and convinced him that it would be a kindness to get Ellen into Hiltingbury House, too. She didn't specify to whom—it would be a kindness, I mean—but he was pretty quick on the uptake and between them they pushed it through before Ellen or her daughter could come up with any objection. A room fell vacant and Matron and her crony leapfrogged Ellen to the top of the waiting list. It's always who you know...."

Drowsing in the glow of the firelight Harriet knew Sam was remembering, as she was, the damp, gray December morning when Christiane Marchant was finally sent to her rest.

"What a sad, injured soul she must have been," reflected Sam, looking momentarily unhappy as he considered the warped and twisted mind of the woman who had caused so much pain and misery.

"Oh, Sam." Harriet looked at him with affectionate exasperation. "Don't go all broody about it. There was nothing you could have done for her, even if you'd known. She wasn't the type to let anyone get close." Knowing his tender heart, Harriet decided to keep her real opinion of Christiane Marchant to herself. *I don't believe,* she pondered, *that even such an appalling event in her past could have turned a normal woman into a monster. Sad or angry, certainly, insane even, but such a bitch? I don't think so.*

She upended the champagne bottle over his glass. "Here, get this inside you and pass me that tin of Quality Street. It's Christmas Day, let's just thank God it's all over and we managed to get out of it unscathed."

He grinned at her and nodded. "Happy Christmas, Old Hat," he said, raising his glass to her. "Here's to us."

* * * * *

REQUEST YOUR FREE BOOKS!

2 FREE NOVELS
PLUS 2 FREE GIFTS!

MYSTERY WORLDWIDE LIBRARY®
Your Partner in Crime

YES! Please send me 2 FREE novels from the Worldwide Library® series and my 2 FREE gifts (gifts are worth about $10). After receiving them, if I don't wish to receive any more books, I can return the shipping statement marked "cancel." If I don't cancel, I will receive 4 brand-new novels every month and be billed just $5.24 per book in the U.S. or $6.24 per book in Canada. That's a saving of at least 34% off the cover price. It's quite a bargain! Shipping and handling is just 50¢ per book in the U.S. and 75¢ per book in Canada.* I understand that accepting the 2 free books and gifts places me under no obligation to buy anything. I can always return a shipment and cancel at any time. Even if I never buy another book, the two free books and gifts are mine to keep forever.

414/424 WDN FEJ3

Name _____ (PLEASE PRINT)

Address _____ Apt. #

City _____ State/Prov. _____ Zip/Postal Code

Signature (if under 18, a parent or guardian must sign)

Mail to the **Reader Service:**
IN U.S.A.: P.O. Box 1867, Buffalo, NY 14240-1867
IN CANADA: P.O. Box 609, Fort Erie, Ontario L2A 5X3

Not valid for current subscribers to the Worldwide Library series.

Want to try two free books from another line?
Call 1-800-873-8635 or visit www.ReaderService.com.

* Terms and prices subject to change without notice. Prices do not include applicable taxes. Sales tax applicable in N.Y. Canadian residents will be charged applicable taxes. Offer not valid in Quebec. This offer is limited to one order per household. All orders subject to credit approval. Credit or debit balances in a customer's account(s) may be offset by any other outstanding balance owed by or to the customer. Please allow 4 to 6 weeks for delivery. Offer available while quantities last.

Your Privacy—The Reader Service is committed to protecting your privacy. Our Privacy Policy is available online at www.ReaderService.com or upon request from the Reader Service.

We make a portion of our mailing list available to reputable third parties that offer products we believe may interest you. If you prefer that we not exchange your name with third parties, or if you wish to clarify or modify your communication preferences, please visit us at www.ReaderService.com/consumerchoice or write to us at Reader Service Preference Service, P.O. Box 9062, Buffalo, NY 14269. Include your complete name and address.

WWLI1B